Water Wings

Water Wings

Kristen den Hartog

Alfred A. Knopf Canada

PUBLISHED BY ALFRED A. KNOPF CANADA

Copyright © 2001 by Kristen den Hartog

All rights reserved under International and Pan-American Copyright
Conventions. Published in 2001 by Alfred A. Knopf Canada, a division of
Random House of Canada Limited, Toronto. Distributed by Random
House of Canada Limited, Toronto.

Knopf Canada and colophon are trademarks.

Parts of this novel have appeared in different form in *Other Voices, Blood and
Aphorisms, Prarie Fire, The 1997 Journey Prize Anthology* (McClelland & Stewart),
and *The Turn of the Story* (Anansi).

Canadian Cataloguing in Publication Data

den Hartog, Kristen
    Water wings

ISBN 0-676-97285-3

I. Title.

PS8557.E537W37 2001   C813'.6   C00-932435-6
PR9199.3.D46W37 2001

First Edition

Visit Random House of Canada Limited's Web site: www.randomhouse.ca

Text design: Valerie Applebee
Printed and bound in the United States of America

10 9 8 7 6 5 4 3 2 1

For Mom, Dad, Tracy and Heidi,
and for the many branches of my family tree.

Stories never live alone: they are the branches
of a family that we have to trace back, and forward.

ROBERTO CALASSO,
The Marriage of Cadmus & Harmony

Water Wings

Hannah

The windshield is dirty, smudged with the tiny bodies of spent insects. Early on Hannah had been taught that insects were beautiful, even ordinary flies, though they began as swarming maggots. It was her father who had pointed out the metallic blue and green of them, their huge eyes and their legs that bent at the knee, things she may never have noticed on her own. How long since he'd died? Nine, Hannah was when it happened, so fourteen years without him. Funny to think. After that there was only the three of them: Hannah, Vivian and their long-haired mother, Darlene. And yet all this time the ghost of their father had hovered like a transparent umbrella, there but not there, just as he'd been there but not there when he was alive.

The anniversary of his death had passed silently last month, as though it were any other day. Blue Thursday this time. The day and the colour camouflaged, changing every year. Hannah woke as usual to a radio song, ate cereal, showered, went to work at the flower shop, came home, ate dinner, watched television and readied herself for bed. It was not until then that she saw him. Just a glimpse. He appeared briefly in her mirror, his face replacing hers. He had his mouth open in song, and he was wearing his mock-serious opera face. And then he was gone and her own face was there. She said aloud, "He died today."

She had tried to remember the funeral, as she has often attempted to do, but all that had come to mind were the flowers, deathly gladioli, common and unlike him. Two stiff arrangements flanked the coffin, and a wide ribbon bore the hand-written words, *R.I.P. Mick Oelpke.* In her memory she could not see anything clearly but these flowers and her own finger in the wrinkled lower blooms, touching the velvet centres. If he had only waited to die, she would have made beautiful bouquets of reeds and wildflowers and weeping willow that spilled to the floor. It was easy to know what he would love.

It would be harder to choose flowers for Darlene, which soon she must do, because out of the clear wide blue, Hannah's mother had announced her engagement to Reg Sinclair, a man who had never meant anything to any of them. A stranger, as much as anyone can be a stranger in a town as small as theirs. And this is where Hannah is headed, back home for the wedding.

Ottawa is less than three hours from the town where she grew up. She should visit more often, needing no reason to come, such as this wedding. Her gift will be the bridal bouquet and two large arrangements to frame that same altar. She must also make a boutonniere for Reg and a basket of petals for Brie to carry. Beautiful Brie, a flower girl. On the passenger seat the basket sits filled with florist's supplies: pins, tape, wire, wire snips, filmy organza ribbon in two shades of green and a spritzer to spray Darlene's bouquet before she walks down the aisle. Darlene had wanted common red roses and baby's breath because she hadn't got them the first time around, but Hannah had said no. It was unlike Darlene to back down, and Hannah had been surprised when she'd said, "Okay, Girly," in her nonchalant way. "You're the expert." And she was. Hannah knew her flowers.

Still, she was afraid of failing. She had made many wedding bouquets, but Darlene's would be different. She had looked through all the books at work, hoping for a magical idea. Stood staring into the cooler, making imaginary bouquets from the flowers there, and in the end she had come up with nothing. What suited Darlene? What suited the lapel of Reg Sinclair, whom she barely knew?

In her mind she conjures Reg Sinclair's shoe store. The Footworks sign and the yellow circle of lights all around it. Inside and out, it was glitzier than the other stores in town. A band of mirror running low along the fake wood walls so that you could see your feet everywhere you walked. Reg Sinclair measuring Hannah's foot with a foot-shaped ruler, sliding its metal knob to cup the place where a bunion has since grown. From him Darlene had bought Hannah and Vivian sandals in summer, school shoes in fall. Once, patent-leather shoes that smudged when Hannah touched them, holding the print of her finger. Back then they would never have guessed he would marry their mother. That they would one day have Lily, his half-Chinese daughter, as a stepsister. Suddenly related to a girl they hardly knew. Lily was between Hannah and Vivian in age. Rumour said a mysterious wife had given birth to her and returned to China, leaving Lily motherless, a horror Hannah couldn't imagine. Even before Mick had gone, she'd had nightmares about losing Darlene.

What would Mick think of Darlene marrying Reg Sinclair? Hannah wonders if he knows, if he is somewhere out there, watching. He hadn't believed in an afterlife, but smart as he was, he may have been wrong. No one would be more surprised than Mick to discover himself in heaven, looking down. He might now know everything and more.

She is nearing home and there is that smell in the air, of cut grass and river. In her rusty VW Bug, a convertible, she turns off the Trans-Canada and onto the tar-mended road into town. A sick, childhood feeling sweeps hotly through her and is gone. The water tower, with its missing letters, seems small now, but it's true that a boy once jumped from there, plummeting not to his death but to a state of vegetation. Mick had explained what that meant. She used to think of the boy every time she ate vegetables. His brain curly like cauliflower, but wet and bluish-grey. She can't remember his name. Had she actually known him? Or was his leap something that had happened far away, something she had seen on television and absorbed into her own life? Briefly she closes her eyes to see the no-name boy climb the tower. Night. No cars. Just a rogue transport roaring in and out of town. The boy's shoes clanging on the metal frame. Higher and higher. His hands smelly, like when you grip monkey bars. Chips of mint green stuck to his sweaty palms. At the top he stops and wipes his hands on his jeans. And then he lunges. In her head he falls in slow motion, almost floating. His hair fans out, the red strands glinting. His smile gets bigger the further he drops, long legs spread in the splits.

Hannah opens her eyes to find herself sailing through an intersection. Lucky for her there are no cars coming. Sometimes only luck keeps a body from harm. She rambles down the hill and towards downtown. There is Reg's Footworks, *Sorry! We're Closed.* And beside it the snack bar, still called The Snack Bar. Kids she can't know lurk outside, leaning against bicycle racks and smoking. There is the chip truck, still yellow but with new red stripes. And something else—a depiction of steaming chips in a paper bag. What's meant to be steam looks like wisps of curling black hair growing up from the chips. Everything the same, but different.

Hannah weaves through town and onto her old street, where she first learned to tell left from right, no matter which way she was facing. Past the stop sign that faces the other way. Past the Ferguses'. The Hannah Tree dwarfs the For Sale sign in her mother's front yard and now blocks most of the picture window. A stupid place to put a tree. Darlene surely picked the spot.

"Right here," she would have said to Hannah's father, Mick. She would have trampled the grass with her smooth feet to mark the chosen place. Held her slim arms out at each side, tree-like. "It's gotta go right here, Sweet Boy."

Darlene had made him cry, and he had made her cry too. That was love. For him Darlene had cried until her eyes were raw, stuck shut, and Hannah, looking at those eyes, had felt the sting in her own. People are soft and bruisable, she had known this even then. But what could you do with a heart once it had landed in your hands? It seems unlikely now that Darlene might ever sob and break down over Reg Sinclair, but maybe that's the way love should be. Tearless, pain-free.

Hannah pulls into the double driveway and parks over an oil splotch. The only fancy thing about this little bungalow is its puzzling two-car garage. Before Hannah has turned off the engine, Darlene emerges, screen door banging behind her.

"Girly!" she squeals, reaching in, hugging.

Hannah hasn't yet unbuckled her seat belt. She keeps her foot on the brake and hugs back, breathing in the scent of Darlene's thick hair and also Darlene's own secret fragrance—lavender, sweat, mandarin oranges.

Angie

Darlene's sister, Angie, tries to understand why Darlene might want to remarry. Sell her house and move into someone else's. Change her name once more. She sews Darlene's dress and thinks of her own, yellowing in her bedroom closet. The write-up in the paper had been like the write-up for a movie star.

The bride wore a gown of white chiffon over peau de soie,
styled with a rounded neckline outlined with appliquéd
rosettes, fitted bodice and short sleeves. The bouffant skirt,
sprinkled with matching appliqués, extended in a chapel train.
A coronet of rhinestones and pearls held her fingertip veil of
silk illusion, and she carried a bouquet of feathered white
mums, pink rosettes and ivy.

They didn't do that any more for ordinary people. Darlene
had been Angie's bridesmaid, too ravishing in knee-length blue
taffeta.

⁓

Angie and Charlie Hill had not been married long when
Angie's periods stopped. Elated and doubly alive, she right away
felt the baby flutter, and to Charlie she said it was as though
she'd breathed in a live butterfly. Vicariously pregnant, he slept
with his hand on her stomach. Much too early he began to listen for the baby. He pressed his ear to Angie's stomach, and
Angie placed her hand on his other ear to hold the precious
sound in, even though she knew it to be food digesting rather
than the baby growing and gurgling.

To Darlene, Angie said, "I'm pregnant," and Darlene said,
"Aha!" and pinched the skin beneath Angie's chin. "I thought
you were looking a bit puffy lately."

Darlene had just given birth to Vivian and did not look puffy at
all. Throughout her pregnancy her limbs had remained toned and
slender. From behind, it had not been apparent she was pregnant.
Only her stomach grew, first small and smooth like a child's pot
belly, then rounder, harder, but never grotesque. Baby Vivian was

as lovely as Darlene and her husband Mick, though at first to Angie
she had seemed somewhat alien, with bulging green eyes and white
goose-feathery hair that would not lie flat.

Early in Angie's pregnancy her elation dwindled. She was sick
night and day, and thought she might be throwing up happiness.
She stopped wanting Charlie to touch her, a thing she had loved
and craved, and if they did make love she moved mechanically
and did not kiss him.

"What's wrong?" he whispered.

She shrugged. "I'm tired."

And it was true, she was. Always tired to the bone.

Like Darlene she gained little weight, but was surprised at
how miserable this made her. Her breasts were hard but small
like apples, sore to the touch. Her belly was distended. She
began to feel heavy, swollen, not herself. In the thick July heat
she slept often on the itchy chesterfield, dreaming weird baby
dreams, a whirring fan aimed at her sprawled, bloated body.
She dreamed her skin was a jumpsuit, its thick metal zipper
crossing her stomach like a mouth. Slowly she pulled the tab
and peered inside. Something long and sticky swarmed in
there. An eel, maybe. A wet rat. She chose not to touch it.
Closed the zipper and waited.

Each afternoon Darlene arrived in one of her many outfits—
orange hot pants, a pink daisy-patterned mini dress—baby
Vivian clad to match her. Hearing the stroller, Angie parted the
heavy drapes and peered out into the brightness of the day,
where it was now too hot to go. When Darlene and Vivian
entered, a powdery berry smell came with them, freshening the
stale air. Sweet sweat shone on Darlene's brown chest and
shoulders. Together they watched soaps and game shows in the
dark living room while Vivian cooed on a blanket on the floor.

Angie made constant trips to the washroom, heaving happiness and swallowing the thought that something might be terribly wrong. On stifling days Darlene spritzed herself and Vivian and Angie with lemon water. The fragrant burst of mist brought such exquisite relief that Angie closed her eyes to savour it.

Sometimes Darlene suggested they go to the beach.

"A swim would cool you off, Angel."

Which was true, it would, but the very thought of walking there made Angie hot and worn out. So they stayed in the house and watched TV with Vivian, who now had a tooth and was smiling.

And then Wren was born. In the hospital Angie's own baby lay among the healthy ones. Angie watched at the window in her slippers and robe, hand pressed against her flat, slackened stomach.

Before she'd discovered what had gone on within the womb, pushing the baby out had been a joyous relief. But then she saw its hands—joined florid fingers and tiny half thumbs. Angie was horrified. The baby's whole self was ugly. Organ pink. Scrunched up. Wet slime coating its body, matting its sparse, dark hair. The nurses cleaned it, weighed and measured it, and later laid the child in Angie's weakened arms. Angie wanted not to look and touch, but to sleep and sleep. Charlie, in his inside-out T-shirt, slipped his shoes off and lay in the hospital bed with Angie and Wren. He smelled of coffee and dirty hair.

"Flowers fell from heaven when Buddha was born," he told Angie. "He had webbed fingers and toes. It was considered a sign of greatness."

Charlie stroked the baby's cheek with his big finger. He held his face in a false smile and looked at Angie, who turned away. It hurt to see him, to look into his sad cow eyes. It hurt to see that baby. Angie tried to imagine it might be magical and gifted, the owner of some unseen special power. She tried coo-cooing and googly-gooing but the noises came out flat and slow, and she passed the baby to Charlie and pretended to sleep.

Eyes closed, she thought of all the things she had ever wanted to change about herself. The sound of her voice. The shape of her earlobes. Always she knew that, given the choice, she would change nothing in the end. But now, if she could, she would change everything about this baby. She would trade it in without hesitation. She thought of fair, lovely Vivian, with her one-tooth smile, and of Darlene, who used her tongue to kiss her husband in public. Perhaps true love produced perfection. Perhaps she and Charlie hadn't loved fiercely enough, and lazy love had ruined Wren. There was no way to know for certain.

The baby came home swathed in a butter-coloured blanket bought earlier for the happy occasion. Wrapped this way, it looked enough like the others. Angie held it tightly in the car and Charlie drove without speaking. They toured the town slowly and parked for a time at the waterfront to watch the boats. She wondered if he, like herself, didn't want to go home. She didn't ask, or even look at him, though Charlie looked at her. He sighed repeatedly and shifted in his seat, bare hairy legs squeaking against the vinyl.

The air was thick and humid. Milk spilled from Angie's weighted breasts, and she felt it pool against her stiff brassiere, then trickle down her belly. She thought she'd like to walk through the long grass to the water, sit at the edge with her feet dangling, immersed in coolness. Lay that baby on a lily pad and watch it float away.

"Never you mind," Darlene told Angie. "What's in a hand?" she asked, holding her own out at each side, palms up. She took

Wren's hands and kissed each ruined one, kissed too the baby's strange bony forehead, leaving a bright lipstick print there.

But Angie knew the value of hands. Hers were long and slender, piano player's fingers. She painted the nails on special occasions, wore an engagement ring that sparkled in the light next to her wedding band. And even when she'd been swollen with Wren inside her, her hands hadn't looked so bad. Wren would never wear a ring. She'd never pick her nose properly or make a peace sign or cross her fingers for good luck.

And it wasn't just her hands. Wren was not right. Her face was an adult's in miniature, pinched and hard. She lacked Vivian's soft roundness—flushed water-balloon cheeks, pouty lips. Even Wren's eyes were narrow, dull grey, not blue like Angie's or brown like Charlie's. But how Charlie loved Wren! Angie wanted to feel what he felt but could not. Lugged herself through the days and nights, guilt heavy in her belly.

At night Charlie wheeled Wren's crib into their bedroom, casters squeaking. He held Wren to Angie's breast—awkward for everyone—and Angie lay with her eyes closed, once more feigning sleep. Not grimacing, though the pain was intense and the milk came too slowly. Once Angie had seen the milk spurt out of Darlene's full breast and into Vivian's open mouth, which had been inches away, preparing to latch on. There was nothing Darlene had to work at. "Hi, Sweet Pea," she'd sing-song to Wren, pretending nothing was wrong. To Angie she'd said, "Don't fret, Angel. At least she's even," perhaps suggesting that two deformed hands were better than one. But Angie had heard her tell Mick it had better not run in the family. Angie had seen her sister shudder. And Angie had prayed, *Let her get hers,* an evil prayer, although she knew better than most that what went around did not always come around.

Charlie took the baby back to its crib and kissed it good night. He climbed in with Angie and held on, as though she were cold; but she was not cold, she was hot, and his skin stuck to hers. On her back he drew I L-O-V-E Y-O-U, to which she did not respond.

Light from the street lamp gleamed through the crack in the curtains, shining all night on Wren. Angie looked and Wren looked back with her steady adult's gaze, lips pursed as if holding something in, and Angie for the first time thought of going to Wren, perhaps touching Wren's patchy hair or the tender hollow on her head, a dangerous spot. She thought of that joke: *Why do babies' heads have indentations? So God can carry them five at a time.* There could not be a God, not now. She looked again at Wren and thought, If she cries, I'll pick her up. But Wren wouldn't cry. She only stared blankly at Angie until she drifted once more into sleep.

Angie slept soundly, dreaming that a man in a top hat had come to claim Wren. Angie hovered somewhere in the sky above them. Wren grew and grew, looked less and less normal in an array of frilly pink dresses that hung on her awkward body, her meaty hands huge, ugly against lace cuffs, oiled like muscles so they gleamed in the light. Wren stood in a row of freaks, and the onlookers ogled. The man in the top hat used a pool cue to point out the freaks, one by one, dotting their foreheads with blue chalk as he went. Beside Wren was a fat lady, then a set of conjoined twins. Another man's unformed brother hung from his chest— just a baby pair of arms, legs, a skinny limp body. Wren stood among the freaks, held her hands high and slowly turned them.

When she woke, guilt, then loathing, welled inside her. She waited. The feelings passed, and dull emptiness set in. Her body ached and she remained again in her milk-stained robe and slippers. Marvelled at Charlie, who'd begun to take Wren for walks in the neighbourhood. He wrapped her in the same butter-coloured blanket, tucked her into the pram they'd bought when they were still excited, wheeled her down the street. Angie watched from the window.

"You should go along, Angel," said Darlene, watching with her, but Angie couldn't imagine: everyone staring, wanting to see.

Angie herself had the urge to inspect. One day she stripped the baby, laid it on the carpet. Ran a finger down its chin, neck, belly. The skin was smooth, white now, except for the reddish hands. Below the left knee she found a tiny patch, pale pink, a birthmark. Angie checked the toes. Pressed her finger deep into the space between each one. And then, bathing Wren, poking into the folds of skin with a warm soapy cloth, she found herself weeping, surprised by these sounds that were hers in the silence.

Charlie readied himself for work and Angie lay in bed watching. He stood at the closet in loose underwear, holding the sleeve of a blue shirt in one hand and the sleeve of a white shirt in the other. Choose blue, she thought, and closed her eyes. She liked him best in blue. His suit at their wedding had been blue, feet bare to make a statement, and she had loved that about him, his muted whim-sicality. She'd stood beside him at the altar, arm muscles clenched to keep her bouquet from shaking. Smiling, she had watched his toes throughout the ceremony wishing she too had gone barefoot, as he'd suggested. She was always regretting.

Now she watched him drop the blue sleeve and take the white shirt from the hanger. An omen. She wanted to sob out loud but already he thought she'd gone crazy. He hadn't said it. Only said, in his soft, even voice, that the wife of Chief Fergus had felt strange when baby Stuart was born. Acted different.

"It's normal," he'd said.

She'd wanted to scream that there was nothing normal about Wren, about hands like lumps of flesh, about a baby who made no sound, no fuss, just stared. And she had seen that Fergus baby, with whom there was nothing wrong. When she'd been pregnant with Wren she had touched him.

"His name is Stuart," the Fergus woman had said. "You can hold him if you like. For practice."

And Angie had taken the fat pink baby from the woman, cupping its floppy soft head, and she had rested its warm foreign body against her stretched stomach, where Wren kicked.

No, she did not feel kinship with Mrs. Fergus, who had no reason to feel strange. Instead she felt kinship with the silent Chinese wife of Reg Sinclair, who'd borne the breathtaking baby Lily and then returned to China alone.

Charlie leaned into the crib and pulled Wren into his arms. He hugged her small body and laid her next to Angie in bed. He kissed both of them in turn, and Angie wanted to grab his sleeve then, ask if he remembered when it had been just the two of them, when they were perfect, when her nipples weren't huge and cracked and sore and when only he sucked them. But she said nothing. Watched him leave, wiggling his fingers in a silly wave.

Angie looked at Wren, so close she seemed blurry. She could hear Wren's heartbeat, or perhaps her own. Smell the sour milk of Wren's breath, a smell that came from Angie's own body.

Three babies had been the plan. All as lovely as Vivian, as lovely as Darlene's next baby would be too. Hannah, yet to come, with fine fair hair and invisible eyelashes. But Angie would take no more chances. She had read about babies born blue, strangled by the very cord that fed them. About babies born with twisted spines, or red birthmarks that blotch the body

like lakes on a map. Babies born too early, too small, heads soft
and bruised as peaches. Everything out of a mother's hands.

What's in a hand? Darlene had asked.

In Wren's there are bits of nail in odd places, sharp, needing to
be clipped. Wren with little scratches, some that bleed, but still she
does not cry. Not until today, this day that stays with Angie always.

Angie wakes with a pain in her head, behind the eyes. She
tries to sleep again but Wren beside her lies awake, watching,
keeping Angie alert and edgy. Off and on it rains and Angie
hears drops hitting the screen, smells the soil dampening. The
rain makes her drowsier still, lids heavy, mouth slack, and just
as she is sinking into sleep, Wren cries. Loud, wailing sobs, and
Angie sits up. She looks at Wren. Her head throbs. The muscles
in her neck and shoulders are tight and knotted. Wren cries and
cries, a new sound, and Angie's headache swells. She squeezes
Wren's cat-thin arms above the elbows and hisses, "Stop it!" but
Wren keeps on, wails harsh and crackly, narrow eyes bulging.
Angie tries to take full deep breaths, in through the nose, out
through the mouth. The thing to do would be to pick Wren up,
walk her, cradle her, whisper *hush-hush* or sing a song. But Angie
has read about mothers who've shaken their babies to death.
Tiny bones in the neck snapping.

Angie is outside in her fitted blue wool skirt, and she has not
brushed her hair or her teeth. The skirt itches and is too tight.
There will be red lines when she removes it. Sore wiggly ones
around her waist and down her hips where the seams dig in.
Last year it had fit perfectly. Wren was inside her then, the size
of a lima bean, no deformities apparent.

Angie squints in the sunlight and smells the musty fall air. Wren
is silent in her pram and together they make their way to the river.

Angie avoids looking at Wren, though she can sense the baby's weird eyes on her. The wind is cool and damp. It has been some time since Angie was outside. Fall still reminds her of school, new binders and a pencil case with a stiff zipper. Angie thinks of Judith Dean, who was obese and had a club foot. At recess Judith played tag with the others, always It. Angie can almost touch the memory. Fat Judith lurching after them on a built-up shoe. Wren too will be It. Will chase, arms outstretched, shiny hands keeping the others running, squealing, hearts racing with fear and elation.

At the shore Angie parks the pram and removes her shoes, hoists her tight skirt up around her hips, where it stays put. She takes Wren in her arms and wades into the water, warm for fall. She can feel Wren's breath on her neck, smell the milkiness of it. In the water Angie's feet are magnified and astonishingly white. She spreads her toes wide and digs them into the sand. Wren's blanket slips from her shoulder and a corner of it dips into the water. Angie moves further out. The water is thigh-high now. She looks at Wren's curled-up hand and wraps her own hand around it, around the tiny fingers and the long-neglected nails, paper thin. With her teeth she peels the soft whites of Wren's nails from one hand, then the other. Slowly she lowers the child into the water, her pink sleeper deepening to fuchsia. She dunks Wren under and Wren stares up at her from below the surface, bubbles escaping her thin lips. And then, as quickly, Angie pulls her out, numb with the shock of what she has almost done, a secret weight she will now carry always.

More shocking still is Wren, who laughs and laughs for the first time ever. She is only three months old and has never even smiled before. Angie has the strange feeling this laughter is impossible, a miracle. She watches Wren's thin lips stretch into a glorious O and release once more a gurgly laugh, high then low, filling the quiet.

Wren

Wren has since watched her own daughter laugh, and she is watching that now, Brie laughing. There is a bird, a sparrow, trapped in the house and it is flying frantically from room to room, searching for the way out. Delilah, the dog, yaps and pants, circling. Brie doesn't see the bird's desperation, only its wild wings flapping. She squeals, chasing it and Delilah, and Wren follows, opening wide all the windows and doors, wishing, trying to help. She grabs Delilah's collar and holds her back. She cannot show that she is crying inside.

Brie doesn't know that Wren was named after a bird. Not by Angie, but by Charlie, who'd had some hope she might fly.

"A wren is a tiny singing bird," he'd told his daughter, "and your hands are beautiful wings."

Alone in the backyard where no one could see, Wren had flapped her arms gracefully, then eagerly, then frantically. She watched birds and mimicked them—poised, leaning forward, chest filled with air. She craned her neck, tilted her head as birds do and looked at the sky. She blinked big popping blinks with her narrow eyes wide, alert. The breeze lifted the tiny hairs on her arms and she imagined they were feathers. But still she remained grounded. Dismayed, she began to see her hands the way her mother first saw them. Mangled. Raw pink. She hid them in her pockets, in sleeves, in mittens. At school she sat on them and in bed she hid them from herself, beneath the pillow.

Until finally her father suggested her hands might not be wings but rather cocoons in which pupae were metamorphosing into butterflies.

"I should have named you Sara Orange Tip," he told her, "or Dreamy Dusky Wing."

Wren agreed, for even the oblong shape of her hands was pupa-like. A pupa is grotesquely ugly, but beneath the cocoon comes the whir of change. Wormy green caterpillars transforming, taking on thin, bright wings and slender bodies, antennae and long drinking-straw tongues that unroll to reach deep into the centres of flowers.

That's what she was, a butterfly. But his name for her, Bird-Girl, remained.

The sparrow is gone at last. Through the back door and out into the sunny day, soaring slowly away. Delilah yowls and shakes her head, tags jingling. Wren's heart beats less rapidly. She stands on the step watching Brie, who runs into the yard and waves good-bye to the sparrow. Already she's wearing her flower-girl dress, though Darlene's wedding is days away. There's a little grass stain on the skirt, but against the floral pattern it barely shows. Still, Angie would moan to know it, unable to delight even in Brie's love of the frilled sleeves and ruffled skirts, which Wren herself had loathed as a child. Brie is the girl Angie longed for. Eight now, and beautifully normal. Spinning and flapping her arms, she soon slows, and weaves with dizziness until she sinks to the grass in limb-weakening laughter.

Wren, too, had once laid in the grass in Bo-Peep dresses, knowing that if you lay long enough some unafraid creature would crawl on you, never guessing you were human. Maybe a white ladybird, still spotless, freshly reborn. Ladybirds are everyone's favourite beetle, but only a few know the seven-spot ladybird brings good luck. Only a few know the ladybird's blood is a surprising yellow, and that it spews from secret pockets in her knees when she's in danger. Fewer still have seen this happen. Wren was one. It was because she had patience. There should have been a badge for that in Brownies, the way there were badges for knitting or dishwashing. Looking back, she supposes all those badges were for patience, and who could fault that? But at the time she had hated Brownies. She'd never asked to go, and yet suddenly there she was, dressed to match the others in that brown pleated shirt dress with its awful tam and orange scarf. As uncomfortable as her fussy everyday clothes. An Imp, she was, one in a group of five others—Deborah, Lisa, Paula, Kim and Adrienne—all of whom she vaguely knew of from school. It was strange to see them elsewhere, in matching costumes. Not wanting to look into their eyes, it was difficult for Wren to distinguish who was who, and she came to think of them as one person, one overlarge Brownie. Yet, for the first time, she realized everyone knew who she was, whether she knew them or not. And no one wanted to touch her. Which, of course, she had expected. Long before coming she had dreaded the time for holding hands.

"I don't want to be a Brownie," she had told Angie, though even if her mother had asked, Wren would never have told her why.

Wren stood on the table in her uniform while Angie pinned the hem.

"Sure you do," Angie said after a pause. She did not look up. There were pins in her mouth and the words were a mumble. "Quarter turn," she told Wren, and kept pinning, and Wren secretly wished she'd been born to Darlene, whose daughters were never forced to do anything.

Charlie drove Wren to her first meeting. Anxiety ballooned in its quiet way. He kept looking at her, which she wished he would not do. "I'm proud of you," he whispered, which she wished he would not say. He reached over and stroked her hair, hanging long and black from beneath the strange beret.

All she could think was *How could you?* though she had not once asked him not to make her go, never wishing to say out loud what she knew would happen.

What happened was this: you stood around a big fake toadstool made from papier mâché, and you pretended to be a creature of the forest—Imp, Pixie, Sprite, Elf—but surely such creatures were not dressed like this, in brown pleated skirts. Like butter-flies, they would come in all colours and have elaborate embel-lishments, antennae that bobbed in the breeze. When Brown Owl asked them to join hands, she lifted hers out, just slightly, from her body and waited for them to be taken. There passed a long and painful moment until a girl, unaware, folded her hand around Wren's. But then, feeling that strangeness, she looked and screamed and let go. The others began to giggle. Their laughter spluttered forth and spread contagiously from girl to matching girl around the circle. Out of the corner of her eye, Wren watched the girl wipe the hand that had touched Wren's on the skirt of her uniform, and then shake the skirt, now laughing along with the rest. Wren, frozen, waited. She did not cry. There was the angry clap of Brown Owl's hands, and then her sharp words, but Wren did not listen. She kept her head high and looked at the overlarge clock on the gymnasium wall, watching time move slowly. She stood with her arms still lifted until she felt an adult hand on either side, and then the whole circle moved in unison, singing some new song. It felt miraculous, the singing. Wren's voice emerged wobbly and strange, a bird's warble, and she thought, Never mind, you are the Bird-Girl. You're a butterfly. These girls are not strong enough to hold hands with you; so great is your wish to be airborne, you need to be held by adults. Else you'd rise up and float away.

On the drive home she told her father nothing of the hand-holding. Only of the pond in which they'd found their reflections, the enormous fleshy toadstool with its brown stem and the strange, untouchable dolls placed around it. Every pretend thing seemed simply that, pretend. The pond unlike a real pond, only water from the bathroom in a plastic pool. The papier mâché toadstool shiny merely with varnish. Even her own reflection was unlike herself, dressed as it was in a passed-on outfit, little stitch-holes on the sleeves where someone's badges used to be. Brown Owl, too, was only Mrs. Fergus in disguise, wife of the chief of police. Hannah and Vivian's neighbour chanting, *Taa-wit, Taa-wit, Taa-wooo!* and rounding up on the balls of her feet with each hoot. She sounded nothing like an owl. This Wren knew. She had listened to real owls. She told Charlie the pretend things were silly, since the real ones existed not far from here, as she knew from the places he had taken her, and even from the times she had ventured no further than the back-yard. What was the point in a fake school-gymnasium forest when the real forest was just down the street?

"I don't want to be a Brownie," she said matter-of-factly, making sure no spot on her face quivered to give her away, not her lip or her nostrils.

But week after week she was delivered there. Always at the beginning and end was the circle and the long moment, a ritual now. Brown Owl looked the other Brownies hard in the eyes, silently willing two to come forward and set an example for the rest. Wren looked only at the loudly ticking clock and wished the moment over. Each time it would end with adult hands in hers. Brown Owl's fingers secretly tickling her palm.

Until once.

The hand that folded around hers was warm, and softer than Brown Owl's. Softer than Vivian's too, and more slender. Wren felt the warmth transfer to her own cool hand and then rush up her arm and through her whole self, feet included. She turned to look at the girl beside her, who was smiling and had long dark hair, almost like Wren's, but thick and shiny. The golden brown of her skin shamed the drab brown of her uniform. The hat sat just right on her head.

"I'm Lily," the girl whispered.

"I'm Wren," whispered Wren.

Afterwards Brownies seemed less awful. Lily didn't ever try to speak to her, or befriend her in any ordinary way, but Wren didn't mind. What did she know of ordinary? At least Lily stood faithfully on her left each time they formed the circle. For that Wren thought she probably loved Lily, and felt sure that in time they'd be closer. Bird-Girl, Flower-Girl. Meanwhile, she concentrated on getting her badges. Soon the shining gold emblems ran down each sleeve. Vivian scoffed, showing her jealousy, and Hannah, only little, drew on her own sleeves with marker that would not wash out. Wren had never been copied before.

She began to look forward to Wednesday night Brownies, until the night Lily was not there. Nor was she in school the next day or the next. It was said she had pneumonia, that she was wasting away, and Wren imagined her lying wan against white sheets, her blue-black hair sickly tangled.

"I want to send a card," she told Charlie, and she set about drawing. She curled her strange, malformed hand around the pencil and beautifully drew herself and Lily, holding hands, wearing brown. Brown saucer hats on their heads at jaunty angles. Inside she wrote, *To Lily, Get Well Soon, From Wren*.

The card was delivered to Lily's large brick house on the rich side of town. Wren's own hand pushed it through the slot in the door, which she held open briefly and peered through. Seeing only plush green carpet and a dining-room chair with arms.

But Lily did not respond. Two weeks later she returned to school, and to Brownies, but she did not take her place in the circle beside Wren. She looked wan and fragile, all the more beautiful, still with her easy smile and her xylophone laugh. She has amnesia, thought Wren, from the pneumonia.

The humiliating image of the card stayed with her. She could see the rough blue paper and the figures, too carefully drawn.

That night in the car she cried, a thing she did so rarely that Charlie sat stunned and speechless behind the wheel. He grabbed her hand and held it, even while he changed gears, and he did not drive home but rather all around town, along the waterfront, all the way up to the highway, and then back down again, taking Townline Road, her favourite for the many dips, and the fact that you could best hear crickets there.

"Bird?" he said softly.

Wren just sobbed. She leaned her head back in the seat and knocked her hat off by accident.

"What happened?" he asked.

All at once Wren ceased crying. She looked at Charlie with a blank, tired face and he pulled the car over to the side of the road.

"They think what I have is contagious," she said, because that seemed the simplest way to explain it.

Charlie sighed. He squeezed the hand he was holding and kissed it. "They should be so lucky," he said.

Wren did not catch his meaning and so smiled with her mouth only. Inside she felt an overwhelming sadness, greater than the one she had had before telling him. What was sad was that he couldn't help, not the way he used to, when he told her about the tiny singing bird, and then later, about Sara Orange Tip. She had never before noticed how powerless he was. Now, as she thought this, there came the sick, guilty feeling for thinking it, piled onto the sadness. But it did not show on her face. She lifted her head so that her neck grew long and slender. She smiled again at Charlie, crinkling her eyes this time and urging warmth into them, and she turned to look out the window at the road ahead, a signal that he should drive on.

The skin around her eyes was tight from crying, but that was all. In minutes the tightness would be gone, and only the two of them would ever know this had happened.

That night in bed she lay listening to her parents in the room next to hers.

"I just don't see why she has to go. She hates it," Charlie said.

"She doesn't hate it. She's got badges up and down her arms, for crying out loud."

"But she doesn't want to go. She *never* wanted to go."

"Don't be ridiculous. What little girl doesn't want to go to Brownies?"

"*Our* little girl, Ange."

"Nonsense."

"Hannah and Vivian don't go. They don't seem to be suffering."

"Look again, Charlie."

"What does that mean?"

"I am not my sister."

"What does *that* mean?"

"Ssshhh!"

Some nights, like this one, it seemed there was less air inside. So Wren crept along the hallway, past her parents' room, and down the carpeted steps that made no sound and out into the night, where she found the dome of stars and the moon shining down in its varying forms of roundness. Her Uncle Mick had given her this idea. He would lie outside with her cousins, Hannah and Vivian, and point out all the constellations, which he knew by heart. Hannah said the stars smelled metallic, and Wren thought that, although it sounded crazy, on cold nights she might just be right.

The owls and the crickets made sounds in the darkness, speaking a language unknown but familiar. That was her favourite night pastime, to lie and listen, closing her eyes to tune in the sounds more keenly. Once she opened them to find a raccoon staring down into her face, black eyes shining and black nose twitching. It held an egg in its hands, which it turned and turned, looking all the while at Wren, unblinking.

"Hello," she said.

It was hard to believe raccoons were vicious. This one did not seem so, and she wondered if, like people, some were gentler than others.

Vivian

As Hannah's VW pulls into town, her sister Vivian is still miles away, riding from Toronto in a rust-and-blue Dodge, wide as a boat. She has taken the long route, zigzagging up and up and up, edging northwest instead of northeast, cruising the lake country in her old jalopy. Windows down, she smokes cigarette after cigarette and enunciates with a fitting accent each place name on the population signs she passes.

The names pull her forward, determine her route. Last summer she did a prairie trip based only on names. Map spread on the seat beside her, she went where the words took her, arching north along the Bruce Peninsula before hopping a ferry to Manitoulin Island, where there were Kaboni and Buzwah and Tehkummah, and not just Wikwemikong but Wikwemikonsing. The smaller the place, the better the name. From here she moved west through Manitoba, following the Yellowhead Highway, which showed as a yellow head on the map, and on to Saskatchewan, where she came upon Eyebrow and Elbow. She thought she could have stayed there, in Saskatchewan, so bewitching were the rolling hills and the sagebrush and the ever-swaying grasses. Vivian, who could usually remain impassive, here could not do so. She sat in her car on the side of the road and watched a storm blow in all the way from Alberta. She found herself thinking of Mick. Of how he would have stood in open-mouthed wonder in such a place. But in his thirty-five years her father had never made it this far, not for lack of enthusiasm, she now realized, but for a glut of it. Any place he went was a wonder to him. He had to see it inside out before he could go elsewhere. He could have lived in the Ottawa Valley forever, lost in dendrology, and in the end, he did. A short forever.

In this way, she was not her father's daughter. As soon as she knew it was possible, what Vivian wanted was to be as far from the Valley as she could be. In a place where trees grew from holes in the sidewalks, or from enormous concrete planters, not nearly enormous enough for roots that longed to spread every which way. Where the prevalent birds were pigeons and wailing, scavenging gulls.

Why, then, had she felt this surge of warmth? For it had not only come in Saskatchewan, but also at other times, unexpectedly. An unfamiliar tenderness invading her when she could see both the front of a population sign and the back of its twin just down the road. That a place could be so tiny.

And yet she would not live anywhere but a city, the bigger the better. She even likes the noise and the hot summer smell of exhaust and softening pavement. Longs for that now, as she meanders north through Catchacoma.

Sorry I couldn't make it to the wedding, Mom. I caught a coma.

There would be no surprise on Darlene's part if Vivian didn't make it to the wedding. Lasting anger, certainly, but no surprise. Just as there would be no surprise on Vivian's part if her mother didn't make it either. Who knew, she might call off the wedding at the last moment for love of melodrama.

The story went that on the day Darlene had married Mick, she locked herself in the bathroom moments before the ceremony and refused to come out. Refused also to let anyone in, not Angie or even her own dismayed mother. Mick waited in the yard with the guests, under a rented marquee, Charlie beside him. People coughed and whispered.

Eventually, Grandpa Gillis appeared, brideless. He walked alone down the shorn-grass aisle to where Mick stood, and he held his palms out to the air.

"Sorry, son," he said, "she's not up to it today."

And that might have been it, it might have all been over, had Mick not emerged fuming from beneath the marquee, had he not taken the stairs to the bathroom two at a time and pounded both fists on the door.

"What did she say?" Hannah and Vivian asked.

"Nothing," Mick told them, grinning. "Just *boo-hoo-hoo*. You know your mother."

"And what did *you* say?"

"Let me IN!" he boomed in that voice he saved for manliness.

"And did she?"

"Of course!"

"And then what did you do?"

"I threw her in the tub and ran cold water all over her."

"With her dress on and everything?"

"With her dress on and everything."

"That's where Vivvy came about," Darlene added, giggling. "In the tub at Grandma's place."

Mick would tell that story with the wry smile of someone joking, and afterwards he would hug Darlene and call her a real piece of work.

"What!" Darlene laughed. "I just wanted to see how much you loved me."

Oh, he loved her. All her stalling caused her red-rose posy to wilt and droop, and when she saw it was ruined she almost started crying all over again.

"What did you do?" the girls asked him.

"I grabbed her hand and took her out to the garden and picked a proper rose for her, thorns and all. That was all she carried. One bloom."

Vivian thought of that story every time they drove six towns down the highway to Grandma Gillis's. And, once there, the tub glowed white in her peripheral vision whenever she walked by it in the hall. It was strange to know the very place you were created, and stranger still to bathe in it. She often wondered, what if he had given up and gone home instead of climbing into that tub?

Once she asked him, "How different would we be now if you had married someone else?"

He thought a moment and then said plainly, "Well, you wouldn't *be* at all. Even if you'd been conceived on a different day, by the same parents, you'd be someone else completely."

He always told the very naked truth to Vivian and gave Hannah the better version.

Vivian turns east, through Algonquin Park, with the Oxtongue River running along beside her. This is so close to home, and yet they had come here only once as children, daughters though they were of a silviculturist. Vivian smirks at the word. What Mick did was nothing fancy, tending trees at the forestry and following the orders of the scientists there, like Uncle Charlie, who strove to help nature make a better, stronger tree. And yet the job was part of who Mick was, his rough hands with ever-present soil in the prints of his fingers and under his nails.

She thinks, *Reg Sinclair,* and laughs at how silly it seems that this peripheral man, this shoe-store man, will marry her mother.

Unrolling her window, she breathes in pine, a smell that brings the scratch of their needles to her skin, and also the memory of herself and Hannah and Wren in miniature, wearing tiny clothes and shoes, and taking many tiny steps to get around. Closer to the ground back then, and so looking there more often, inspecting spotted ladybirds and slugs and June bugs that crunched like hard candy when you stepped on them. When Hannah was a baby, it was just Vivian and her cousin Wren, holding hands, a mangled and an ordinary one, palms pressed together. Wren's hand was narrow, clammy, yet so often in Vivian's, it felt wholly normal. Two daughters of forestry men, they'd moved like dryads through the woods, which from outside looked impenetrable, but inside held paths that sneaked maze-like between the trees. The floor springy, spongy, below small bare feet, layers of leaves and bark and rusty pine needles and soil. Vivian in stretchy size 6X shorts and a T-shirt, and Wren dressed up, as always, carrying her buckle shoes and wearing a blue checkered dress with extra-long sleeves and a slip underneath, and in her wispy dark hair a blue checkered bow, meant to keep the strands in place but slowly slipping off.

Beneath the rocks and soggy leaves they found faceless worms and hard grey beetles with lines on them. Wren told Vivian, "If you cut a worm into seven pieces, he'll heal himself and become seven new worms," and Vivian, skeptical, dangled one from her fingers, looking for something sharp to slice him with. When she found a sliver of stone Wren cried, "No! You have to know just the right place!" but Vivian went ahead anyhow. When they returned the next day they found the annelids hardening, purplish in places, all the life vanished through open wounds.

It had pained Wren, the killing, but life went on. Vivian had known that even then. The death of a worm—of seven worms—was no great misfortune.

The year before that, when Vivian was five, Darlene gave birth to Hannah, and Vivian gave birth to four babies of her own beneath a bally pink blanket in Wren's room, two boys and two girls. She kept the blanket pulled up to her chin and slid the babies out the side, handing them to Wren, who was nurse, husband and father, and even though Wren didn't feel like playing, she tenderly wrapped each baby in patterned paper towel and lined them up on the bed beside Vivian.

Mick planted a tree in Hannah's honour and called it the Hannah Tree. It grew more slowly than Hannah, who, though weed-tall and toothy, remained for a long time almost bald, with only a fine fan of stand-up hair that changed from red to blonde to red again.

"What if it never grows in?" said Darlene to Mick.

"Don't be ridiculous," he told her. He ran a hand over the spray of hair, and as the hair bounced back, his smile spread.

"Don't you care if she's hairless?"

Mick rolled his eyes. *"Hairless,"* he scoffed. "You make her sound like some kind of exotic dog."

"I'm asking you!"

Vivian heard the change in her mother's voice, a stridency that came as quickly as it went. She touched her own hair, white-blonde, not thick but covering as much of her scalp as a hat would. She looked at Hannah, who had quickly become Hannah Banana, then Banana, then Bee, and Hannah looked back. Her tuft stood up and her eyebrows did too.

Maybe Mick moved out all those years later because Darlene was ridiculous, as well as for that other reason, left undiscussed.

Once he was gone, even though he had only moved downtown, everything changed. For a long while they ate wieners for dinner every night, sometimes with buns, sometimes without. Darlene stopped combing her hair, and Vivian's too, though by now Vivian was ten—old enough to comb her own hair but often choosing not to. Even Hannah's hair, which had grown surprisingly thick, hung in a long, knotty ponytail from which the bauble would sometimes have to be cut free.

It was Angie who suggested dating. But Darlene, true blue, blew out a long sigh and said she never wanted another man.

"I love my husband," she told Angie, and she blinked her puffy eyes slowly.

"I hate to say this, Dee, but I don't think he's coming back," said Angie. She said Darlene should at least come to a beach party for Charlie's work.

"For Charlie's work?" screeched Darlene. "What if Mick is there?"

But Angie shook her head. "It's only for the scientists," she said. Of which Mick was not one. She said a man named Tim would be there. It wouldn't be like a date. She could bring a jellied salad. She could bring Hannah and Vivian and just see.

"Well," said Darlene, "I suppose."

She perked up as the days passed. She took Hannah and Vivian to Footworks and bought them each new shoes—platform wedgie sandals for herself that tied high on her calves, and for Hannah and Vivian, stiff patent-leather shoes with buckles, all wrong for the beach.

"These have more class than a flip-flop," said Darlene, and Reg Sinclair, who owned the shoe shop, agreed. He said they could wear them to church as well, and Darlene said, "True enough," though they had never been to church in all of their lives.

Vivian glowered at Darlene, who smiled too much at Reg Sinclair and wiggled pumiced toes on the foot ruler, toenails gleaming. She let her skirt slide high on her tanned thighs, insisting Reg measure both feet, just to check that all was as it should be, which of course it was, Darlene being perfect.

In the days leading up to the beach party, Darlene bought three new perfumes—one thickly musky, one sweet and berry-ish, one fresh as squeezed lemons. Fragrant clouds wafted around her as she walked up and down the hall to break in her new sandals. Hannah walked too, to soften the leather, taking gentle steps to avoid cracking it.

"You should break those in, Vivvy," said Darlene, but Vivian's distaste for the shiny shoes was enormous.

On the day of the party they walked to the beach because Darlene felt the extra time in the sun would give them that healthy glow.

"We'll have a bit of an edge on the others," she said.

But during the walk, a blister quickly grew on Vivian's foot and throbbed and throbbed. She took off her shoe to look, and all around the watery bubble was pink achy skin. Vivian sank down in the sand, twisting her leg so that her heel touched only air. Darlene struggled on, not noticing, holding Hannah's hand, and when finally she turned she was so far away that Vivian could feel but not see her green eyes narrow.

"Come on, Viva! *Vite-vite!*" she sing-songed. She let go of Hannah's hand and wobbled a step closer to Vivian.

"I can't," whined Vivian. "It hurts." She watched Hannah kick sand and saw the sun glint briefly on her patent-leather shoes.

"Just a bit further, Sweet Pea! You can do it!" Darlene stood with her hands shading her eyes. Her wraparound sunglasses rested on top of her head, holding her hair in place.

Vivian shook her head. She looked at the blister, now throbbing so intensely that even the air around it hurt.

"Vivvy!" called Darlene, less musically. "Come on!"

Again Vivian shook her head. It was hard to know if dipping her foot in the river might make it feel worse or better. She spread out on the sand. She could sense Darlene moving quickly towards her.

"*Get up,*" hissed Darlene. "Now." She leaned over Vivian and the freshly trimmed ends of her hair brushed Vivian's cheek. Darlene's eyes darted back and forth, looking together into one of Vivian's, then the other. She tightly grabbed Vivian's arm above the elbow and pulled, but Vivian pulled back and away. "Get up," she said again, and she spelled out n-o-w to show she meant it.

"*N-o,*" said Vivian, knowing as she spelled it that she'd gone too far.

Darlene's eyes widened, then squinted. She sat in the sand in her blue wrap skirt and grabbed Vivian's ankle in one hand, the hard new shoe in the other. Her face tightened as she rammed the shoe on, slapping the base of the heel with the palm of her hand. Vivian felt the full blister burst and the slippery water ooze out. Her foot and her heart and the backs of her eyes stung. Darlene's face softened. She lowered Vivian's foot on to the sand and rubbed her calf. Then she put her hand in Vivian's and pulled her up.

"Come on, Viva. The party's starting."

Vivian took in Tim. He was not a strapping man. His hair was dark greasy brown and his skin had a yellowy cast. Today he would burn in the sun. His shoulders sloped and black hair grew on them. There was hair on his chest and back too, the blackness a contrast to his sallow flesh. He had breasts. Small, true, but unmanly. Big nipples pointing. Darlene lapped him up. She sprawled beside him on the sand, one leg crossed over the other, foot swaying in its new wedgie sandal. She laughed so loudly, so often, that hot shame bled into Vivian's face and neck.

Charlie roasted wieners.

"No," said Vivian boldly, when he offered one. "It's all my mother ever cooks."

She reached in front of him and took three buns from the grill, ate each of them slicked with mustard. She looked at the jellied salads with their trapped, suspended fruit and shreds of carrot. She ate a devilled egg. Eggs were abortions, she had read that. She picked up another and tongued the lump of red-sprinkled yellow, placed the firm white back on the platter. Inside her shoe was sand and raw skin. Water would wash it away. Water would soften the shoes, like with buffalo sandals. She limped to the shore and walked along it, stepping on soft dead minnows. She let the blistered foot slip in, and after three steps heard her mother's high, false laugh.

"Viva!" Sing-songy. "You'll ruin those shoes!"

A pause.

A giggle.

What was funny?

Cool water swished between Vivian's toes.

"Come out, please, Sweet Pea."

Vivian turned and stepped the other way, letting the right foot slip in, because now that heel was raw too.

"Vivian!"

With each step her shoe made a splurching noise and a footprint appeared and dissolved in an instant. And then, just as quickly, Darlene's wedgie sandals were beside her own shoes, water splashing up around them, the canvas wet. Polished toenails peering out.

"Get those shoes out of the water." Top teeth and bottom teeth clenched together, all lined up. "You're making a fool of me." Hands around Vivian's wrist like an Indian sunburn, then long fingernails pinching the fat part of her arm. Darlene's now-unpretty red face was close to Vivian's, sweet breath and too many mingled perfumes.

Strangers and the man named Tim sat staring. Wren, out in the water, stared. Angie stared. Charlie burned four wieners, staring.

Vivian pulled the awful shoes from her feet and threw them one by one through the air. That was a beautiful moment. Everything stopped. The shoes seemed to move in slow motion and everyone's eyes followed them. Except Hannah's. The shoes flew high over her head and never once did she look up from her castle, though her cheeks flushed dark with hot blotches.

Hannah

Hannah was four then, or five—she can never remember—but she remembers the day itself clearly, especially the castle, which had a moat and a bark drawbridge. With her finger she scooped out an arched doorway and then three more just like it. Passing time. What she needed to do was take her bucket into the water and fill it up with the wettest sand, but Darlene was there with Vivian, and they were splashing around. Hannah wanted to be small, out of the way, so she stayed beside her castle, making doors and windows with her finger. Sand seemed bigger when it was wet, the individual grains more permanent. Some of them sparkled. She drilled a window in the roof for watching stars. A bird flew over her head and then another bird, following close. They landed behind her, *thud, thud.*

Everything was quiet now. Hannah looked at her pail. She could take it and rinse it out, fill it up again. Instead she got up and turned away from the water. She walked to where her Uncle Charlie was and stood beside him. The wieners were scarred black and there were new raw ones beside them. She walked further up the beach, past Angie and the man named Tim. Soon a voice might call out, *Hey, Missy, where do you think you're going?* That's what Mick would say. If he were here he would catch her, sneaking off in her sandy, broken-in shoes, grab her under her armpits and whirl her in too many circles, then back the other way to let her unwind. That was what she wanted now. She disappeared from the beach and hurried up the tree-lined path to the street.

From here she wasn't sure of the way to his place, but if she had to she could find him by smell. She was made from him. Soon she would be sitting on his blue plaid chesterfield, watching the blobs of the lava lamp that moved the way the blobs inside her did when things went wrong. They were moving now. Swelling and deflating in her stomach with the wieners. She could poo when she got there, and then she'd feel better. He would set a place for her at the marbly red table with chrome legs, laying down the plastic placemat that said *Hanna*, spelled wrong in flowers, and he would pour lemonade and not ask questions, even if she cried, which she would not do, not if she was there. He would tug her pigtails. On his half-fridge would be pictures of her and of Vivian. Some of Darlene. And three fridge magnets—a V, an H and a D—which he had stolen from their fridge, saying, *Ssshhh,* and pressing his finger to his lips.

Sometimes Hannah didn't know: did she remember a thing happening, or just the photograph because she had seen it so often?

But in his apartment there was nowhere to go. The kitchen was in the living room and the bedroom was in there too. There was a big window, but only the small bottom part of it opened, and so the place was hot and stuffy. The air that came in was like someone blowing on you, nice but not enough.

Where could she go? She stood on the sidewalk and watched the passing cars. She was wearing just her orange swimsuit and shiny new shoes. She looked at her legs, now starting to marble with sunburn. She pressed a finger to her thigh and made a white spot that quickly reddened again. The sand had scratched her shoes. She licked a finger and squatted, rubbed at the scratches. The scratches would not rub off and now there were smear marks too. She could see a blurry version of herself in each shoe, pieces of her missing near the toes, where the cut-out diamond shapes were. She had almost cried but the urge for that was over. Even her stomach had settled. Now it just felt like a regular poo in there, waiting, not one that moved and swelled inside her.

She would return to the beach because they would be worried. Perhaps they'd already called Chief Fergus and were hunting for her. A special police dog sniffing her left-behind dress.

No one had noticed.

Hannah slipped off her shoes and wiggled her feet into the sand. Wren was in the water and Vivian was further out on the raft, where she was not supposed to be. Darlene lay on a towel, and the man named Tim was spreading lotion on her back. Pressing hard, like kneading dough. Hannah circled around behind everyone, the way she had left, and went back to her castle.

Today was Saturday, so pink, her least favourite. The colour was milky, opaque, and it hung around all day—from the time she woke, just before she opened her eyes, right through to bedtime and on past it, when she was dreaming. Even by Sunday, which was black, that Saturday hue often lingered till breakfast, like a dream you could and could not remember.

Wren

The fight was ugly, but nothing new.

Wren waded into the river, and the shouting grew faint. She listened to the *lap-lap* of the water against the string of plastic floats that marked the drop-off, and watched two damselflies flutter by in tandem, one with red wings and one with wings that were colourless. She floated on her back and felt the sun heating one side of her while the water cooled the other. Her ears were submerged and she noticed that the water itself had a sound, like monotone wind. She could hear herself breathing. Then she squatted in the water, so that only her eyes and the top of her head rose above it, the way a frog's do.

From here she could see that Darlene had hold of Vivian's elbow. Her new shoes, as well as Vivian's, were in the water now, which made the fight seem crazy, and uglier still. Wren watched, froglike, as Vivian lifted one leg, then the other, and pulled the shoes from her feet, not bothering to unbuckle them. First one, then the other shoe flew twirling through the air and arced over Hannah, who sat building a sandcastle. Everyone but Hannah looked and looked away. Darlene and Vivian watched the flying shoes, then turned back to each other. Vivian's wiry body was stiff and unflinching, but Darlene released a long sigh. Wren could see that by the sudden droop of her tanned shoulders. Her mouth was gently moving and she put her hand out to touch Vivian's hair, but

Vivian jerked her head back and waded further out. Darlene watched her for a moment and then she, too, turned and walked away. Left the shoes lying sole-side-up in the sand.

Wren frog-legged a few strokes and floated on her stomach, face down, eyes open. There were trails in the sand down there, paths that shells had made themselves. Just as she lifted her face from the water, she saw the damselflies land near Vivian, releasing their eggs. Vivian reached forward and flicked the insects with her finger. Startled, they flew apart and then turned and flew into each other and away again. Wren swallowed the need to react. She ignored Vivian and watched the damselflies dance through the air, not the straight-ahead buzz of the dragonfly, but butterfly flight, slow and tangential, coming to rest with their wings uplifted.

"You're lucky you didn't hurt them," she said after a while, not looking at Vivian. "It brings bad luck. If you kill one, it means someone in your family is destined to die." It was both true and untrue at the same time. The omen wasn't about the damselfly but the dragonfly. Anyway, Vivian did not know the difference, nor did she deserve to.

Vivian rolled her eyes, dunked herself in the water and rose out with her hair slicked to her head.

"Everybody's destined to die, Wren." Spoken with a flat, cruel voice.

Wren thought that Vivian must be the person she loved most in the world, but also the person she most hated. When Vivian was angry she held herself so tight that her bones and raised veins seemed too close to the surface. She looked like that now, tiny but strong and wiry, her eyes mean green.

For a time they floated side by side on their backs. The water was flat, waveless, until a motorboat passed and set them swaying. The water stilled again, and Vivian stood and spoke.

"It's a public beach," she said, looking at the long stretch of sand. "My dad could come by any time, even if he wasn't invited. You don't have to be a scientist to come to the beach. And look at her with that gross man."

Vivian shuddered and dove into the water. She swam under the floats and made her way out to the raft, where she was not allowed to go.

Wren, heart racing, glanced to the beach to see if Darlene had noticed. But no, she was laughing with the stranger. There was something about Darlene that could make your body heat up when you watched her, causing you shame for watching, and so Wren looked away to her own mother, and then to the shoes on the sand, to Hannah's castle. But where was Hannah? She searched the beach with her eyes and tried to suppress the lurching feeling that something bad had happened, or surely would. She thought of the damselfly and the half-lie omen, perhaps destined to come true because her own mouth had spoken the words. What was awful was that Vivian's family was Wren's family too. She had cursed them all.

And then she saw her: a speck of orange emerging through the trees, standing gangly in only her shoes and bathing suit, holding the tip of a long, hanging willow branch. Wren's heart filled up. She had a special love for Hannah, who lived in some world of her own. A special fear that she could easily go missing.

Now she surveyed the beach again, just to check that everyone remotely connected to her was there. Her Aunt Darlene, her own mother and father, and Tim, who did not seem the awful man Vivian saw but was no Mick either. Mick whose beauty matched Darlene's, Mick who was always smiling. Almost. She thought of his ashen face that night he had come to her house with sleepy Hannah and Vivian, who'd been livid and wide awake.

She shook the thought away, plunged into the water and frog-legged under the floats and back, not emerging until she was on the allowed side. Angie made her be careful but she was a fabulous swimmer, seeming surely to the minnows like some strange new form of mermaid, a distant relative of the little mermaid, from that story Vivian had once read aloud. Ever since she could read, which was early, Vivian had loved to read aloud, and the stories drifted in and out of Wren's mind, but this one had stayed. She'd called it up when she'd first learned to swim, and ever after when she was in water. Wren, some lovely hybrid creature. It was the only way she could have got through swimming lessons, which at first had been excruciating, but now she was glad to have taken them. Better than Brownies in the long run. You bit your lip through the hard parts, was all, until soon you were underwater, where there wasn't anything strange about strange hands. Look at ducks. The flappy hands of fish, too close to their bodies. There were even people like that, armless, so Wren was lucky. Underwater it was fine to have webs; better, even. And though Wren's hands were not webbed, exactly, they might look that way moving quickly as she swam.

The worst part of the lessons had been standing tall and skinny in the sand, so exposed. There were no pockets in a bathing suit. If she'd had the kind that was a dress with panties, like baby-doll pyjamas, a lovely frill around the edge, she could have tucked her hands beneath the loose skirt while she stood on the beach with the other small swimmers, listening to the droning instructor. She could have stood casually that way, no one noticing. But she did not have that kind of bathing suit. Instead she had a red bikini, its top decorated with three buttons that buttoned nothing. She had chosen it herself, not thinking.

Hanging on its little plastic hanger, it had seemed beautiful. She had not stopped to picture herself in it. Her mother had not approved, perhaps knowing, but Wren had pleaded, and at her first lesson had stood wearing it. The stretch of her long torso making too big a space between top and bottom. Nowhere to put her hands. The other bodies were so tiny with their curved and golden limbs. *Can you guess which one is not like the other?* Dressed always in her dark hair and white skin that would not tan, not ever. Black, white, red she was. Stark and ugly.

Please let us go in the water. It seemed he might never stop talking, that instructor who on regular days was just another boy.

In the water her red suit became beautiful again, changing from tomato red to crimson. She could hide her hands in the river, and anyway, they were special in there. Mermaid hands. Not her legs joined but her fingers, webbed in a way, made for swimming. Little Mermaid. She heard Vivian's croaky voice tell the sad, sad story.

> *The little mermaid drew back the crimson curtain of the tent, and beheld the fair bride with her head resting on the prince's breast. She bent down and kissed his fair brow, then looked at the sky on which the rosy dawn grew brighter and brighter; then she glanced at the sharp knife, and again fixed her eyes on the prince, who whispered the name of his bride in his dreams. She was in his thoughts, and the knife trembled in the hand of the little mermaid: then she flung it far away from her into the waves; the water turned red where it fell, and the drops that spurted up looked like blood. She cast one more lingering, half-fainting glance at the prince, and then threw herself from the ship into the sea, and thought her body was dissolving into foam.*

Wren imagined she swam with the grace of that mermaid. How could she not? All that water joined to her, moving with her, made her more like a sea creature than any old bird or butterfly. *Nameless little mermaid, that's who I am.*

But when she climbed out, she was shivering. Sand caked her long, flat feet and her white body pimpled. So skinny and tall was she that her belly button was oval, not round. The top of her bikini, with its useless buttons, gaped soggily and there was nowhere, not one safe place, to hide her hands.

Smock-and-panties was the kind of bathing suit she had now. It was yellow with large pink flowers, and like most of Wren's clothes, it had been sewn by Angie. If she could have, Wren would have worn it all summer, like a dress. But her mother would never allow such a thing. If Wren pointed out, as she had often done, that Hannah and Vivian wore whatever they wanted, Angie would just shrug and say, "All the more reason."

Still, the suit was the first outfit Wren had loved in all of her ten years. The first thing she'd had that made her like the way she looked, despite her hands. Staring into her river reflection, she wondered if she might be beautiful.

Hannah

Hannah carries her bags down the hallway, and with her toe softly pushes open the door to her room. In here old sorrow hangs in the heavy, humid air. The room is Saturday pink, the colour of Pepto-Bismol, always unsettling. Pink wallpaper. Pink paint. How badly Hannah had wanted blue.

"Pink's cheerier, Girly," said Darlene. "Blue would only bring you down. That's why they call it 'the blues.'"

Darlene soaked her roller in the pool of pink and spread it on.

"See?" she said. "Gorgeous!"

She dipped her finger in the paint and touched it to Hannah's nose.

"Plus, you're a bit of a blue Sue already, Banana. You could use some cheeriness in your room."

Tim was in charge of the wallpaper, a boy job. Because the big pink flowers turned this way and that, it was hard to tell which way was up, causing Tim to roll one panel on upside down. No one noticed right away. Not until the end, late in the day, when Vivian came in and immediately pointed at it.

There was a silent moment.

"Oops," said Tim. He bent and picked at a stuck-on corner.

Vivian laughed out loud at Tim, and Darlene glared at her. Hannah stared at the mismatched flowers and at Tim's hand touching them.

"It doesn't matter," said Darlene.

But it was plain that it did. Darlene's cheeks flushed their own shade of pink and she slapped Tim's hand away from the seam, a long length that now glowed in a way the rest of the room did not.

"You'll never notice it," said Darlene to Hannah. "Not after a while anyway."

Which was untrue. There was rarely a day she didn't notice it, maybe never a day. She even noticed it in bed, in the dark, when she herself was in a way upside down. She ran her hand along it, feeling its wrongness.

It is the first thing she notices now, so many years later. The pink matches the pastel pink bedspread but not the cowboy curtains she loves, which billow in the breeze. Now, with the door open, the breeze moves the air in the room, stirring up the sadness. Some of Hannah's things are packed into give-away boxes and others are where they always were. Tucked into her mirror frame is a square school picture of her grinning self, high pigtails in plastic happy-face baubles, small teeth, big teeth, one tooth missing. What had made her smile that way? Perhaps she had been a happy child, after all.

Hannah takes the picture with her to the living room, blowing the dust from it.

"Look how cute you were!" says Darlene, peering over Hannah's shoulder, resting her chin there.

Hannah's mind holds pictures of all kinds of things that maybe did or didn't happen. She closes her eyes and calls them up. Sees through these boxes of Darlene's, through all the things inside them, to the faint ketchup stain on the carpet from one of the times she faked her death. Her heart aches for her younger self, as though now she is someone else. For their lives packed into boxes the way his life was when he died.

"Most of it's going to charity," says Darlene, motioning with the hand that wears her diamond. "Reg has pretty much everything we'll need."

In Hannah's mind is a picture of the grocery-store boxes from which she pulled her father's things, and now there will be a picture of these boxes too, added to visions of a pale green house with yellow doors, the Hannah Tree, the rickety lobster trap, the pot of weedy chives, the rhubarb patch, the trailer under which no grass grows. And her sad, square room painted Saturday pink.

Hannah has always seen the days of the week in colour. Synesthesia, it's called, though if not for Vivian she would never know this.

"There are all sorts of manifestations," Vivian told her recently. "Some people taste shapes. Or they might connect colours with names or words, or even days, like you do. I only read the article because the headline caught my eye and made me think of you. It said, 'Friday is Green.'"

"No, it's not," said Hannah. "It's white. White Friday, pink Saturday, black Sunday, green Monday, light-blue Tuesday, orange Wednesday, blue Thursday."

It wasn't something Hannah had ever thought much about. The colours that came with the days had existed since she had. Now, when she remembers a momentous day, she recalls the colour too, clues that transport her backwards.

Monday, pear green, was the day the divorce came through. Hannah was seven then, or was it eight? It had been three years since he'd left, because that was how long you had to wait for what Darlene called a "friendly divorce," the kind where no one had done anything wrong, and no one had. Though there was a dim memory of wrongness, of a sad and ugly night.

"We just grew apart, Sweet Pea," said Darlene. "That's all."

Sweet peas didn't grow apart. They grew together. They curled their fine green tendrils around each other and the fence out back. They grew like weeds, Darlene said, which in this case was a good thing because sweet peas were not weeds, they were flowers. When weeds grew like weeds it was not so good, though why Hannah did not know.

That Monday Darlene sang twangily about her d-i-v-o-r-c-e. She clicked her fingers and swivelled her hips, pretending to be overjoyed, but her green eyes were puffy and red-rimmed, and eventually she laid a thin slice of cucumber on each one and stretched out on the couch with the afghan and a large bag of ketchup chips. Hannah stood at the edge of the couch and combed Darlene's hair, twisting one lock into a bun, braiding others, and tying in trailing ribbons. Sometimes Darlene moaned, either because it felt good or because she was sadder than sad. Hannah loved to touch her mother's thick hair. She loved to touch her father's hair too, but got to less often. There was less she could do with his, so really it was just as well. Mostly she combed it, blowing out the bits of dandruff that were not cooties but dry skin, and parted it straight down the centre. Vivian said the style made him look pompous and Johann Strauss-ish, but to Hannah he was tidy and handsome this way.

Why didn't they want to be together? Could they not see how perfect they were for each other?

Through the long hot days that followed the divorce, Hannah looked up to keep her tears from dripping. She looked at the puckered tops of curtains, at a cobweb. She could see the fine hairs of her eyebrows. It hurt her eyes, looking up too hard, and it didn't work when she was lying down. Tears in her ears to think of Mick in his tiny apartment with only a hot plate for cooking. Now that the divorce was official there was no chance of him returning. Hannah let all the hope go out of her. For four days she ate only Cheerios.

"Good God, Girly, you're gonna turn into one big O!" said Darlene, mustering some humour.

But she did not. She stayed her same old Hannah way, no matter how little she wanted to be Hannah Oelpke. What she really wanted to be was a Fergus. Hannah Fergus who lived next door with a mom and a dad and a brother. She had always been a Fergus, in a way. Left out of the games that her sister played with Wren, Hannah had been oddly paired with Stuart, the only other child on the block, ever since she could remember. Every spring she helped the Ferguses rake their smelly wet leaves and pick up the flamingos, and the dwarves with their little hats on, and she and Stuart would wipe the dwarves' faces, dirty from lying out all winter.

Stuart Fergus was almost Vivian's age, and Vivian said he was sinister and darkly crazy. Loyal anger welled in Hannah, but she couldn't deny he was strange. Once he'd stood trancelike over their toilet, peeling paper from Darlene's tampons and dropping them in. The tampons had swelled so much they'd plugged the pipes, and the plunger had to be used. Stuart's own mother, Mrs. Fergus, said it wasn't Stuart who did these things. It was the Visitor.

"Uh-oh," she'd say when Stuart went weird. "We have a visitor." She pronounced the word slowly, enunciating *vi-zit-oar* so it buzzed in Hannah's ears. And with the buzz came an icy numbness that quickly spread from her head to her toes, as though she were diving into cold water.

Three years before, when Mick had first left and Darlene had come unstrung, the Ferguses took Hannah everywhere, like a cherished daughter. Chief and Mrs. Fergus collected her at night and took her on pyjama rides to watch bears at the dump. Hannah and Stuart shared one seat belt stretched across their bony, soft-skinned bodies. Hannah wore a purple nightgown that had an itchy lace collar and cuffs, and a gathered pocket large enough for only three fingers, which she kept curled in there. Stuart wore two-piece pyjamas, like a small man's, blue with dark blue piping. Propped by pillows and blankets they watched the road, a long pie lifter with stripes of school-bus yellow down its centre. They kept the windows down, and the cool, lapping air fluttered their pyjamas and made their own hair tickle them.

Sometimes the dump was on fire and there were no bears.

"A bear can smell a fire from miles away," Stuart told her.

They stayed anyway, on those nights. Rested their chins on

the open window and watched flames leap up around the things no one wanted, shadowing them golden. If there were bears, they had to roll the windows back up again, because a bear might maul or at least bite you if it had the chance. Through glass they watched the bears and raccoons rummage through rusted tomato-sauce tins, torn lawn chairs, broken bottles. They watched a bear pick up a peanut-butter jar and swirl his tongue around inside.

"Bears will eat anything," Stuart whispered.

Hannah could feel his breath on her ear. In the dark his eyes glowed like hard marbles.

The same summer that Mick moved out, a neighbour's cat had kittens. Stuart chose one and let Hannah name her Princess Tiara, a name she had picked out long ago in case she was ever allowed to have a pet, even a fish or a hamster. Stuart called the name "high-falutin" and shortened it first to P.T., then down to Pete in one rapid afternoon. Pete was white with blotches of black and orange, and the padded parts of her paws were both pink and black.

When Hannah and Stuart played dress-up they dressed Pete up too, pulling old clothes from a metal trunk in Stuart's basement. Hannah in a shiny pink bridesmaid dress and underneath a dented bra. On her head a half-slip, like a long mane of hair. Stuart in discarded checked golf shorts that reached to his ankles, cinched at the waist with an old pair of nylons. On top a ruffly tuxedo shirt. (For boys there was less to choose from.)

They dressed Pete in a butter-yellow doll's dress with red smocking, and tried to wrap her in a blanket but she began to hiss and scratch. Stuart's eyes went hard and glassy, his mouth a thin, tight line. Hannah felt the churn of panic. Pete's yellow eyes widened and narrowed. She stretched out her paw, and with her claws, made three long slices in Stuart's arm. These puffed up instantly. The cuts shone with blood, but the blood did not drip. Hannah saw the colour leave Stuart's cheeks and lips. She saw his hands tighten around Pete's squirming dressed-up body—its kitten head flopping back and forth—and she thought she saw Pete's eyes look into her own, but the little head was moving so fast now, it was hard to know.

Hannah tasted tears before she knew they were there. She tasted snot and bright pink Avon lipstick.

"Shut up," hissed Stuart, and she knew she was crying out loud.

Stuart stuffed Pete into his shirt, beneath the ruffles which bulged out anyway, and grabbed Hannah's wrist.

"Come on," he said. "And quit blubbering."

In too-big blue high heels it was hard to keep up, but he pulled her up the stairs and outside and through the backyard, over the fence that needed painting and that would give you long painful slivers if you weren't careful, down the grassy slope, across the unpaved New Road, through the cleared lots where sprawling houses would soon be built, and into the woods beyond. Hannah could smell soggy bark and moss and rotting leaves. She could hear her heart beating.

Stuart lifted a rock and revealed scurrying bugs with striped grey shells. With his hands he dug a deep hole in the soft, wet earth and as he worked the lump of Pete swayed in his shirt. Hannah stood watching, scrunching with sweaty hands the satiny skirt of her dress. When he finished, Stuart pulled Pete from his shirt and placed her in the hole, smoothing her yellow dress before pushing dirt over her. Though she was only a kitten, this was Pete's ninth life; Hannah knew it by instinct. She kneeled and helped Stuart, because the faster it was done, the sooner it would be over.

On the way back he stopped at the edge of the woods and waited for her, and she saw that he looked like himself again. He pushed the slip back from her forehead and wiped her face and snotty nose with the long sleeve of his shirt, and he bent down and took the blue high heels from her feet. With his dirty hands he cleaned off what he could of the mud, and when he saw that he might be rubbing the mud into the satin, he put a shoe into each pocket of his voluminous checked shorts and took Hannah's hand and smiled at her.

"What matters most is we didn't mean to," he told her, and over and over she mouthed the words.

They moved through the lots, across New Road, over the fence, through the yard and down into the dark clammy basement where the dress-up trunk still yawned open. They took off their muddy costumes and put on their real-life clothes, and all the while Hannah mouthed, *What matters most is we didn't mean to,* but she did not say one word out loud.

Stuart told Chief and Mrs. Fergus that Pete had disappeared. He cried and he broke out in red blotches. He wandered the house wailing, "Pete! Pee-teee!" He looked under the chesterfield, pulled the cushions off and looked there too. There was not a place in the house he didn't look. He looked in closets and in the laundry basket and under each bed, and even up inside the chimney where a bird had once died. He looked in the piano bench, although Pete could not possibly be there, and in the bottom of the china cabinet too. Hannah got caught up in the looking and the lie. Tears welled, but like the blood on Stuart's arm, they did not drip down. She looked through the blur of them into radiators, behind the bookshelf, under the TV. She lifted curtains and looked along window ledges, because at her own house these were the places she found foiled eggs at Easter, when the rabbit remembered to come. She thought of Pete's curled body in the ground, of the little beetles she had seen in the freshly dug hole. How long would it take them to gnaw through Pete's skin, where you could feel thin bones below the surface? Wren would know. But Hannah couldn't ask. This was one thing she could never, ever tell.

The day stretched on in its washed-out Tuesday way. Mrs. Fergus said she couldn't bear the thought of Pete lost, meowing, and so Chief Fergus led the way as the four of them went out and called for her. They moved along the street in a familial line, tallest to smallest, past Hannah's own house, where sunglassed Darlene lolled in a lawn chair, missing Mick. They called for so long that Hannah drifted in and out of remembering Pete was actually dead.

Later they made up posters—LOST! One Precious Spotted Calico Kitten, Pink Nose, Three Months Old. Dearly Loved, Deeply Missed—and stapled them to the telephone poles in the neighbourhood. In the fall some posters were still there, rained on and wrinkle-dry. Sometimes just a corner of paper and a staple, causing the seasick memory of Princess Tiara to once more surface and dip.

Wren

Mick left home and arrived at the Hill's, two blocks away, with only a hard grey suitcase. Charlie told Wren that Mick had been his friend for a long time, and that Mick needed him. "He'll need us all," he said. Wren had never thought of Mick as someone in need but suddenly he was a smaller, different man. He slept on the pull-out couch in the basement, saying he would stay just until he could organize something else. But he did not seem to be organizing anything, except the stars, which he lay under night after night, past midnight. Wren could not go outside, not with him there, in the shape he was. It was embarrassing simply to be near him. The handsome man he had been had given way to a raw, more basic version. Reverse metamorphosis, Wren thought to herself.

For the first week he did not go to work at the forestry, nor did he come upstairs during the long hot days. Angie would call, "Mick, breakfast!" and later, "Mick, lunch!" but never did he emerge until dinner, appearing haggard, though he had done nothing all day. His silent presence stifled their own conversation, and there were only the sounds of chewing and breathing, of clanking forks on plates. Partway through the meal he pushed his plate away, half full, and smiled a watered-down version of his lopsided grin.

"Thanks," he said.

He stood, pushed his chair in and returned to the basement, not to be seen again until late, past bedtime.

Wren thought, watching nightly from her window, that he had become nocturnal. A still, colourless moth. He sat in the backyard in a plastic chair and smoked cigarettes, which he had never done before, not that she'd seen anyway. The firefly end glowed each time he puffed, and then came the blue release of smoke into the air. He crushed the cigarettes beneath his slippered foot and left the butts there, a little mound. Angie gathered them up during the day. She said that, though it was rude, it was unlike him, and so, forgivable.

Everything, just now, was forgivable. Darlene was forgiven for tearful appearances in the middle of the night. Wren in her room heard the frenzied knocking, and Angie's feet on the stairs.

"I'm sorry," cried Darlene, choking out the words. "I need to see him. I need to see my husband."

My husband, she said now, while before she had said *Mick*.

"Where are the girls?" asked Angie, alarmed.

"They're sound asleep, Ange. Nothing will happen. Please. Let me in."

Wren could see the top of Darlene's head, her bird's-nest hair that showed she had been tossing and turning.

"What's gotten into you?" Angie hissed. She pushed open the screen door and slipped outside. "You can't just leave your children alone, Darlene. They're *children*."

There was a long pause.

Darlene's head drooped forward and after a time her shoulders shook. Wren thought of that song: "Ladybird, ladybird, fly away home. Your house is on fire and your children are alone." But Darlene did not fly. She stood and cried. Her head inched slowly forward, towards Angie, but Angie did not embrace her, not even when the head flopped uninvited on Angie's shoulder.

They stood that way for more than one full minute. Wren heard the flip of a number-card inside her clock radio, and then another flip, and as though Angie had heard it too, she grasped Darlene's arms and gently pushed her away. She looked into Darlene's face and shook her head slowly, in that exasperated way Wren had seen herself, many times. And then she slipped off Darlene's jacket and put it over her own shoulders.

"I'll go stay with the girls," she said. "Don't be long."

She hurried down the street towards Hannah and Vivian. It wasn't something Wren ever thought she'd see, her mother outside in her nightgown.

"Thanks, Angel," called Darlene, brightening.

She disappeared into the house and Wren listened. For a

long while there was no sound. Wren lay, thinking of the disar-
ray that had arisen so suddenly. Of how strange it was that her
Aunt Darlene was here, while her own mother was down the
street with Hannah and Vivian. Soon there came the sound of
sobbing. Not just Darlene's, which was familiar, but Mick's too.
She had never heard a man cry.

Wren guessed she must have slept after that, because in the
morning she did not know whether Angie had returned. She
crept downstairs and saw Mick and Charlie at the kitchen table.
Mick had his head in his hands and was crying. She wondered if
he had cried all that long time, from last night to now.

"I don't know what to tell you," said Charlie. "But if you love
her—"

He looked up, saw Wren and smiled awkwardly.

"Morning, Bird!" Charlie called, and pulled a chair out,
patting the seat.

Mick wiped his eyes and turned to face her. He was combed,
at least, and washed. He was not his same old self but he was better, she could see that. Better than he'd been all week. He
smiled, and there was almost that light in his eyes, which faded
when he heard Darlene emerging from the basement.

She was sleepy. Mussed up but happy. She smiled at Wren
and Charlie and put her finger to her lips, thinking she was
sneaking up on Mick. But Mick had heard her. Wren could see
that in his blank face. Darlene slid her hands around his
shoulders and chest and whispered, *"Boo!"* with her lips barely
touching the rim of Mick's ear. Her tongue darted in and out
again, and she slipped a hand between the buttons of his shirt
to touch his bare skin.

"Let's go home, Sweet Boy."

She squeezed him with her arms and smiled with her eyes squinted shut.

Wren looked away. Charlie rose and wiped the crumbless counter.

"Come on," said Mick quietly. "Let's go outside."

Wren looked up and saw that already Darlene's face had fallen. All the brightness gone. Mick stood and thrust his hands in his pockets. He went outside and Darlene followed. Wren leaned back in her chair, on the two back legs. They were standing with their foreheads pressed together, a lopsided teepee.

"Bird!" said Charlie. "It's not your business!"

Then the smack of skin on skin made them both look. Mick stood with his hand on his face, and Darlene walked slowly back home.

After Mick made up his mind to leave, it was Darlene everyone felt sorry for. She was a wreck on and off, appearing some days so distraught that she could not leave her room, and had Hannah and Vivian bring her bowls of sweets and pretzels on a tray from the kitchen. Other days she seemed even more like herself than she had done before. Knowing Mick would be there, she'd show up at the Hills' dressed in her green halter dress, her hair long and gleaming, and with Hannah and Vivian in tow she'd call through the screen, "Yoo-hoo! We're going berry-picking. Anybody wanna come?"

Wren was startled by her beauty. Her eyes glowed when she wore that dress. An emerald version of Vivian's eyes, which were washed-out green. She must have brushed her hair a million times to make it shine so. And yet she had the casual aura of someone who looked that way by accident.

Mick, these days, offered only a curt "Hello, Darlene."

"Hey, Mickey," said Darlene with her dazzling smile. *Hey,* as though he were any old flame.

While she chattered non-stop to Angie, never once looking in his direction, Mick picked up Hannah and flopped her over his shoulder and called her a sack of potatoes. He kissed the top of Vivian's head and smoothed her white-blonde hair.

"Okay, Girlies," called Darlene, "nobody's coming. They don't know what they're missing, do they?" Now she looked at Mick, sending some message. His straight face as lovely as her smiling one.

Wren watched Mick watch his family disappear down the road. Hannah twirling.

Charlie said, more than once, "Don't you think you're being a bit rash?"

And each time Mick replied, "No."

He moved out around the time school started, into the only apartment building in town. Five storeys, almost a high-rise. Hannah, Wren and Vivian walked by it twice each day, on the way to school and on the way home again. Some days, knowing he'd be at work, they'd stop and look in his first-floor window. Vivian hoisted Hannah up by her armpits and let Hannah's bum rest on her knee. The little muscles in her arms bulged, and it must have been hard work, holding Hannah there, but Vivian let her have a long look.

It was one room. There was a cushy chair, torn at the arms, and a mattress on the floor.

"Are you sure it's his place?" asked Hannah, gripping the window ledge.

"It's his," said Wren.

And Vivian added, "Look." She pointed at the hard grey suitcase that sat on cinder blocks and served as a table.

"Oh," said Hannah.

All three of them stared. It was unlike a home and yet his things were there.

Needing to say something, Wren said, "He hasn't had a chance to fix it up yet."

Vivian glowered at her.

"It's only temporary," she said. "He's not planning on fixing it up."

But week after week the little place changed. A table appeared and the grey suitcase was gone. There were three chairs, fine but not matching, and the bed was raised off the floor in some mysterious fashion that could not be detected because new sheets draped it, bright leafy green. Next came a couch, blue plaid, with a rag rug laid in front of it. Hannah stared, unsmiling, and Vivian held her.

For Wren's part, she could not wait to get away from that sad little window, and from the sorrow of Hannah and Vivian. At school, instead of swinging with Vivian alone, she played a form of tag in which she was always It. She zipped around after the others because she was the most wanted. The one they least wanted to be touched by. Pink tip of her hand poking out from stretched sleeves. When she did touch the others, when she brushed her hand against a back, she saw it arch and recoil. As in Brownies, she was contagious here. She ran with skinny arms outstretched, black hair flapping in strings. She was an excellent runner. Long, strong legs. Her shoes, brand new Adidas, royal blue with yellow stripes and a thick tread. She liked most, and hated most, chasing Lily Sinclair, whose half-Chinese hair was heavy, satiny, black too but with shimmery streaks of blue. Wren held her hand there longer than she needed to, not pulling but closing her mitteny fingers on the luxuriousness of the hair, and from behind she could see Lily's shoulders hunch with revulsion. Lily grabbed her hair away with her own lovely gold hand, and she shook and shook her head to rid it of deformity germs, of Wren-ness. She emitted panicky, giggly squeals as she shook, because it was both funny and not funny to be tagged by Wren Hill. Just as it was joyous and not joyous to be It.

Lily still spoke Chinese then. Her mother had left when she was only a baby, but Lily said mothers could teach babies things well before they were born. It was especially true with musicians, she said. Play Mozart to an unborn baby and it might come out a musical genius. When she spoke Chinese the short choppy sounds that came from her pretty mouth were like music. Wren still loved the sound and the look of her, though the thought of that get-well card slipped through the mail slot brought a fresh wash of humiliation. Lily had eyes so dark you could not see the black in the centre. Bangs that fell thick and touched the tops of her fine, pointed eyebrows. Beneath one eyebrow was a small mole, and Wren cherished even this, a perfect flaw.

Sometimes when she was It, Wren saw Vivian leaning up against the oak tree, watching, her washed-out eyes gone angry.

"You shouldn't partake in such antics," said Vivian, speaking in her fancy way.

"Why not?" said Wren.

"Because they're making a fool of you. Can't you tell?"

Wren felt her face go hot. She held Vivian's gaze and lifted her head high.

"It's only tag, Vivian."

"Oh yeah?"

"Yeah."

Wren leaned against the oak tree, beside Vivian, and watched the game. Fat Nicky Lewis was It, and he had no hope of ever catching anyone. They watched him wheeze and run but get nowhere. Lily and the others wove all around him, lunging close then away, and Nicky grabbed for them, always missing, grabbing air, laughing an idiot's laugh, his face nearly purple. And suddenly Wren saw herself there. In his purple face. His dirty, too-small sweatshirt. There was goose-pimply flesh where his top and jeans parted, showing the crack of his bum. She wanted to cry, but didn't.

The break-up had made everyone unhappy. Not just Hannah and Vivian. Not just Darlene and Mick but Wren's own parents too, and therefore Wren. It seemed strange: if everyone was so unhappy, including Mick, why didn't he move back home?

More than once, as Charlie drove her home from ballet lessons, Wren saw Darlene's car parked in front of Mick's apartment building. She saw that Charlie had noticed too, and later, lying in bed, she heard her mother's response.

"Don't give me that, I know what it means. It means she left those kids alone again."

"Give her a break, Ange. She's doing her best. She wants him to come back home."

"He's a fool if he does."

"Why?"

"Oh, come on!"

"Seriously, why? People make mistakes."

"And his would be going back home."

Best was being away from all of them, walking enchanted through the woods that half-circled the town and held things together like a cupped hand. Here Wren squeezed leaf buds open, lifted knitted green moss. Stood so still that a ladybird could alight and wash herself on Wren's thin shoulder. She spent her time watching, never collecting, unless the specimen was already dead, because how could she bear to kill a thing and then put pins through its body and wings? Ladybirds died like crazy in the fall. Once she counted thirty-four of their vibrant dead bodies on the way to school, never looking up for fear of missing one.

Vivian

Once, just after Mick's abrupt departure, Vivian awoke in the middle of the night and made her way to the washroom to pee. Darlene's door was wide open and there was no sign of Darlene. Vivian looked at the rumpled bed. The sheets had been tossed back hastily. On the bedside table was the bowl of pretzels Hannah had brought earlier in an attempt to pacify Darlene's misery. All the round edges had been bitten off and only the straight Y centres were left.

Vivian thought, now they were truly on their own. Like Pippi Longstocking or Huckleberry Finn. Hannah was no Huck but Vivian could be, were it required.

"What are you doing?" whispered Hannah, peering out from her bedroom door.

Vivian put her finger to her lips. She pulled closed the door to Darlene's empty room.

"I was just checking on Mom."

"Is she crying?" asked Hannah, starting towards the door.

"No, she's okay now. She's sleeping. You should be too, Banana."

She put her hands on Hannah's shoulders and turned her around, marched her back into her room. Then she climbed into bed with her and stayed until Hannah had fallen asleep, breathing with her mouth open.

All the while Vivian's heart pounded. Where was Darlene?

Pippi's mother had died when Pippi was just a baby, and Pippi didn't miss her at all because she couldn't even remember her. And later Pippi's sea-captain father, Efraim, had been blown overboard, disappearing in the wild spray of a storm. But Pippi had survived. She set up house in the ramshackle Villa Villekulla. She strapped scrub brushes to her feet and cleaned her floor that way, skating. As though it were an adventure to be on her own. But that had been in Sweden, in a different time and place. Pippi had had endless gold coins. And she had been only Pippi, with no little sister.

Vivian looked at Hannah, who was sleeping with her pigtails in. Hair was wound around the baubles and the look of her crooked part-line unearthed that strange tenderness in Vivian, along with the surprise at feeling it. People talked about a heart as though it really was the place you felt things, the way they talked about a mind as though it were a brain. Which Vivian knew to be bull. Mick had said as much himself; he told her everything. And yet, when Vivian felt this surge, it was there in her chest. She could feel the heart swell and deflate again, though she knew it to be hollow muscle.

She eased out of Hannah's bed and walked down the hall to Darlene's room. She focused on the door to see if she could sense Darlene, having a bright hope that she may have silently returned. But Darlene never did anything silently, and Vivian knew, sensing no presence, that the room was still empty. The house without her had a different vibe, as though it were in hiatus. Like the silent coloured stripes that showed when the TV cut out, now was a heavy moment of nothingness. For a brief but awful instant she thought of Darlene's dead body, a cadaver. It was possible that a hideous crime had been committed while the chief of police slept next door. It would not be surprising. All the chiefs and Brown Owls in the world couldn't make a place safe.

She pushed Darlene's door open. Now there was a chill all through her, and an inviting warmth emanated from Darlene's bed. Vivian climbed in and began to pull the covers over herself, realizing that the electric blanket was on, even though it was summer, and that it was cranked to nine. It was then that Vivian knew the extent of Darlene's sadness. Her need to be warm when it was warm already. Vivian, too, had that sudden need. She pulled the blanket to her chin and fingered the hot cord that ran through the wool. Darlene's smell was in the sheets and pillows, and Vivian breathed it in. She ate a broken pretzel and lay in the dark.

When the robbers had come to steal Pippi's gold pieces, they had asked, "Where are your parents?" And Pippi, unafraid, had answered frankly, "They're gone. Completely gone."

Vivian woke to Angie's hot hand on her hot face.

"Poor thing," said Angie. "You're sweating like crazy."

She peeled the electric blanket back and switched the dial to zero, then lifted the sheet, fanning Vivian. It felt delicious, but Vivian lay still.

"Your mom'll be back soon. She wanted to see your dad."

Vivian nodded, as though she had known.

"You were worried, huh?"

Vivian shrugged with one shoulder, looked away.

Angie sat down on the bed again, too close, and touched Vivian's cooling face. Vivian wished she would not sit watching her that way.

"*This* is a difficult time," said Angie. "You're a big, strong girl for ten. Everyone's very proud of you, you know."

All in her too-soft voice.

Vivian rolled her eyes and still did not look at Angie, but she could feel Angie's eyes on her, burrowing in.

"It's nice that you came looking for your mom. I hope you weren't too worried."

Vivian turned and glared at Angie.

"What's the big deal? I just came in here to eat the pretzels. She took the last of the bag."

It went on, her leaving. Not often, but often enough. For even after Mick had moved into his own apartment, even after she had met the sallow man named Tim, Darlene still longed for her husband. You never knew when she might start sobbing. She'd slump down in her chair and let her head fall forward, and no sound would emerge for the longest time. Not from anyone. They would all just watch, waiting. Darlene's mouth open in anticipation. And when she let go it was a low moan that slowly rose higher and higher. Afterwards she'd lie on the couch, depleted, and Hannah would stand behind her twisting and styling her hair. Leaning forward at intervals to give butterfly kisses, her pale lashes brushing Darlene's flushed cheek.

Vivian would give her mother no such thing. Many nights she heard the screen door close, knowing that Mick might let Darlene in, time and again, but he would never take her back, not ever.

Hannah

Hannah and Darlene hold dinner for as long as possible, hoping Vivian will show. But Vivian is in no hurry to return, Hannah knows that, and Darlene probably knows it too. Still, she works at looking happy.

She beams and tells Hannah excitedly, "Tomorrow I'll take you to meet Reg."

Hannah wants to say that she's met Reg already, twice a year since she can remember, in spring and in fall. She also wants to ask the very plain question, "Why are you marrying him?" But she cannot imagine a very plain answer, like "Love."

Eventually they eat cheese melts and settle into the green-and-white striped chesterfield, which still smells faintly of grass and dirty feet. On television there's a program about a man who, at times, has no memory. Not just amnesia but some sort of brain malfunction so severe that often he cannot recognize himself. Hannah leans back into the cushions and closes her eyes. Her own recall has always disturbed her. She is unlike Vivian, who has the sharp tongue and long memory of every oldest sister. Hannah remembers things Vivian says never happened. And there are several memories she keeps to herself, knowing they can't possibly be true. Pierre Trudeau, for instance, could never have come to the little Oelpke bungalow, but in her mind he is there in their driveway, wearing his red boutonniere.

Hannah opens her eyes. The bland face of the man with no memory fills the screen. He tells of being at a party, having to pee. He moved through the crowd, looking for a washroom. Around a corner, down a hall. So many people! He stepped aside to make way for another man approaching, and the man did the same. This side, that side, until they were both embarrassed and laughing. He reached out to touch the arm of the man, and the man reached out too. Both with surprise touching glass, their own reflections.

"Ha!" says Darlene. "Imagine not recognizing yourself! I'm sure I'd recognize myself from a million miles away!"

She points the remote towards the television and begins the long, confusing routine of switching channels. Hannah looks away. She cannot watch a thing that flashes and vanishes so quickly. Finally Darlene drops the remote on the carpet and sighs.

"Maybe Viva won't come at all," she says.

"What?" says Hannah. "Why would you say that?"

Darlene shrugs. She smiles her fake smile but her eyes well up.

"I wouldn't put anything past her," she says.

That's funny, Hannah thinks. I've heard her say the same about you.

Darlene stands and stretches. "I'm off, Girly. I need my beauty sleep."

She bends and kisses Hannah's forehead, and there is that smell again, of lavender and sadness.

Another smell stays once Darlene has gone, and Hannah lies still, trying to find the source of it. When the scent comes, a numbness comes too.

Outside the window is a crooked row of petunias in pink and white and purple. She is amazed she can smell them inside, their fuzzy spiciness floating up to her through the screen. Petunias were the only flower ever planted here, though a garden like this, wide and facing south, could have been glorious.

The smell of petunias was on her hands the day Mick died. Hannah had been sitting on the garden's rock border, squeezing the sagging blooms and pulling them off. That was why her hands smelled like flowers when they flew to her face upon hearing. The day was Saturday, opaque pink. Her father had been caught in a boat's propeller, like seaweed. Parts of him were chopped off and bleeding. Hannah was nine, she knows that for sure. She was the same height as the Hannah Tree he had named in her honour.

To the funeral Hannah wore a yellow sundress with straps that tied over each shoulder, and yellow flip-flops, a plastic flower on each, like something you'd wear in your hair if you were born in Hawaii. She also wore the red hood from her snowsuit, the string pulled tight in a triple knot under her chin. Vivian said this was ridiculous, to wear an unzipped snowsuit hood in July, especially to a funeral.

"Puerile," she added, shaping her lips to the word.

She tugged the hood angrily, but Hannah held it close around her face and screeched. Vivian yanked, pulling Hannah's hair too, pulling hair right out of her head, but Hannah hung on. Vivian pushed Hannah out the door and into the driveway, where Tim, now Uncle Tim, waited in the car, adjusting the rearview mirror. Hannah's head throbbed. Each hair hole stung. She rubbed the hood against her scalp.

Vivian came close but didn't touch her again.

"You're just like her," she whispered meanly, nodding towards Darlene. "Look at her, trying to look all lugubrious. She's making a show of herself and a mockery of him."

Together they looked at Darlene in her scarf and dark glasses.

"He would have hated that scarf."

Hannah, though silent, disagreed. She could conjure his rough fingers on the smooth silk, slipping inside to touch

Darlene's yellow hair. He would not hate the scarf. She hoped he would not hate the hood either. The last thing she wanted was to disappoint him.

"*Vite-vite,* girls!" called Darlene.

They rode in the back seat of Uncle Tim's Rambler convertible, one on either side of Darlene. Their mother's dress was short, tight, and she sat with her feet on the hump, bony knees close together, the freckles there fading into her tan. One hand held her scarf in place, the other squeezed a wad of Kleenex. She looked at herself in the rearview and kissed the Kleenex, muting her lipstick. Then she leaned back between them and sighed. She seemed stronger now than she ever had. Sad, but suffering boldly. She took Hannah's hand with the one that held the tissue, and Vivian's hand with the other.

"Remember this is nobody's fault, my girls." A tear fell from beneath her glasses and her tongue slipped out to lick it away. "Not your fault or mine or Daddy's. Accidents happen."

Hannah looked at the four hands lying in Darlene's lap. At Vivian's unholding fingers. She had not been thinking of faults. Not of theirs anyway, but an accident meant there was no one to blame, not even Eyebrow Chuck, who had been driving. Hannah briefly closed her eyes to see Chuck. One white eyebrow, one black one. Muscly tanned torso. Hands gripping the wheel. Leaning forward over the tiny motorboat window, leaning into the turns.

It was hot inside the snowsuit hood, and hard to look sideways. Hannah's head turned but the hood wouldn't. She peered partly outside and partly at the crisp red lining. Children skipping rope stopped and pointed, half laughing, as the Rambler rolled by.

She wore the hood for seven days.

"You'll get pediculosis," Vivian said, "if you don't wash your hair." To Hannah's blank stare she added, "Cooties."

Some of the kids at school had cooties. Bus kids, mostly, who lived on the outskirts. Cooties were living beings, bugs so small they were almost invisible. They jumped from head to head, so it was best not to sit next to a bus person in class, or even hang your coat too close, or you'd have to have an oil-and-vinegar treatment and wear a plastic bag on your head.

"You'd be a walking salad," said Vivian.

Hannah's head itched, thinking of cooties. Uncle Tim scratched her head a lot, now that she wore the hood, but it didn't take the itch away. His fingernails against the nylon bugged her. Uncle Tim's nails were too long for a man's, with slivers of dirt underneath. Hannah didn't like him touching her, not even with the hood between them. His toenails were long too—yellow and curled down at the ends like ugly hats for his toes. And hairs sprouted from the skin there—black and wiry like the hairs on his arms and legs. Hannah didn't know if Mick's toes had been sliced off in the accident or not. In life his toes had been long and slender, the nails wide and clean, unlike his hard-working hands. She could picture these. His bony nose and blue swimming-pool eyes. But she couldn't see him all at once. He came to her in pieces. There were probably bits of him still floating in the river.

A bright day. Hannah squinted in the sun, head pressed into the screen, pushing it out, making it lumpier, looser, which would anger Darlene but Hannah didn't care, she kept pushing, watching, listening for her father's old Alfa Romeo to buzz around the corner so fast it might topple over. He always drove too fast, and on the highway he let you roll the windows down, front and back, and get all blown around, even if you were eating ice cream and your hair got sticky.

Hannah watched the empty street and put his car there, pulling into the driveway. He leaves the keys in the ignition because who'd want to steal his old heap anyway? He gets out, stands in the street and waves, hair sticking up in front where his cowlick is, like Hannah's, and Hannah waves back and pushes the door open and hollers across the lawn, even though she just saw him yesterday and the day before and the day before that.

Hannah listened. Any time now. Just to say hi and pick up the mail. There was always a stack of it for him, even still, sometimes with his name spelled funny, though really it wasn't that different from how it sounded—*Oelpke*—but people were always getting names wrong that didn't come from England or Scotland. It might come as *Okee* on the envelope, and he would laugh and bellow that tune, "I'm proud to be an Okie from Muskokie," and then just when they were having fun, *Gotta go!* and Hannah would hop on his back and flop out to the car and slide off him. Waving and waving until he'd gone right around the corner and out of sight, and he'd wave all that time too, looking in his rearview and not even watching where he was going, that's how great a driver he is. Was.

Hannah waited.

Only Stuart appeared, a teen now, so too old to bother with her, and mean as well. Loping down the street in too-long jeans. He saw Hannah and looked away. Hannah thought of waving and calling out to him. She pressed hard into the screen. The pattern embedded in her forehead.

Once Mick was gone for good they began to visit Uncle Tim more often. He lived on the outskirts with the bus people, where the grass was so patchy and dry you didn't need to mow it.

To get to his house you had to drive out on the highway, past the population sign that faced the other way, and turn right on a gravel road with no name. His house was little and lopsided, not the kind of house a proper scientist should have, said Vivian. Under the chesterfield, and even beside his bed, were dirty dishes, sometimes puffy green with mold, and Darlene gathered them up, shaking her head and giggling. Pretending to be tidy herself. Uncle Tim shrugged and guffawed and said, "What can I tell ya? I'm a bachelor!" And then, quietly, "Not that I wanna be." Kissing her ear.

Hannah wandered through the house, trying not to touch things. If there were cooties anywhere, there would be cooties here. Uncle Tim's bedroom smelled musty and sour, like unwashed sheets. Short black hairs were scattered over his bathroom sink. Nose hairs? Ear hairs? Mick's hair had been strawberry blond. The red in her own hair came from him; she was the only one who had it. Darlene's hair was so blonde it was yellow, and Vivian's was almost white. Uncle Tim was too big, too dark. Too dirty to be one of them. And yet others had come and gone since her father first left, but Uncle Tim remained. He had even become related, though Vivian would not call him Uncle. Used no name at all to get around it. Hannah thought of Batmobile Ned and his Batmobile car. Of White-Shoe Joe, who sang Italian songs, slipping in *Napanee* for *Napoli* and causing Darlene to laugh so hard she snorted. Even blameless Eyebrow Chuck had driven Darlene around on his motorcycle a few times, and once he'd stayed over, but that had been before the accident. Then there'd been Mr. Unwin, who lived with his mother and couldn't sleep over. Hannah and Vivian had called him Mr. Onion, plugged their noses when he came around. Mr. Onion was jittery, almost bald. Wore socks inside his sandals.

He loaned Darlene a stereo, and when Darlene dumped him, she put the stereo outside on the step, a note stuck to it flapping in the breeze. Darlene and Hannah and Vivian had to duck behind the chesterfield when Mr. Onion arrived, but Hannah could see him from her hiding place, struggling with the stereo and two big speakers. She could see the note too, standing up in the wind, stamped at the bottom with her mother's Fire and Ice lipstick. She watched him lug the stereo all the way to his car, then turn around and bring it back. She heard the whispered *Yesss!* hiss between Darlene's teeth, saw her slim, tanned hand curl into a victory fist that punched the air. Now Darlene played Uncle Tim's records on Mr. Onion's stereo. Twangy country tunes about cheating and falling to pieces.

Today they stayed at Uncle Tim's for what felt like forever. Vivian hogged the hammock, swaying, reading the dictionary, swatting blood-filled blackflies and flicking their squashed bodies from her bare pink legs. She was too heavy for the hammock. Her bum a big round melon stretching the twine apart.

"No one just *reads* a dictionary, you know," said Hannah.

"Erroneous," said Vivian. "Some do."

Hannah picked at tree bark. She gave the hammock a shove, but Vivian ignored her.

Inside, Darlene and Uncle Tim lay at opposite ends of the chesterfield, feet touching. All day the fan blew on them as they giggled and whispered. Hannah was beyond bored. Only six houses on Uncle Tim's road and in every one of them were bus kids.

By the time Darlene was ready to leave, it was almost dark. The sky hung navy blue, the air damp on Hannah's skin. She stretched out on the back seat, head against one door, feet flat on the other. Vivian climbed into the front seat and rested her feet on the dashboard, as usual, because the AstroTurf floor mats were rough and itchy. Outside, Uncle Tim's arm circled Darlene's waist and pulled her in. Hannah stared up at them. Upside down they looked like cartoons whose eyes and noses and mouths got drawn on after the rest of them had been made. Uncle Tim kissed Darlene long and sloppy on the mouth, then gave quick pecks to her nose and forehead. Darlene's hand touched his sweaty yellow face, not something you'd touch if you didn't have to.

"Wave to Uncle Tim," Darlene told them as she moved the green Nova down the lane.

Hannah held her hand up and lowered it again. She listened to the crickets, to the tires rolling on the gravel. Watched Vivian's hand slip out the side window with her long middle finger held high and still. Darlene chattered on, not knowing, and on the highway she switched on the radio and hummed along off-key, fingernails clicking against the steering wheel. Hannah stared at the tiny holes in the ceiling. With a pen she could connect the dots. The ceiling looked like a big insole for a shoe. Soft and cushy. If the car rolled it might protect them, their three pale heads stuffed against it.

Orange Wednesday, and the sky brightened behind the cowboy curtains in Hannah's room. Hannah lay in bed, the sheet pulled up to her nose. Inhaled. Sucked cotton into her nostrils. If she concentrated she could open the curtains without ever touching them. Without moving from the bed. She held her breath, flexed all her muscles until her head tingled and orange spots like the orange day blurred her vision. Once, she had moved her dresser this way. Just a smidge, but she could do it again if she tried hard enough. Mick said anything was possible.

Hannah pressed two fingers to each temple. If she had been there she could have stopped it. Used her powers and zeroed in on her father spraying to pieces in the water. She closed her eyes. Saw it before it happened. Wild Eyebrow Chuck at the wheel. She squinted. And her father sprang from the water in maroon swimming trunks with white stripes, spun through the air like a baseball, landed beside her on the beach, wet, laughing.

If she had been there she could have stopped it. *Anything was possible.* She should have gone afterwards, when Chief Fergus came to the door—dressed not as a neighbour or as Stuart's dad but as chief of police—and she knew right away something was wrong. She should have gone because you never know, it might not have been too late. Darlene bending down, freckled knees cracking, and Hannah feeling the something-wrong feeling, like when he left the first time. Her skin hot blotches, head twitching. Stomach light, fluttery, then heavy and rolling like she had to poo. Darlene holding the ends of Hannah's pony-tails—*something awful*—and Hannah running, screen door banging, feet burning on the pavement, all the way to the beach, big strides, knees high, arms working.

If she concentrates, she can see him on the sand, parts missing, flooding blood, and Eyebrow Chuck is there, pacing and holding his hand to his head where a deep gash is reddening his one white eyebrow. If she concentrates harder she can locate the pieces, gather them up with her mind muscles and stick them back on where they belong.

The first time her father left—though Darlene claimed she couldn't possibly remember—Hannah saw him from the back, walking down the hall with his shoes on (a no-no), a hard grey suitcase in his hand.

"You've lost your marbles," said Darlene. "You were at Wren's, and we didn't have the carpet then."

But Hannah does remember. She can see herself at the hall's end, watching him go. Her dad getting smaller and smaller, not turning to wave. Into the kitchen and around the corner, and she hears the door open, close, and the Alfa start up, its muffler dragging on the driveway, tied on but falling off. She stands still till she can't hear it any more and then, in her room, cries and cries into her bedspread, so hard and so long there are sore creases on her face when she gets up. And later she tells the Ferguses, No, he didn't really leave, not like that. He was too tall for the house so he had to move away to where the ceilings were higher, but he still comes to visit every day, so really it's just like normal.

And at school the teacher smoothed wide sheets of pale grey paper on their desks and said, "Draw your house," and Hannah drew on both sides, her own pale green house with yellow doors and the Hannah Tree, chives poking out of a pot by the side door, and then the place where Mick lived, a big apartment building downtown with polka dots of every colour.

Hannah was in the bath, sloshing in warm water, bubbles up to her neck. Darlene sat on the tub's edge in a shortie nightgown, stuffing cotton balls between her toes and painting the nails cherry red.

"What do you think, Banana?" she asked. "You'd get to ride the school bus every day."

Hannah thought of cooties, combed her fingers through her hair.

Vivian leaned in the doorway, arms crossed.

"No way will I share a room," she said. "He'll have to build an extension so I can have my own space."

Hannah scooped bubbles. Uncle Tim didn't look like a man who could build a house, or even part of one. She pictured his square-box place with a piece added on. Hannah a bus kid. Riding to school with fat Nicky Lewis and his scarred sister, Dodie, or Roberta Hay, whose nose dripped dark snot. Kids who smelled stale and wore stained bally clothes with frayed cuffs. Hannah rubbing up against them on bumpy gravel roads. Catching germs. Stretched socks sagging down around her ankles. Cooties and moths gnawing tiny holes in her T-shirts. In the mornings, before she brushed, she'd have to splash water around the sink to wash the mystery hairs down. And black Uncle Tim hairs from every part of his body might wind up woven into her sweaters. Hannah dunked her face cloth in the bath, sucked water from it.

"No," she told Darlene.

Darlene half-smiled. She wiped polish from a flap of toe skin.

"The truth is, I'm lonely," she said.

Me too, Hannah wanted to say, for that was how she always felt with Mick gone and Stuart grown mean.

"And Daddy's not coming back," Darlene added. Her voice became warbly. "You have to realize that now he's gone for good."

Hannah knew. She didn't need to be told. She looked at Vivian, and Vivian rolled her eyes so dramatically it seemed one eyeball rolled separately from the other.

"Sooo," Darlene continued, "what if Uncle Tim moved here?"

"No way," said Vivian without pausing.

Hannah followed the lead. She shook her head slowly. "No way."

Darlene fake-laughed, cheeks pink beneath her freckles.

"Okay," she said, shrugging.

She put her foot on the blue furry bath mat and blew on her toenails.

The house was messy. Little piles of Hannah's father's things on the chesterfield and the dining-room table. Hannah pressed her hand into a pillowy stack of shirts—navy blue, royal blue, sky blue, robin's egg blue, swimming-pool blue. Everything of his was here now, back where it started. Only rolling dust balls left in the apartment downtown—clumps made from his hair and belly-button lint and the tiniest flakes of his skin. Hannah smelled the shirts but his smell was gone already. Darlene had washed the clothes. What fit would go to Uncle Tim, she said. He could use a few things. Hannah shuddered. Uncle Tim's sweaty skin staining the collars, the underarms. Tufts of his back hair sprouting from her father's T-shirts.

Even the Alfa was here, oil staining the garage floor. Hannah sat in the driver's seat, stretched to reach the pedals. In here it smelled of him, so strong it hurt to breathe. Hannah closed her eyes. Winter and Darlene's rusty Nova won't start, so here he comes, saves the day, and the four of them pile into the Alfa to drive downtown, and in the parking lot Hannah leans forward between the two seats and says, "Kiss! Kiss goodbye!" and she sees their faces from the side, half-smiling. "Girly!" says her mother, but her father tilts his head, kisses her mother's cheek with Hannah's face right close to theirs, and Hannah says, "On the mouth!" Her mother laughs and her father laughs too, and even though it's just a quick kiss, a peck where the lips stay closed and the tongues don't touch, Hannah sees Darlene's cheeks flush and is sure it's the start of something, something starting all over again.

Hannah opened her eyes. She could see just her cowlick in the rearview mirror. Tiny baby hairs that never grow, dipping down on her forehead.

Sometimes, from the side, she could see Uncle Tim's tongue rolling in her mother's mouth.

Uncle Tim began appearing in her father's shirts and staying over. Darlene didn't ask if it was okay. Sometimes he came for dinner, which he said shouldn't be wieners, or even noodles with Cheez Whiz, and so Darlene shook chicken parts in a bag of spiced powder and baked them in the oven, which heated the house and made the air meaty. Hannah hadn't known her mother could cook real food. She boiled potatoes and army-green canned peas, then laid them on the plates with the chicken so that no group touched another, but the pea water leaked, inching over.

They began to eat a lot of meat. Uncle Tim brought his barbecue and set it up in the backyard. He wore an apron stained with grease from steaks and burgers. Hannah didn't like meat that was still on the bone. Didn't want to eat someone's leg or wing, chew on a rib. When he finished his own serving, Uncle Tim grabbed the bones from all their plates and gnawed the remnants.

"What a waste," he said, mouth greasy.

Late at night, Hannah could hear them moan and murmur. She sneaked to the bathroom for cotton balls, stuffed them in her ears, but the balls fell out and she heard the moans again. She lay on her side, hands pressed against her ears, and that worked for a while; but when she started to sleep, her hands slid off, and she heard the noises again. She put the cotton balls back in, covered her head with the snowsuit hood, tied tight, and tried not to think of cooties or rolling tongues. If she thought of something else, she could barely hear anything.

In the morning, Uncle Tim was still there, a sour smell all around him, hair crushed on one side, sticking out on the other. His pyjamas were her father's, white with blue stripes. Dingier now, stretched at the knees and elbows.

On Canada Day weekend, a man came and asked for Darlene, who appeared in her pink kimono. She squealed and pushed Hannah aside, hugged the man. The man's striped, wrinkly pants rode up at the ankles when he wrapped his arms around Darlene, and Hannah looked at his socks, lemon yellow with designs where the bone jutted out. His hair was smoothed back with something greasy, and it shone blue-black in the sunlight. Darlene made Harvey Wallbangers and sat outside with the man, laughing, her hair hanging over the back of her lawn chair.

"That was Darrell," Darlene said later, beaming.

Hannah knew that on the inside cover of Darlene's high-school dictionary—blue, loose at the binding—D & D was scrawled in big, loopy letters. Darrell & Darlene. Darlene & Darrell. Dare & Darl 4-ever 2-gether.

He was a photographer, Darlene said. He took pictures and made them into postcards and travelled around, selling them. Hannah thought of her father's Polaroid camera, now hers, and the many pictures left untaken.

Darrell came back the next day and took them all to the Canada Day parade in a rusting white sports car that smelled as though he lived in it. On the floor and in the back window were stacks of blurry postcards, held together by elastic bands. Vivian rested her dirty feet on them, pressing down, flattening her toes on autumn leaves and the faces of strangers.

The parade seemed the same as last year's, bagpipes and flags and a man with a drum strung on, thumping in slow rhythm. Other men in robes and jingling, curled elf shoes meandered, some on puny bicycles. Lily Sinclair, with a maple leaf on each cheek, led the baton twirlers, and other girls cartwheeled. There was Wren, cartwheeling too. Spinning by, her slim body longer than the other bodies, fine strings of black hair flying loose from a tiny bun. Upside down and then right side up, she smiled at Hannah and whirled off.

"Call me Dare," said Darrell, handing Hannah pink candy floss, blue for Vivian. He pressed a corn dog to Darlene's lips and Darlene said, "Oh no, Dare, I couldn't possibly. I'm not the girl I used to be." She wore a tight shortie T-shirt, a crescent moon of sweat beneath each boob. She rested her hand lightly on her belly, pretending to be fat. Dare laughed a low ha-ha-ha laugh, muttered into Darlene's hair something Hannah couldn't hear. He laid his hand at Darlene's rib cage, too close.

That night Dare stayed over. Hannah stuffed the cotton balls in and tied on the rustly hood.

Hannah wondered if now Uncle Tim would stop calling and coming around. She thought of him out there, sweating in her father's clothes. She'd like to get the clothes back, but then Dare might end up in them. Dare was bigger than Uncle Tim. Even his own clothes pulled apart between the buttons.

Dare kept coming over and cooking shish kebabs on Uncle Tim's barbecue. Stabbing pieces of onion and green pepper and mushroom, floppy cubes of pink meat. He taught Hannah.

"Make a pattern," he said, showing her.

She watched his mouth, lips thick but pale. The same colour

as his skin. Hannah had seen Darlene kiss the lips, stain them with her lipstick.

They ate outside at the picnic table, because Dare said they should enjoy the summer weather while they could. Hannah found it too hot, dizzying. Through the fence she could see long slats of Stuart. She watched him as she slid the pieces from her skewer, pushing the now brownish-grey meat aside. No bone, so she didn't know what part of the body this was, what animal it came from. She thought of Pete the kitten and of the pieces of her father that didn't go underground. Fish feeding on him. Soft mouths nibbling on a finger or a toe.

Later she lay in bed and waited for Dare to go away. She wiggled two loose teeth with her tongue and thought of the new ones that would grow in. Vivian said all that should have happened already.

"You're developmentally delayed," she told Hannah.

And all Hannah could think to say was, "I know I am, but what are you?" which she realized too late was wrong.

The night before Mick died they had stayed with him. He had leaned over to kiss them good night, and when his mouth pressed down on Hannah's she winced, thinking it would hurt her tender gums.

Vivian had propped herself on her elbow and smirked.

"You should get Dad to tie a string around those and pull them out. It's taking way too long."

And Mick had smiled just for Hannah.

"She's a late bloomer is all," he said. "Nothing wrong with that."

Now she pictured that pull-out couch, blue plaid, up for sale at the Sally Ann, where someone grubby would buy it. A bus kid sleeping on it. Maybe two bus kids, bringing in toe jam and cookie crumbs and pebbles from outside. Never knowing that Hannah had slept there, with Vivian warm beside her. Dad snoring across the room. Deep breaths, in and out, rattly but steady, nice to hear. And then in the morning, fried eggs with soft centres, toast cut in fingers for dipping. Coffee too, a treat. Half coffee, half milk, heaping spoons of brown sugar stirred in, blowing and sipping from blue plastic tube glasses. And then into the Alfa, all the windows down, weaving through town over the speed limit, taking the long way, up to the highway, past the population sign and back again.

Wren

Wren was fourteen the year Mick died. He had been her only uncle. They were not connected by blood but by some sort of sameness she had no word for. He had been the only other one able to call a butterfly to his finger.

"Not call," he would have corrected. "A butterfly has no ears, so there'd be no point in calling."

Which she knew. For that reason it was always in danger. Deaf and dumb, it flew by day. Moths had ears. Could even speak in a frequency people could not hear. Nocturnal, they had special reflective eyes that shone like a cat's in the darkness.

Mick knew all that and more. One day he was here, telling her, and the next he was not, gone for ever. There was the funeral and then a time when they stood outside the church, shaking hands. Wren did not want to stand in that line, but she did it for him. She was at the very end, beside Charlie. For every person she put her hand forth, thinking only of Mick when she had the panicked urge to withdraw it. She was glad that once he had lived with them, though it had not been for long, though he had not been himself that summer.

They followed the long box that held him and watched as it was lowered into the ground. Wren looked at everyone and felt proud. There was a strangely peaceful dignity that hung around his grave. Darlene had never looked more beautiful, with her movie-star scarf and glasses. She was not his wife then, but she had loved him. She was not making a scene, which made Wren wonder if perhaps she was sadder than she had ever been.

Angie, too, seemed to sense this. After the burial she said to Charlie, "You and Wren go home. I'm gonna go to Darlene's for a while."

Wren thought her father would circle the town in that way he did when things went bad. She had no desire just then for driving, so it was a heartening surprise when Charlie drove up and out of town to the bog. Here there was no one but Wren and Charlie and all the beings whose home this was, breathing in the rich peat. Charlie had often brought her here when she was younger, pointing out the gentle, arching branches of the water willow, the bog rosemary with its pale pink bells. The sticky bug-trapping sundews.

The bog was a sacred place. She collected nothing. She left it all where it was, as it was, knowing there was a reason for it being there. If she saw a rock she admired, she held it in her hand and rubbed its smoothness. She memorized its markings and the rough patches where rock had chipped from rock, and then she placed it back on the soft earth floor and moved away, Charlie trailing behind her.

Sometimes there were things she badly wanted. Once an uncommon leaf, shaped strangely, missing points. She could press it between the pages of a book and the leaf would dry just as it was, only the colour changing. But it would not be the same to own it. To have this keepsake in her room where there were triangular felt pennants and a crescent-moon pillow, things not born from the earth.

Today what she wanted looked at first like a toy, because it was so unbelievably small and had no feathers—peach plasticky skin, a bright yellow beak too large for its head, swollen-shut eyes. Two tiny half-wings, tinged mauve like buried veins. This she wished to take and keep.

"Don't touch it!" shouted Charlie, rushing forward.

Wren widened her narrow eyes at him. His quick movement caused hidden creatures to scurry in the long grass and leaves.

With his shadow around her Wren touched the bird anyway, and Charlie did not try to stop her. She lifted it gently, though maggots crawled out from under it and onto her hand. Already they had eaten the hidden half of that bird, so small it seemed unborn. She held it in her palm and then she laid it back down, rubbed her hand on the ground to brush the maggots off.

Maggots would eat that bird. Later the maggots would become furious flies with see-through wings, perhaps even bluebottles, their bodies that startling sapphire, metallic.

They wandered until the sun went down, and *then* in the car they did not drive off but sat watching. Charlie let his tears stream down. It had not occurred to Wren that Charlie may have wanted to come here not for her but for himself. So that he, in his own way, could honour Mick, who had been a friend and almost-brother. She watched the tears rolling and leaned and kissed his salty cheek. The only other man she had known to cry had been Mick himself, during those painful days. Sobbing loudly.

Angie

Angie hand-stitches glittering spangles to Darlene's wedding dress, which is a far more elaborate style than the one she had the first time around. Angie is embarrassed for her. For Vivian and Hannah, even Reg Sinclair, for whom she does not care. The dress is gawdy, too young. And white! How many years since Darlene was virginal?

As girls, Angie and Darlene took turns kissing Dare Jackson, asking, "Who tastes better?" His lipsticked face like something violated. Dare felt both their breasts, Angie's with his left hand, Darlene's with his right. Angie's were pillowy, he said, and Darlene's were firm and thick-skinned. Dare said this was strange for sisters.

Who smells better?

Who's prettier?

Who kisses better?

Who's taller?

Who has softer hair?

Better breath?

Angie thought she might love him. He had long fingers, and the springy veins in his hands and arms throbbed like a real man's would. He called Darlene and Angie bookends, though truly they did not look much alike. Still, they were always on either side of him, propping him up. In the cinema he let them take turns touching his surprising penis, which pointed straight up when let loose. Angie recoiled when Dare first spewed semen. Darlene rubbed the milkiness between her thumb and fingers.

Then he began to grow long underarm hairs on his square heart-throb chin, spoiling things for Darlene, and so for

Angie as well. Darlene suggested he shave, but he didn't do it often enough. If there had been more hair, Darlene said, enough for a beard, it might have been sexy, but these sparse ones were unappealing. To Angie she said she wasn't interested any more in kiddy-style fooling around, and it seemed that, without her, Dare was not interested either. Angie went twice with him to the movies. She squeezed what she thought was his penis, rubbing and rubbing but afraid to go in alone, and unsure in the end—it may have been the hard fly of his pants. Dare kept his hand on her breast, just resting there. Having as much interest in it as you would in a soggy sack of nothing.

It was later, after they had all finished school, that Dare and Darlene started up again, and this time they were truly a couple. Darlene acted as though this was a whole different Dare, not at all the Dare they had shared, and after a while it seemed that way to Angie too. She couldn't wait to get away. She moved six towns down the highway and took a job at the forestry, typing reports about trees and the unpredictable routes of forest fires. It was there she met Charlie, and life was fine for a length of time.

Before long Darlene showed up crying on Angie's doorstep. Dare had gone. The town was too small for him, he'd said. The whole damn valley was too small, and no, he couldn't take her along because he didn't know where he was going or when he'd be back, and she deserved better than that.

She moved in with Angie and took a job as a waitress. Angie had to unplug the phone because of all the men who called. Darlene flirted but dated none of them. "I'm waiting for Dare," she'd say, eyes filling.

Until she met Mick. Angie had never seen her so in love. Not with love this time, but with him. She barely mentioned Dare again, except to refer in jest to that younger Dare they had shared.

And when all those years later Dare showed up, in his seer-sucker suit and fancy socks, Angie was relieved to finally find him extremely distasteful. Yet it seemed wrong that Darlene should take up with him so soon after Mick's death. True, she and Mick had already been divorced, but surely it meant something that Mick had been the love of Darlene's life. And there was Tim, too, who had long been waiting.

But Darlene was smitten anew.

She brought Dare to see Angie. To say hello.

"Hello," he said.

"Hello," said Angie.

Dare grinned at Wren and pumped her hand without flinching. He said, "Pleased to meet you, young lady," and to Angie it was obvious Darlene had prepared him.

Darlene beamed for three weeks. She lightened her hair and piled it up on her head, pulling tendrils loose to give it that tousled, natural look, as though it had somehow pinned itself up on its own.

"It's just as well the girls put the kibosh on living with Tim," she told Angie. "Obviously I wasn't ready."

Angie's own sore heart ached for Tim, who had rapidly fallen in a love he could not climb out of.

"He wanted to make you and the girls his family," said Angie.

Darlene shrugged. "I know." She twisted a tendril around her finger. "But I think Dare'll want that too, don't worry."

Angie thought of Ned Norman and Joe the Italian from Napanee, and also the man who lived with his mother. All this Tim had endured, sad-eyed.

"Besides, I think I *love* Dare, and I can't say that for sure about Timbo. I don't get that *zzzing* from him, you know?"

Darlene smiled, showing bright perfect teeth, and gazed up at the ceiling. "I *dare* to love Dare."

These were the times Angie loathed Darlene. But perhaps she was just as bad. Hadn't Charlie once loved Angie desperately? Hadn't she pushed him away? She remembered the words on her back, his fingers there. Now the words were not even spoken, let alone written on her skin.

Hannah

In front of them all, Dare talked about the way the sun or moonlight fell on Darlene, depending on the time of day. He said her gold hair swayed like wheat in a prairie wind.

"He gives me dyspepsia," said Vivian. "He makes me want to spew vomit."

She rubbed baby oil onto her already burned skin as she imitated Dare and Darlene for Wren and Hannah. She played both parts, using a low rumbling mumble for Dare and a sweet giggly voice for Darlene.

"Oooh, Dare," said Vivian's Darlene, peering above blue sunglasses, fluttering her lashes. "Kiss me, hug me, pull and tug me!"

Wren laughed, so Hannah did too, although it seemed anything but funny.

"Well, hon-bun, that would be my pleasure," said Vivian's Dare.

Vivian's Darlene let loose wild moans.

Hannah looked away. She leaned further into the shade of the maple tree, wiggling hard on one loose tooth and then the other. Any day those teeth would come out. Would there be blood? Roots?

"Truth or bare me! Double Dare me!"

Hannah felt her cheeks go hot. She watched Wren laugh and practise double-jointedness. Wren could clasp her legs behind her head. She could do sideways and frontways splits. She could cross her legs, Indian-style, and walk like that on her knees.

"Bite my corn dog, baby," growled Vivian's Dare.

It was better not to listen. Hannah picked dandelions and buttercups and Indian paintbrushes and formed them into a posy edged with maple leaves. Dandelions were said to be unbeautiful because they were weeds. To get rid of them you had to dig them up by their roots, not just lop their heads off. Weeds were not flowers. You had to plant a flower, but a weed was something that grew where it wanted. It came up as part of nature. But to Hannah the cheery spiked circles of yellow held more glory than Darlene's petunias, which sagged and folded sloppily in on each other. Next door Mrs. Fergus planted marigolds in two measured rows, and every day she pulled at the fine green weeds that poked above the surface.

In the picture Dare took, Wren stands upside down and red-faced, black hair coiling on the grass. Her shorts buckle at the tops of her thighs and her long sleeves make tents for her hands. Vivian, in a seldom-worn sundress, is caught in mid-turn. The dress billows out at one side, lifted by wind, and her matted white-blonde hair blows veil-like across her face. Hannah sits cross-legged on itchy grass, a bracelet of Indian paintbrushes wrapping one wrist. This year her hair is more red than blonde, unless it's just Dare's camera. She has two braids springing out from her head, too tight and crooked, but she smiles anyway, a crazy, wide, giddy smile showing gaps where teeth should be. The teeth had come out at the same time, on the same day, and she had rasped her tongue running it across gap and gap, feeling the hard gums, and later, the tiny beginnings of new bone breaking through.

Dare made the picture into a blurry postcard and mailed it from Montana. It was as though the image was more than one image, each laid on top of the other and knocked slightly askew. It was hard to look at for the blurriness. It made your eyes hurt. The grass was a smear of yellow from all the dandelions. The smear faded the tiny flowers on Vivian's dress too. Hannah's Indian paintbrushes glowed a bright, blurry orange, unrecognizable, and further back the fan leaves of the rhubarb patch were just a smudge of red and green.

At the post office, Darlene held the postcard limply and began to cry. Everyone looked. Hannah watched the postcard shake with Darlene. She tilted her head to read Dare's slanted writing.

> *Hello from Montana! This is Big Sky Country, and let me tell you, the sky is BIG! Thanks for putting me up, Dee. Wasn't it just like old times? Wish I could've stayed longer but I gotta go where the wind takes me. Hugs and long kisses, Dare.*

Hannah couldn't imagine a sky bigger than the one that was here. She wanted to ask what he meant, but suddenly Darlene sobbed out loud, snorting. She clutched the edge of the junk-mail table, where unwanted coupons piled up, and let her head flop back. With two fingers, Hannah reached up and stroked the soft inside of Darlene's elbow, but Darlene seemed not to notice. Bluish-black mascara streaked crookedly down her face. Hannah watched one dark tear slip from her chin and land in the hollow of her collarbone. Darlene leaned forward onto the table, pressed her face into the coupons and scrunched them and the postcard too. Hannah watched people watching, stared hard at them to make them look away. One hot-pink sandal had slid from Darlene's foot, and with her own foot Hannah slid it back on again. Darlene quieted. She wiggled her foot into the shoe. She kept her face on the table, blew a long sigh that lifted a lank of hair, and from the space it opened she looked at Hannah, sad-eyed. She slowly pushed herself up from the table and dug a tissue from her purse. Wiped at the streaks of mascara and honked loudly. The wrinkled postcard lay looking up at them and Darlene smoothed it, half-smiling. She tweaked Hannah's nose.

"You take a good picture, Girly."

They did not go home, but to Angie's.

Darlene stood leaning on Angie and cried and cried. Angie just let her. She did not speak at all and soon Darlene stopped. They sat at the table and Hannah sat too. Darlene pulled the postcard from her purse and slid it over to Angie, who, smiling, looked first at the blurred image and then read Dare's message without expression. When she was finished she looked at Darlene. She opened her mouth as though to speak but Darlene held up a hand.

"Don't tell me you told me so, Ange," said Darlene. "I knew it. _I_ told me so."

"Fine," said Angie. "Okay."

She made a pitcher of iced tea and poured a glass for each of them. Hannah watched the lemon seeds swirl and float on top. She wondered why that might happen. They were made of wood, maybe. Wood floated.

Darlene sat at Angie's kitchen table, with her bare feet on a chair. She looked at herself in the toaster and said, "He's not just any man, you know."

"Oh, I know," said Angie.

They shared a mysterious look and laughed, and Hannah laughed too, pretending to know what was funny.

Around Darlene's eyes the skin still looked red and sore.

"No, he's not just any man," she said again. "He has to go where the wind takes him. I wouldn't want it any other way."

And to Tim—who came that night when Darlene beckoned and held her in the crook of his arm and kissed the top of her head—she said, "Where would I be without you, Sweet Boy?"

Wren

Darlene felt down when Dare rode off, but she was not the mess she had been when Mick had left home. Still, she took on a tragic beauty when she suffered, and Wren found it hard not to stare. She wondered about beauty, if there was a secret. Her own mother was Darlene's sister, and there was a strong family resemblance. Yet no one would call Angie beautiful.

Wren, these days, looked long at her own face in the mirror. Her black hair and her pale skin might be considered striking. Especially if she lived in the West Indies, where the women wore fireflies in their hair. The thought at once delighted and dismayed her. She wouldn't want them there if they'd rather be flying.

There was no end to the assaults people inflicted on creeping things. Wren had read that, to test their endurance, insects were boiled and frozen. One entomologist kept a ladybird underwater for more than a day to see if it would drown. It didn't. Another dripped dark wax over an ant's eyes to see if the ant's antennae would lead it home again. When it seemed the ant relied more on its antennae than its eyes, the entomologist—just to be sure—captured the same ant and snipped its antennae off. The ant was immediately lost.

Wren loved all insects, but butterflies especially because they were undeniably beautiful and unmarred. At first wormlike, slug-like, crawling through dirt and grass, foraging. And then growing delicate wings, dusted with powdery scales of colour. *Lepidoptera* is Greek for "scale-winged." If you hold a butterfly's wings, the scales rub off on your skin. Beneath them the wings are transparent.

Lily Sinclair had gone through her own metamorphosis. She no longer spoke pretend Chinese, and her blue-black hair was kinked in a perm that had not quite taken. Her golden skin was pocked and tinged pink with foundation and her eyelids sparkled blue. Wren had once swooned in her glorious presence. So what was beauty? Something you wore and took off at night, or something inside you? Around you?

Wren herself had tried makeup. Darlene spreading smooth perfumed creams onto Wren's cheeks and eyelids, blending the blushes and shadows with tiny sponges or with just her thin, strong fingers. "Tricks with makeup can make anyone beautiful, Wrenny." Darlene's sweet breath, warm and moist on Wren's face. The pencil on her eyebrows. Hannah and Vivian leaned in, watching, pursing their lips when Wren did, readying their eyelids. Wren felt a change taking place. She saw her reflection in six eyes and smiled at it with darkened lips. Three pretty mouths smiled back. Darlene touched mascara to Wren's lashes, turning them stiff as the legs of spiders.

"Have a look," she whispered.

And Wren rose slowly from the bed, expecting to be enchanted, but there she was, a tall, frightening doll. Grotesque. Herself but painted. Her ugly, dull eyes with an outline around them. Her ugly, thin lips shining. Each ugly feature accentuated, shouting out its ugliness. Tricks with makeup could not make everyone beautiful.

Blue eyeliner mingled with the water in her eyes, and through spidery lashes Wren looked down at her stretched body, where breasts had started growing. Tricks with makeup could not separate the mounds that were her fingers or turn these tiny nails, curved and pointing, into ten flat, crowning ones, each with a pink partial moon at its bottom.

Hannah

Hannah's teeth had grown in looking Chiclety and out of place, too large for the rest of her. Darlene called this her gawky stage. She lightly slapped Hannah's knees and said the knobbiness was also part of that stage, but that it would pass.

"Don't worry, Banana. You'll be a beauty yet."

Darlene pulled out the old brown photo album that held her history.

"See?" she said, pointing. "I was gawky too."

But Darlene had not been gawky. She had been as lovely then as now. To Hannah it seemed unlikely that she might ever be anything other than what she was right now. But she would not have called that gawky if she hadn't first heard it from Darlene.

Stuart called her Stretch because she was only ten and already almost as tall as he was. She still went to the Ferguses', though less often, and never because Stuart had invited her. He had moved into the basement, a place that stayed dark all day. He called it his apartment and allowed no one else in, except to do laundry. He'd moved down there last year, into the dank, smelly room that once was a guest room, and his territory had spread until he owned the hallway, the rec room, even the tiny bathroom with the metal shower stall and no window.

In the rec room was a long bench, maroon, where the dress-up trunk used to be, and here he lifted weights that changed his body. To Hannah, peering secretly from the stairwell, the bench seemed too narrow to lie on, but Stuart grunted and strained there, his skin gleaming with sweat, even the muscles in his hard face working.

For so long he had seemed too young for his age, and now he seemed too old. But there were still days she could talk to him. Days she could say, "What are you doing?" and he wouldn't shoot her a look that said, "Fuck off, you moron," but rather would answer her pleasantly, perhaps even smiling. When he smiled long creases ran from the edges of his eyes to his jawbone, and dimples dented his skin. His eyebrows, a smooth, rich brown, arched high above his eyes, and if you said something silly or unbelievable, one would shoot up in surprise. Other days his eyes were a colder blue. He said that Eyebrow Chuck had pulled her bleeding, dead father into the motorboat and given him mouth-to-mouth.

"Everyone knows that," he told her.

He said that even though he was dead, her father kept puking into Eyebrow Chuck, making Eyebrow Chuck puke too. He said the breath Eyebrow Chuck breathed into her father leaked out through the gashes the propeller had made.

Hannah didn't want to see this, but it played in her head over and over.

Once she had brought a caterpillar to the Ferguses', striped black and brown with hard hairs like in nostrils. It was okay, Mrs. Fergus said, so long as he remained in his jar during dinner. Hannah sat him beside her glass of milk and watched him climb his stick, sniffing the lid, hairy body arching. Stuart ate and watched with dead eyes. He chewed with his mouth open. When he was finished he pushed his plate away and stretched out a grimy hand, wrapped it around the jar.

"Ahhh," he said. "I'm still hungry."

And before she could stop him, he twisted the lid and grabbed the caterpillar, held him above his open mouth and dropped him in. Hannah simply sat, dumbfounded.

"Mm-mmm," said Stuart, and the memory of Princess Tiara surfaced and moved inside her.

Chief Fergus's hand cuffed the back of Stuart's head and out flew the caterpillar, twirling through the air gymnastically, curled into a terrified ball but whole, at least, and alive.

At home in her bed, in the hazy space between waking and sleeping, Hannah saw Stuart bite the feet off toads so their skinny legs dripped blood. He scooped the eyes out with his dirty fingernails, tossed them from one hand to the other, slurped them down. Bit into their round, squishy bodies too, halving them, and yellow jelly squirted out, dripped down his chin like custard. Stuart laughed, turned to face her. Opened his mouth wide to show all the things inside it—spiders and flies and goldfish and pieces of bloated worms.

Pink Saturdays Hannah went to the graveyard to be with Mick. She looked at the crooked graves of strangers too, at the twisted roots of oaks and maples that pushed at the stones, as though the bodies beneath had rolled in panic. Her father's place was marked by only a small square of granite set into the ground, and she sat right on it, partly because she liked the feel of the stone on her legs, and partly because she did not like to see his name there, carved in, the dates of his birth and death below it. Every year the date of her own death passes in secret, just as every year before her father died the date of his death passed too. People were always dying. She had never noticed it before, but now the dead were everywhere. Each week they listed them in the paper, right alongside the names of the newly born.

When Mick died, Darlene and Uncle Tim had packed his apartment into cardboard boxes from the grocery store, and Hannah and Vivian had pulled out the things they wanted. There were so many things it was hard to choose, and Hannah often worried she'd chosen poorly, or not chosen enough. She'd wanted to keep it all—the T-shirts and hockey socks and chipped dishes and blue plastic tube glasses and ratty rag rugs still with dirt in their braids. The smell of him rose up from the boxes and made her throat ache. She pulled out his passport, which inside held an unsmiling picture of him, and she retrieved a set of cork coasters she had given him one birthday, and also his Polaroid camera. Film for a Polaroid camera was expensive, but Hannah's father had snapped photos like there was no tomorrow, and of course, in a way, there was not, not for him. Before he'd moved out, the fridge was covered with photos of Hannah and Vivian and Darlene, held on by A to Z fridge magnets, and afterwards there were only A to Z fridge magnets, minus three, and sometimes a grocery list.

Hannah put the passport and the coasters into her sock drawer, where she couldn't see them but would know they were there. She held the camera up to her eye several times, but it hurt to know that his blue eye had often been there and never would be again. She could not press the button that made the pictures slide noisily out, and eventually she put the camera in the sock drawer with the passport and the coasters.

Stuart was gone from her too, for the most part. He was a different boy than the one who had gone on pyjama rides, but she found herself drawn to him for a reason she did not know. Vivian, teasing harshly, gave a reason. She'd caught Hannah watching him from the living-room window and chided, "Is it a crush, Bee? Are you lovelorn?"

"Viva, stop," said Darlene.

But Vivian kept on. "You know why they call it puppy love? Because it turns you into a panting, pathetic puppy dog."

Only one time did she say, in her strange, caring manner, "Seriously, Bee. He's not a nice kid."

Hannah knew that. But she also knew that once he had been. She was as puzzled by the complete disappearance of the old Stuart as she had long ago been by the sudden emergence of the Visitor. Missing the old Stuart, she followed the new one in secret, though it only made her miss him more. She watched him smoke. She watched him steal. She watched him press a girl up against a tree and kiss her in a way that looked painful. One black Sunday she watched him step on a hornet nest, like grey crepe paper, which crumpled beneath his foot. It was the only time she saw him panic. He screamed once, a short wild sound, and Hannah emerged to save his life. Screaming too, jumping and shaking her head and long limbs, although there were no hornets on her. Stuart in shock and unable to move, no sound coming from him. The hornets swarming. Thick on his ankles

like black and yellow socks. In his hair, on his arms and legs, up
his shorts. Though Hannah, by some curious miracle, was not
stung at all, looking at his face she felt the stingers poking in all
over like tiny jabbing needles. She kept screaming. A hornet's
wing brushed her tongue, vibrating. Was Stuart swelling? His
face was puffy, lips ballooned. She shrieked, convulsed,
grabbed her hair to shake free imaginary hornets there.
Screamed loud enough that eventually someone came, a man or
a woman Hannah cannot remember, but who brushed the hornets off Stuart, sometimes slapping him and surely getting
stung too, and then grabbing Stuart's hand. Stuart lifted his
foot from the papery nest, which now was torn and ruined, and
ran out to the road.

In the man or woman's car Stuart wheezed and scratched, his
swollen tongue hanging thickly from his mouth. Hannah sat
between him and the man or woman and held her hands to her
face, smelling petunias. It may have been that very smell that
had kept the hornets from stinging her. Stuart hadn't had that
same protection, and so the hornets had stung him, filling him
up with poison. Any more stings and he might have stopped
breathing. A body could die so quickly. Any time you saw someone it might be the last time.

Vivian

Right now in India it was so hot people's eyes were burning. Here
it was not that hot, but Vivian, preparing to lie outside in the sun,
put on her blue-lensed sunglasses anyway. She looked through
them into Hannah's unprotected eyes and exaggerated her story.

"The sun can incinerate your eyes, you know," she said. "Those little blue-yolked eggs you have in your head." She made a sizzling sound. "You'd better watch it."

She breezed through the house in her bikini, passing Tim and pausing to watch as he removed the screen from the front door and set a big rectangular fan in its place, backwards. He said it would suck the hot air out, keep the temperature down.

"You're a genius!" Darlene squealed, stretching up on her toes to kiss Tim's nose.

Vivian thought Darlene was more likely the genius. She had a way of making people want to do things for her and give things to her without them ever realizing they'd been had. Once she'd acquired a whole trailer from a man, giving nothing in return. There'd not even been a reason for her wanting it. Except, perhaps, to see if she could get it. Now it was a useless fixture in their backyard.

Nearby, Vivian spread her towel. All afternoon she lay away from the shade, even the soles of her feet burning. At night the most tender parts were the small of her back, where the skin felt scraped and raw, and the hollows behind her knees, where the tendons inside also seemed burned. She was so burned that her blonde eyebrows glowed white and her freckles, nut brown, were tinged green.

Darlene disapproved.

"You're not a girl who should spend so much time in the sun, Viva," she had said just this morning. "You're like your daddy that way. Not like me." She pressed her own brown arm to Vivian's burnt one, comparing.

No, thought Vivian, I am not like you.

"You're a white girl through and through," Darlene went on. "And now look at you. You're red." She leaned towards Vivian, peering closely. "You're even a bit green, Vivvy. That can't be good."

Vivian wanted to say without smirking that she might be dying. Of greensickness, chlorosis, a maiden's disease. But Hannah, of late, staged her own death daily, and Darlene had made no attempt to find a cure.

Death might run in a family. Mick had died not last summer but the summer before, also on a hot day. He had strapped broad skis to his feet and let himself be pulled behind a boat, driven by a man who was inebriated, or at least tipsy, Vivian was sure. Mick, too, may have been drinking. He had always been reckless. Still, the event had been called an accident.

Their neighbour Chief Fergus had appeared in his official capacity. "There's been a terrible accident," he'd said, his fat face drained of colour.

Darlene looked as though she'd been slapped. Hannah shook all over, even her tight twisting braids. Vivian waited to be told why and how, what had gone wrong, but no one ever truly said. It was an accident. The day moved slowly on.

Late that night, while everyone moaned and wailed, Vivian went to the scene. Eyebrow Chuck's boat floated out where it always had. An old bleach bottle marked his mooring. Vivian stood at the shore, incredulous. The boat rose and dipped with the waves. It should have been pulled up on the beach, had yellow tape spread around it, but nothing had been done. No one had even bothered to check whether this had been an accident, whether there had been drinking. Vivian kicked off her shoes and swam out in her shorts and T-shirt, telling herself that the current had already carried his blood far away. She reached the boat and gripped the side. At first she couldn't pull herself up. All the strength had vanished from her thin, muscled arms, and so she hung there, staring at the boat's white side. She began to shiver. She hooked a leg over the side and pulled herself in and sat on the seat that faced backwards. This was where she would have been if she'd been spotting. Mick riding in the wake. She could not look there, and looked down instead, held her breath at the sight of his shoes on the dirty floor of the boat. For a long while she sat with her head on her knees, arms dangling. She looked up at the shoes again, reached and pulled them towards her. She slipped one on, then the other, and pulled the laces tight.

The moon was high in the sky when Vivian walked home, wet in Mick's wet shoes. She thought of the huge black shoes Pippi's father had bought her in South America, and how Pippi had planned to wear them forever. And the thought of that old book with its pages worn soft made her cry.

There were boys standing up ahead by the Snack Bar, and she walked past them in her big shoes.

"Hey, Viv—" one began in his loud cruel voice, but another shoved him. She moved into the street lamp's circle of light and out again, and they all stood silently and let her go crying by. She did not look to see how many they were, or who.

When she got home, the whole house was dark. She stood outside and wiped her face with her T-shirt. She changed into her own shoes and put Mick's inside her top and then stole to her room. But Darlene had heard. Just as Vivian slid the shoes beneath her mattress, Darlene came in and strode to the bed and pulled Vivian up by the arms, pinching.

"Where have you been?" she hissed, shaking Vivian. "What were you thinking?"

And just when Vivian thought she'd never made Darlene so

angry, she realized Darlene wasn't angry at all. Was now holding her tightly and rocking and sobbing and rubbing her back, and Vivian closed her stinging eyes to savour the moment.

Now, as she lay in the sun, she tried to shake the memory out of her head. But at some point every summer that other summer returned. Like vomit, like something burbling in a drain, it had to come up. She tried and tried to stop it, but it always flooded in. The smell of the water. The image of the boat with its damp white interior, permanently dirty. Gas rainbows swirling on the river's surface.

Mick once told her that it took half as long as you'd been with someone to completely get over them.

"It'll take me six years to get over Mom," he said. "Seven, if you count the years before we got married. I'm doing my time."

All this he had said with a kind light in his eyes to soften his words, but he meant every one. He was a sad man without her. And when he died, Vivian thought, How long for me to get over you? Half as long as I've known you is half my whole life. And as soon as she'd thought it she'd heard what he had told her the first time he'd gone.

"You're a tough girl, Viv. You can take it."

Even then she had wanted to say no. *No, I cannot take it. I am not a tough girl.* She had not yet known what else she'd be asked to endure.

Now they were three: Vivian, Hannah, Darlene, with Tim and various menfriends coming and going, bringing appliances, beer, often meat for the barbecue. Vivian surveyed from behind her blue-lensed glasses, sometimes sliding them down her nose to check the colour of the sky, or just to give a pointed look with her pale green eyes. She felt sexy with the glasses. Mysterious. Ursa Majorish.

She lay on her back and stared straight at the sun. Some people could not even show themselves to that orb. Porphyriacs, they were. Sunlight could cause their teeth to brown and erode. Hair might erupt on their faces, up high on the cheeks, where a beard was unexpected. The sun could blister porphyriacs so badly their noses might fall right off. Maybe I am like that, thought Vivian. And had an image of herself and Darlene in front of Darlene's big mirror. Darlene with a nose and Vivian without.

"You're not like me, Vivvy."

No, I am not like you.

After the bright outside, inside it was dark, spotty, hard to see. Vivian, oiled and glistening, let her eyes adjust. Sprawled on the carpet was the long body of Hannah, a tangy tomato smell all around her. Ketchup spilled from her ear, her open mouth. There were clots of it in her hair and a thin red line streamed from her eye. Hannah's lashes fluttered. Her mouth twitched.

Vivian stopped and stood above her, pressed a foot lightly on Hannah's belly and jiggled. But Hannah stayed dead, and Vivian moved past in silence, leaving a trail of baby-oil footprints and thinking how odd it was that *ketchup* was originally a Chinese word.

In the bathroom she pulled off her bikini, left it inside-out on the floor. Beneath it was her real skin, like a suit too. White and unblemished, cool and clammy to the touch. Hot water from the shower stung her burn but steamed her pores open, drew the dirt out, and was delicious because it was disallowed. Long, hot showers were expensive and wasteful, Darlene said, as though she herself was not frivolous. Steam moved in a cloud through the screen and into the outside. Everywhere beads of water dripped, swelling the toilet paper to unrollable proportions. In the corner by the door, pansy wallpaper curled away from the wall. Furry spots of mold sprouted on the ceiling. Vivian washed her sore skin delicately, and afterwards patted herself dry with a soft towel. Spread on soothing Noxzema, thick white like a paste.

A towel on her head and another round her body, Vivian moved to her bedroom and stretched out on her bed. Tucked beneath her mattress was her collection: Mick's flattened canvas shoes, a lucky stone worn smooth, the wings of a dragonfly pressed in wax paper and a dog-eared stolen book about dreams and nightmares that said people may indeed spend five years of their lives dreaming. The fact was meant to be astonishing, but Vivian was disappointed. Five years seemed a paltry amount of time, and she believed herself to be an anomaly in this instance, given that she dreamed often, in vivid detail. Lately, with summer, these were shocking dreams with much blood, Mick wholly alive and then in pieces. Vivian woke to her own silent screams, with her mouth stretched open so her sunburned lips cracked, a hiss caught at the back of her throat. Hannah dreamed too. But Hannah was able to call for help. Vivian heard her cries, and heard Darlene wake, her bedroom door cracking open, bare feet padding on the carpet. Darlene's voice in gentle highs and lows. In the mornings, provided a manfriend had not stayed over, Vivian saw that Hannah was in Darlene's bed, an eleven-year-old baby, the lump of her reedy body stretched diagonally, filling as much space as possible.

Vivian kept her dreams to herself, collecting them in the space marked "Notes" at the back of the stolen book. The book was large, hardcover, with a smooth dream-blue jacket. Even beneath her thick baggy sweatshirt the corners had poked out.

Vivian suspected she could steal anything. At times she was invisible, and therefore uncatchable. The book was not the only thing she had stolen. Many times she had fitted tight jeans under her own, tucked long, slim eyeliners up her sleeve. She had even stepped into sandals and left her sneakers, smelly and soiled on the inside, neatly displayed on the shelf beside the New for Summer sign. The blue sunglasses were stolen. Placed on the bridge of her burnt nose, one arm curved over each burnt ear, price tag still dangling. She also stole from girls at school (mawkish diaries, earrings, a tube top, After Bath Splash), from strangers (a set of keys, once a whole wallet), from Hannah (a bag of marbles, an Australian coin with raised kangaroos, several stale Halloween kisses) and Darlene (many dollars, a white dickey that fit nicely under V-necked sweaters). Many of the stolen things lay now beneath her, with the shoes and the stone and the wings and the book. Vivian concentrated, felt their shapes through the mattress, which was soft, lumpy and covered in a navy sheet that was faded in the place her body lay. Vivian could feel the book, hard but soft, between her shoulder blades. The dragonfly's wings fluttered near the centre of the bed, where the thin bluish skin was not yet burned. The stone lay at the base of her head, in the hollow space where her neck began. Sometimes she could feel the stone inside her head, pounding wet against the skull, searching for the way back out. She could feel the tube top and the dickey too, not flat but bunched, a mound of fabric beneath each knee. The shoes were right near the corner of the bed. She touched them each time she tucked in her sheets. Now she sat up and reached a hand beneath the mattress, feeling crumbs and lint and dirt and wadded tissue, and then the tube top. She shrugged the towel off and pulled the top on, rose from the bed and surveyed herself in the mirror. The towel on her head was turban-style, exotic. It pulled her eyes on either side, turned them felinesque. But the tube top flattened her small breasts, and white stripes from where the swimsuit had been rose out of the green fabric and over her burnt shoulders. Below, her belly and hips were also white, and sparse, rough hair sprouted between her burnt legs. She stood looking until she saw herself as ugsome and vile. Darlene said she could be lovely, if only she bothered to try.

"Boys would flock around you, Viva. A little effort and a lot less attitude would go a long way."

Vivian knew better than to trust her. Darlene's arrogance radiated outward. It encircled Hannah and Vivian; to Darlene it was without question that any child of hers would be physically appealing. But perhaps it was true, what Darlene said, that green was Vivian's colour. A match for her eyes, which were not as green as Darlene's but close enough. Vivian kept looking. There was the chance she was Ursaful even now, despite the chlorosis. Mick would have known that word, she thought, for it was not only a sickly maiden word but also a botanical term. Anemic leaves.

All of a sudden she felt swoony. Spots once more in front of her eyes, fuzzy black on either side, like tunnel vision or looking through binoculars. Vivian's head weighed heavy, the stone in there again. She lurched towards the bed and crawled under the sheets in her turban and tube top, blocking out the feel of the shoes and the rest beneath her.

Sunstroke nap, revealing round sea urchins, striped green and white like the sofa. Tiny squirming minnows, a swollen purple starfish. All of these move from the gashes in Mick's opened body. The starfish's meaty appendages pop out one by one, and it climbs with its many hairlike feet along the dead, muscular arm and shoulder, up the neck to the unsmiling mouth, where it stops, perfectly centred. Vivian can hear the starfish breathing through its own little hole of a mouth into Mick's useless one. The energy the starfish exerts in this futile stab at resuscitation turns it brilliant saffron, crimson, cobalt blue, chartreuse.

Tim the genius left and a different manfriend came for dinner. Darlene kicked off one strappy sandal and through the slats in the picnic table Vivian could see her pumiced toes rubbing the man's bare leg. She knew Hannah could also see the game going on. She could read Hannah's thoughts as though they were her own. She knew why Hannah pushed the stubby sausages aside, hiding them with an oily leaf of romaine lettuce. Meat conjured blood, any living thing dying.

Beneath the table there was touching, not touching. Touching again. It was disruptive but not dismaying. Any man-friend who was not Tim was bearable, first because he would disappear quickly, and second because Mick had despised Tim, and for that reason alone Vivian swore never to warm to him. She had witnessed the look on Mick's face when he first saw Darlene with Tim. It had been right here, in this backyard. Vivian had been reading *Huck Finn* under the shade of the maple tree, and Darlene, far across the lawn, lay sprawled on her lawn chair. A pitcher of lemonade sat on the picnic table, and Tim kept dipping his hairy hand into it, scooping out an ice cube at a time and rubbing it on Darlene. She lay smiling with her eyes closed and her head flopped to one side, and Tim just sat staring at her. Vivian heard the Alfa. She knew Darlene had heard it too. They all knew its defining sound. Vivian didn't move. She held her book so that her eyes peered just above it and waited to see what Darlene would do. Which was nothing. She lay swaying one leg, as if she did not know Mick would see her. And after the shouting, after he had squealed off and scarred the driveway, Darlene sobbed like a forlorn child. Vivian stopped watching. She looked back at the words on the page but the words she heard were Darlene's.

"He doesn't want me," she said, "but he doesn't want anyone else to have me either." Portraying herself as a trinket one could swap or stash away.

After dinner Vivian wanted to shower again but Hannah was in the tub, clothed and underwater, eyes bugged open, cheeks ballooned. Her shorts, T-shirt and hair lifted away from her, undulating in seaweedy slow motion. Vivian dipped her hand into the coolish water, reached between Hannah's feet to pull the plug. She stripped and inspected her burn while the water drained.

This next hot shower was less acceptable than the first, but it took a lot to enrage Darlene when a manfriend was visiting. She looked less attractive when angry—green eyes darting maniacally, perfect skin blotchy. From the bathroom window Vivian could see Darlene and the manfriend sipping Harvey Wallbangers from good glasses, their bottoms rounding out the lawn chairs. Darlene pretended to be engrossed in the manfriend's laughing chatter, but Vivian saw her made-up eyes narrow at the steam billowing through the bathroom screen. Read her angry thoughts, mixed with hot, sexy thoughts for the man. Tonight Darlene would *swive* with him. Vivian relished that word, so old it was not even in regular dictionaries any more. It sounded dirty and crude, and so it suited. The crude sounds would eventually wake Hannah, if Hannah did not wake from the terror of dreams alone. And she would not be able to crawl in beside Darlene because someone would be there already.

After the shower, Vivian looked at her face in the mirror. True, it had turned a strange shade. She went to Darlene's room in search of makeup that might change the tone of her skin, and there she found Hannah, sprawled diagonally on the bed, Flintstones vitamins dotting her open palm, the bottle uncapped. Her mouth was open, tongue lolling, a partly dissolved pink Betty stuck to its tip. She was wearing the manfriend's large blue flip-flops, and all around her narrow feet were the grey stains of the manfriend's feet.

"You'll get athlete's foot," said Vivian, "wearing that guy's shoes."

Hannah bolted up and kicked the shoes off, sat chewing the vitamin and watching Vivian in the mirror. Vivian hooked her fingers beneath the handle of Darlene's middle drawer and slid it open. The special powders and potions clinked together in their tiny glass jars, emitting, even before they were opened, heady smells of musk and lavender. She pulled the tray of bottles from the drawer and rested it on the bed beside Hannah, who pouted her lips and closed her eyes, ready. Vivian daubed a hint of blue onto Hannah's lids and frosty pink onto her lips.

"Oooh, Bee!" she said. "You look Ursaful."

Hannah grinned. Jumped from the bed to see herself in the mirror.

Vivian spread foundation on her burnt skin, then green above and below the eye in an attempt to make the eye itself greener. And then mascara, thick black, covering all the blonde. She was sixteen now. Soon she could leave home. Move to where something exciting would happen.

The house was still hot, despite the work of the genius. Vivian lay on the sofa reading, and intermittently Darlene entered through the side door. She came in to pee and reapply Fire and Ice lipstick and mix more Harvey Wallbangers. Each time she was more flushed, giddier, even though her own drink, Vivian knew, was what she called a Shirley Wallbanger, booze free, which gave her the upper hand in male company. And so, when she passed, she smelled not of booze but of heat and raspberries. Her gauzy wrap skirt, in rose-petal pink, was heavily wrinkled, etched on the bum with the weave of the lawn chair, and there was a thick snake of sweat up the back of her white T-shirt, through which her flowery bra was visible.

"Hoo!" she said each time she entered, fanning herself with a manicured hand. "Is it hot!" She pointed to her freckled brown chest, shiny with sweat. "Look—I'm glowing!"

In her strappy sandals Darlene zipped from room to room, and Vivian, lazing on the sea-urchin sofa, watched her go and come again, waiting for her to notice Hannah, this time staging a guillotine death with her head in the kitchen window. Vivian could not see into the kitchen from her place on the couch, but if she closed her eyes she could. She heard Darlene mixing drinks, clinking ice cubes into the good glasses, licking Harvey from her fingers. She lifted the glasses, ready to go, and then, out of the corner of one green eye: Hannah. A gasp.

"Girly!" she said in a panicked voice, and then she laughed uneasily. "You little drama queen."

The ice cubes clinked again and the drinks sloshed over the rims as Darlene set down the glasses. She pinched Hannah's bum in stretchy hand-me-down shorts.

"Whatchoo doing?"

Rubbed Hannah's back.

"Huh? Whatchoo doing?"

Lifted the ponytail of red-blonde off Hannah's back, blew

on her neck. Vivian felt Darlene's fruity breath on her own neck, cooling the skin for a brief, exquisite, vicarious moment. Cool. Hot. Cool again. Hot. The breath ruffled the tiny hairs on Hannah's neck and then moved past her, unsettling the dirt and dead flies on the sill. Darlene ran her fingers through Hannah's knotted hair, loosening the tangles. She rubbed her back again. Picked up the glasses and went outside.

Late at night, Darlene still sat outside, laughing with the man-friend. Vivian lay beside Hannah in Hannah's room. From here they could see the tops of trees, a street light, the starry sky. They had watched stars with Mick, but already Hannah was forgetting. They'd lie on the beach, just the way they lay now, but with his live body between them. Dig their feet into the cool sand underneath and watch the sky, waiting for a star to fall. Wishing one would and would not at the same time because they knew what it felt like to fall, how your stomach separated from its lining and turned at a different time than the rest of you. Some nights they'd lie there for hours, Hannah on one side, Vivian on the other, the fine blond hairs on Mick's arms tickling their skin. To pass time he'd show them Ursa Major, Ursa Minor, not just star names but movie-star names.

"Me and you, Bee," whispered Vivian, refreshing. "We'd be Ursa and Ursa." The s sounds hissed in her whisper. Vivian drummed her fingers on Hannah's hot belly. "If we watched long enough, one always fell, so fast your eyes could only follow it partway down, and then it was like we made it happen. Willed it, you know? The three of us combining our special powers."

Soon Hannah slept. Vivian listened to the steady whisper of her breathing and watched the moon move higher. Still Darlene laughed outside. Vivian moved to the living room, where Just for

Lovers music played on an ex-manfriend's stereo, speakers pointed at the window. She looked out at her mother and the man, then at the trailer. If the trailer had been a proper camper, a Winnebago, she would have ridden out of here long ago. Packed her things and headed down Highway 17 to who knew where. She could have lived in it on the side of any road.

Soon, she thought.

She couldn't leave town yet but she could leave this house. She could be gone all night, this night, and Darlene would never notice. She opened the side door quietly and stepped out. She stayed in the driveway a long while, leaning on the trunk of the manfriend's car, and then she walked slowly out onto the street. She passed the Ferguses', looked through the window at the fat chief and found herself thinking, What is the point of you? She could feel the anger rising. How could Hannah forget all those stars? All that time Mick had spent had been wasted. She passed yard after yard, moving through the night invisibly. The ground dewy, prickly beneath bare feet. She stole downhill towards the beach, where there were more willows than spindly Jack pines. Across Beach Avenue, the road a washed-out pebbly grey with spongy snakes of black gluing the cracks together. *Step on a crack.* And then across the gravel parking lot, which hurt the feet, to the root-snarled mossy shortcut through thick trees and blueberry bushes and pouchy lady's slippers. Smelling the water, feeling wetness in the air.

And then the river. At night you couldn't tell it from sky, except for the places that shimmered in the moonlight. She walked to the water, feet sinking in wet sand, and thought of the time she'd laved her foot there. She could smell the dead minnows. They lined the shore like discarded plastic bait. Once she had stepped on them. With a jackknife she'd sliced one open.

Gently squeezed its tiny head between her thumb and finger to make its mouth open, close, and Wren had protested, although the thing was already dead and stinking.

A breeze rose from the water, lifting the hairs on Vivian's burnt skin, forming goose pimples. She pulled off her T-shirt and shorts, and the places she was not yet burnt glowed bright white beneath the moon. In the water even her red skin was white. She waded in slowly, body cooling, and then was below the waterline, green eyeshadow washing from her lids. The caked black mascara loosened, revealing soft blonde lashes, fine as caterpillar hairs. Tears mixed into the river and flowed downstream, around the bend, where Mick last swam.

Hannah

Though Hannah did not remember falling-star nights, she did remember another astronomical night, when the earth's shadow blocked out the moon.

"I'll come and get you," her father said on the phone.

She twisted the cord's ringlet around her finger. She still was not used to talking to him on the phone. It seemed wrong, as though he were a friend calling up to ask her over.

"We'll stay up late and watch the eclipse," he said.

She waited for him in the Ferguses' backyard, playing cro-quet. Chief Fergus had arranged the hoops in a challenging way, involving the flamingos and hatted dwarves that dotted the yard. Through the slats of the fence Hannah could see pieces of Darlene and Uncle Tim, weeding the garden. Touching some-times. Kissing. It was better to watch the coloured wooden balls, but still she could hear them, Darlene's shrill giggle, and then the Alfa, Chief Fergus muttering, *That damn muffler;* and Hannah dropped her mallet, raced around the house, too late to keep her father from the backyard. His face red when she got there. No one talking. She stood behind him. Looked at the bulging veins on the white inside of his arm. And then Darlene shouting, Mick shouting, Tim shouting, *Stop shouting.* Hannah looked up, not blinking. Stuart peered through the slats in the fence, and far across the lawn Vivian lifted her book in front of her face. Hannah looked again at Mick's arm, at his shaky hand with its blond hairs and freckles.

When he turned to climb into the Alfa he did not look at her. He did not tug her braid or kiss her cowlick. Maybe he walked right through her. He squealed out of the driveway with his veiny arm stretched across the passenger seat, where Hannah should have been, his head craned backwards to look where he was going. Where was he going without her? He left her standing there. A blackfly landed on her eyelash and slid into her eye. Darlene sobbed and snorted and Tim held her. Held her up, Hannah knew, because when Darlene cried alone she slumped right down on the ground and stayed there for a long time.

Hannah cried too. Later, in her room. Cried until her throat ached and snot seeped down into it. Stuart in his pants-and-top pyjamas sneaked in through her window and crept across her floor, avoiding the places the boards creaked. He closed his fingers around her wrist, and she got out of bed and stepped into her flip-flops and followed him back across the floor, stepping where he stepped, trying to hush her breathing and the slap of her thongs. He boosted her up and out the window, and back in his quiet yard they watched the sky until the moon sank into the shadow of the earth, glowing copper.

Was the real Stuart that one or the other? As he grew older, he seemed more and more the Visitor, here to stay. Lots of days it made her sick to know him. When she went to his house she could tell right away who he was from the look of Mrs. Fergus. Shock pulled at her thin eyebrows, raised them high on her forehead and kept them there until the visit was over. A glossy film appeared on her eyes. Not tears or even dampness, but a layer of something. Stuart smashed dishes and used the shards to carve obscenities into the walls of the basement, and once to carve into his own skin. He peed in the garden like a dog, not bothering to hide his penis. He regularly dismantled the phone and the TV and the radio, and someone had to be called in to put them back together again. There was no knowing what he might do. Whether it would be merely bratty and a funny story for later, or catastrophic, a Fergus family secret, with Hannah a Fergus by proxy.

Vivian said he was demented.

"He's a bedlamite," she told Hannah. "Admit it or deny it."

Hannah could do neither because what was a *bedlamite*? A bedbug? A mite? All she knew was that she missed him.

The year Hannah was eleven, Stuart was sixteen, and he began to go everywhere with a girl more his age, Gabby Mirault. Hannah was surprised. He had had other friends before, but these had been fleeting, had come in twos or threes and had always been boys. Never had there been one solitary girl, a redhead, like Hannah. Gabby's hair was copper, with no softening blonde, and it spiraled from her head in a wild halo of curls. She never came to Stuart's door. She sat at the edge of the woods behind their houses and waited, perched in a tree. Some days she waited all afternoon and Stuart didn't appear. Yet she never seemed angry. Instead she seemed as if she didn't care either way whether Stuart joined her. She would have sat in that tree regardless. If he didn't appear, she climbed down, swinging from the last branch, and wandered away. If he did, they walked off together, and Hannah followed in secret. Sometimes Gabby saw Hannah and smiled with shiny lip-glossed lips, but she did not give Hannah away. Hannah liked her for that, and for the tube tops she wore over her bikini, and the cut-offs, which were frayed and cut high up.

That summer was so hot it seemed the grass might at any time ignite from the blaring sun. Hannah squeezed her eyes shut and saw the town ablaze. Evening was a safer time of day. The sun sinking slow into the mountains, glowing pink-yellow instead of fire orange. The pavement still held the heat of the day, so hot it smelled and briefly burned each bare foot that landed upon it. She was following Stuart and Gabby to the beach, and when they got there the dented sand was a relief, hot but cool deeper down. The beach was empty. Hannah sneaked behind a log and stretched out there, fingering the nooks where bugs crawled. She could hear Stuart and Gabby splashing, moving further out past the yellow plastic floats where the bottom dropped off. She peered over the log. Gabby led. She kept her arms up high like someone arrested. Stuart shovelled water at her and she squealed, arched her back, which was bare except for the tiny bikini strap bowed there, blue with yellow stars. Hannah slid behind the log again and put one more dent in the sand with her head. She rubbed her hair into it. Before they'd buried their father for real, Hannah and Vivian had buried him in sand, only his smiley face peering out. In pails they had gathered wet sand from the shore and packed it hard with their hands, and he had lifted himself up out of it, the sand cracking and falling away.

Hannah heard a splash and peeked again over the log. Gabby was on the raft now, and Stuart was in the water, circling. Each time he put his hands on the red wood and tried to pull himself up, Gabby stood on his fingers, laughing. Stuart was laughing too. He swam and circled again. He held the raft once more and Gabby stretched out her leg and placed her foot on Stuart's head, trying to force him under, but Stuart grabbed her ankles and in one smooth movement pulled her into the water, then lifted himself onto the raft. He was breathing hard. The raft swayed with his weight. He shook and water sprayed from him. When Gabby tried to climb back up on the raft, Hannah saw him crouch and put his hands on hers, pressing down. She saw him sit on the raft and watched his leg kick out, as if in slow motion, until his foot landed on Gabby's head. Gabby was laughing but he pushed her under, and her laugh disappeared. She was thrashing and springing up, sinking under again. Hannah looked at the sky. Today glowed green. It was Monday. How long could you hold your breath underwater? How long had it been? She looked back at Stuart. His excitement raised the hairs on her own arms and legs. She felt the muscles tensing in Stuart's long white leg, which rarely saw sun, and as her eyes moved along it she felt a cramp in his toe. She saw Stuart lift his hands and she saw Gabby's fingers slide from the raft into the water. She closed her eyes. She felt Stuart's bony foot on her head, as though her head were Gabby's. Her seaweed hair floated around her, tickled when it brushed against her skin. Between strands of it she glimpsed him, blurred and shimmery. She pressed up against his foot but couldn't get air. Water seeped into her nose and mouth, ears too, filling all her holes. Hannah opened her eyes and breathed a long wheezy breath. Stuart turned slowly towards her, blank eyes locking on hers, and she realized she was standing in plain view, and for a moment she could not move. Stuart's long, muscled body was tinged mauve in the queer light of early evening, his torso a face with eyes only. And then she was gone, running, sand kicking up behind her and stinging her back.

All the way home the trees and road and cars and houses blurred around her, and the memory of Pete the kitten cleared and blurred too. *What matters most.* Hannah's skin itched and tingled like something that didn't belong on her, and when Darlene saw her she let out a soft gasp and reached a hand to touch Hannah's forehead.

"Girly!" said Darlene. "What's wrong, Sweet Pea? Touch of sunstroke?"

Hannah opened her mouth but no sound came out. She looked at Darlene's painted-on lips and felt them pucker and press against her forehead.

"Let this be a lesson, Girly," said Darlene. "No staying so long in the sun without a hat." With a finger Darlene traced Hannah's crooked part-line, hot pink snaking through her hair.

She put Hannah in winter pyjamas and tucked her into bed, with a wool blanket to keep her teeth from chattering. She bent to kiss Hannah once more and the citrusy smell of her made Hannah want to latch on, tell all, but her mouth felt locked into the rhythm of shivering. And anyway, what could Darlene do? How could any bad thing be undone once it had already happened? Gabby Mirault was dead now, and Stuart was too. The old him.

He used to jump through the sprinkler with her. Hannah in her orange suit first thing in the morning, waiting on the front step. Pulling sticky petunias from the garden, chewing grass. Soon came Stuart in his big red shorts that stuck out like a triangle. Slamming his screen door and running across her lawn, past her, his bed hair flat but frizzy, one curved strand flopping. Around to the side of her house, and then the tap squeaked, the water sprang up and arced back and forth. Hannah sat on the sprinkler. Hard sprays of water squirting against her suit. Stuart leaping high above her, flying one way, legs in the splits over her head. Flying back, as if the water was still waving through the air, not stopped by Hannah's bum. She watched his legs when he jumped over her, the skin all white and marbly. Short chopped bits of grass stuck to his ankles. His long toes splayed like fingers.

Hannah thought now of Darlene's sing-song rhyme, no longer uttered since Mick: *Adam and Eve and Pinchmequick went down to the river to bathe. Adam and Eve drowned. Who was saved?*

In the middle of the night, Chief Fergus moved the cherry from his dashboard to his roof and made it flash and peal there. Hannah's room glowed red, then briefly white from the headlights. She lay and listened to the waning siren, which traced her steps in reverse.

Wren

Wren, for once, was sleeping when she should have been, and so the knock was a knock in her dream at first, but it kept on and finally woke her. She looked at her clock radio. It was 2:03. She heard Charlie hurry downstairs, and she stood at her window, looking down. Mr. and Mrs. Mirault were in her driveway. Their two white faces shone beneath the outdoor light. Wren pulled open her screen to better hear their voices. They told Charlie their daughter, Gabby, had gone missing. They called her Gabrielle, and they said that while she had stayed out late before, she had never stayed out this late. She was no angel, they told him, but she was a dependable girl. They said they had a bad feeling. Taking turns, they spoke in calm, low voices that filled Wren with a spreading dread. She, too, had that bad feeling.

"We've called the chief," said Mr. Mirault, "and we've knocked on a few other doors. We were hoping you—"

"I'll be right out," said Charlie. "Angie too."

Wren sat down on her bed. She listened to Charlie's feet take the stairs two at a time, and she heard him tell Angie.

"What are you waiting for?" he asked. "Get dressed!"

"But we can't leave Wren—"

"Ange, she's sixteen!"

"Charlie—think—another girl who's sixteen has just altogether vanished. I'm not leaving mine."

Wren appeared fully dressed in the doorway to her parents' room.

"It's okay," she said. "I'm coming too."

Families set out in teams to search for Gabby Mirault. Wren knew every snaking path, every fallen hollow tree. She led her parents through the woods, and Charlie and Angie called, "Gabby! Gabrielle!" The names from their mouths sounded strangely artificial, like words hollered in a movie. None of them had known Gabby Mirault, and so calling for her in such an intimate, desperate way seemed a gross invasion. Wren stayed silent but her eyes scoured the wood. She did not want to find Gabby but she did not want to overlook her either. Only the light from the moon and their two weak flashlights helped in the search. Wren shone her light down to the carpet of moss, and up, up through the trees to the highest branches. At night there was less colour in the trees. The green of the illuminated leaves appeared silvery, blanched of life. And yet the trees themselves seemed alive, their muscled, shadowy trunks and limbs like the live, breathing bodies of humans. Now she was scaring herself. She thought it must just be the darkness, the fact that it was late, that they were looking for a girl who might be dead. Any step she took might land on Gabby, or near her. *Gabrielle*. She heard the name again, in her parents' calling voices and the near and distant voices of the other searchers, an echoing echo. She looked with growing dread into the thick sprawling wood. Gabby could be anywhere, or nowhere. Murdered, perhaps, but by whom? Someone among them, or an evil stranger passing through? She might now be lying with her throat cut, her raped, bruised body hidden by leaves. Or perhaps she'd been mauled by a bear or a wolf, and that, while sad, would be better. Altercations between humans and animals rose up out of fear, out of no clear understanding of each other's language. It was painful to see, but less painful, less baffling, than the violence that arose between humans.

"Oh, God," said Angie. "This is hopeless."

She stopped on the path and Wren kept walking, until Charlie shouted after her.

"Bird! Wait—stay with us."

Wren turned and looked at her parents. Angie raised her hands to her face and began to sob silently. Charlie stood behind her. He wrapped his arms around her and rested his chin on her shoulder. He took Angie's two hands in one of his and held them. He whispered in her ear and wiped her wet face with his fingers. His flashlight was on the ground, lighting up a new path in the forest. Wren followed the beam with her eyes and thought again of all the places Gabby might or might not be.

At 4 a.m. they heard a shout echo off the water—just one word, *"Here!"*—and they made their way through the bush to the shore. A man held up his flashlight and the long yellow beam reached the raft and a hand sticking out from beneath it. Charlie and the man took off their shirts and their shoes, and ran into the halting heavy water, though there was no need for hurry now. Angie curled her arm around Wren's shoulder and gently turned her away. They passed a tube top and shorts lying inside out on the sand. They walked up the beach to a log and they sat there together, facing away. Wren leaned her head on Angie's shoulder, and Angie combed Wren's hair with her fingers. It was the nicest feeling.

It was still dark when they arrived home. Wren had left her bedroom light on and her screen pulled open, and a flurry of moths fluttered anxiously around the bulb, drawn to the brightness on dull powdery wings. She flicked the light off and lay down on her bed, willing them one by one out the window.

She thought, *Never swim alone,* it is the first thing they teach you.

There was no relief in the fact that Gabby's death had been an accident. Accidents seemed the very worst way to die. If one thing had been changed in the chain of events that led to an accident, that accident might never have happened. Accidents occurred in a flash, and altered whole lives for ever.

Vivian

After Mick died, Darlene went back to waitressing three nights a week. She was a terrible server but got extravagant tips regardless.

"Charm'll buy your way, Viva. Remember that."

She liked the job. Not just for the tips but for the social interaction. The restaurant was on the Trans-Canada Highway, and so peopled not just with locals but with travellers too. She said it was the only job possible for her.

"You know me," she laughed, rubbing her sore feet. "I could never get up early enough for a day job."

Which was true. Darlene loved sleep. When he had been with them, Mick had pulled her out of bed early every morning. Propped her up at the table and delivered cup after cup of thick black coffee. He said it was important not to miss the day sleeping. Even when they stayed up late, Mick woke early. He had been in tune with his circadian rhythm. He had never needed an alarm clock. Without him, Hannah and Vivian overslept repeatedly, arriving at school dishevelled and somnolent.

Summers were especially lazy. Vivian could sleep all day. She began to believe she might have hypersomnia. Often she woke to a sky that was bright afternoon blue, and even then she could sleep longer if she wanted to. Some days she slept until two or three, but more commonly it was noon when she arose.

Come noon the day after Gabby Mirault died, Hannah, Vivian and Darlene were just sitting down to breakfast. Vivian bit into a hot, sweet Pop-Tart and saw Wren ride up the drive on her bicycle. Wren did not grin or wave. She let her bicycle fall beside the lobster trap on the front lawn, though she had always, as a rule, used the kickstand.

"Hey, Peaches," said Darlene. "Want a Pop-Tart?"

Wren shook her head no, though she had never not wanted that treat, forbidden at her own home, and Vivian knew something awful had happened.

Wren sat at the table.

"Gabby Mirault died last night," she told them. All of them looked at her, waiting. "She drowned," said Wren. "It was an accident."

Vivian pictured that girl, her live-wire hair, penny red and springing. Once, while reading in the backyard, Vivian had looked up and seen Gabby sitting in a tree at the edge of the woods. A strange place to be because there was nothing there but trees and more trees. She sat in the V of a maple, her legs stretched up the limb. Vivian thought, *incongruous*. She was like a peacock there, misplaced. Her vibrant hair and her tank top, vermilion, blazed against the muted tones of the forest. Vivian had stared from behind her blue glasses, and Gabby, as though drawn to that stare, saw her and smiled. A brilliant smile, live like her live-wire hair, and easily given. But Vivian had not returned it. Had hidden behind her glasses, pretending not to see. Looked back to her book and read a whole chapter without looking up again, and when she did, Gabby was gone.

Wren told them how all night long they had looked for Gabby Mirault, calling and calling. She said that many families had shone a light into bushes, into alleys and garages, and finally the light lit up a hand sticking out from under the raft.

Darlene gasped.

"Oh, God," she said, "those poor, poor people."

Hannah stood and clutched the edge of the table.

"What is it, Sweet Pea? Is it the sunstroke?"

"I feel sick."

Vivian looked at Hannah. She was pallid. Too white for a girl with sunstroke. But she was quivering. Even her teeth were chattering. Darlene put an arm around her and led her down the hall to the bathroom.

"It was awful," said Wren when they had gone.

"Why?" asked Vivian. "It's not as if you knew her."

Wren paused. She stood and turned her back to Vivian, looking out at the yard.

"You don't have to know a person to feel sad when they die."

Vivian shrugged. "People drown all the time. It's part of life. We of all people know *that*," she said.

When Wren did not respond or turn, Vivian told her that people even drowned in the winter.

"It must be far more horrible," she said. "Once a man and his Ski-Doo went through the ice, and nobody found him till spring. He was still in his snowsuit. It kept him warm, though. His body had actually boiled and turned into mush. Can you imagine unzipping him and finding that?"

Wren left. She said she was tired but she was livid, Vivian could tell. Livid because of Vivian's cruel indifference. *Livid* was a perfect word. It came from the Latin *livere* for "bluish," and it could still mean that. Of a bluish, leaden hue. Discoloured, as by a bruise. Gabby Mirault would certainly have been blue when they found her. Livid, but dead.

Vivian went outside and sat behind the trailer. No one could see her from here, not Darlene or Hannah or the neighbours. She cried hard and she had no idea why.

Hannah

When Gabby Mirault died, the town's Canadian flag was lowered to half-mast, something they'd not done for Mick. Vivian said a child's death was more tragic than an adult's, but Hannah didn't understand that. Weren't you leaving more people behind if you'd lived longer? Didn't more people love you?

All the town went to Gabby Mirault's funeral. Stuart stood

with Chief and Mrs. Fergus, but Hannah could only look once at him, and briefly. His lips were purple and there were purple circles beneath his eyes.

Hannah sat between Wren and Vivian, holding Wren's narrow hand, even though she was eleven now and too old for that. Vivian pointed out Mrs. Mirault, who clutched the sleeve of Mr. Mirault's good jacket. The jacket stiff, like something not often worn. His shirt rubbing his neck, chafing the skin. Hannah rubbed her own neck. She looked at the wrinkled sleeve as Gabby's mother released it to move into the pew, and then she looked at Gabby's mother. She saw Gabby in the woman's face, though her hair was duller red and more frizzy than curly. She saw Gabby in her mother the way she saw herself in Darlene and Vivian. Sometimes an expression formed on Hannah's face, and she could feel that her face was, right then, one of theirs. They were all made from each other. They each had thin lips and large eyes. Hannah was part of Vivian and Darlene, even part of Wren and Angie, as they were part of her and each other. She was always aware of that, though the others seemed not to know.

This funeral was in a different church than Mick's had been. A high-ceilinged Catholic one, with a looming Jesus. The windows that stretched along each wall glowed red and orange, and though outside wasn't visible, the sun streamed through. People piled in and brought wet heat with them. Hannah pulled her sundress slightly open and blew on her own sticky chest. All the parts where skin touched skin stuck together.

Up front was Gabby in a long brown box, Jesus looking down on her. Hannah's father had been in a long brown box, although it was not what he'd wanted. They had put him in a hole in the ground and scooped dirt on top, and now they would do that to

Gabby. Hannah felt tears well up. She looked up at Him. Salty snot dripped from her nose and she licked it away. Vivian pressed a Kleenex into Hannah's hand, squeezing once and then taking her hand away, and Hannah used Wren's hand to squeeze back.

"Catholics are from the wrong side of the tracks," Vivian whispered, cajoling. "At the separate school they have to slow dance with balloons between them so they don't get carried away. They have lusty blood. Even though they take classes in religion and have to pray all the time, they're the ones who smoke and fight and get pregnant and drop out of high school." Vivian grinned lopsidedly. "Dad called them cat lickers."

The sound of his name made Hannah's stomach turn over. Would it always? She could hear him saying it, *cat lickers, cat licks*, cranking up his Valley accent to make them laugh. She could see him too, smiling with one side of his mouth the way Vivian did. What would happen if she blurted it out? Right now, loud. *Cat licker, cat lick*. In her head she said it hard, spitting the *ck* sounds out from the back of her throat. She thought of Gabby's blue-and-yellow starred bikini, her inside-out shorts on the beach. She could stand up right now and tell. But too much time had passed. She had been throwing up for days.

"What a bug you've got," Darlene had said.

That's what it had felt like. A horrible bug crawling around inside her.

She looked in the crowd for Stuart. If she couldn't see his eyes she could watch him. His shoulders in a suit jacket were broad and mannish. She looked at the back of his head and thought that she'd been looking at the back of him for a long time now. She would stop following because, anyway, he really was gone.

The organ music swelled and quavered like an old lady's voice. Wren was an only child, like Gabby. Could two parents with a dead daughter still be called a family? When Mick left the first time they stopped feeling like a family, and in one more year, when Vivian left for school, they would feel even less like one. Hannah alone with Darlene, eating pickle-and-plasticky-cheese sandwiches.

Men in suits carried Gabby from the church to the graveyard, and everyone trudged behind. Hannah held Wren's hand as Stuart passed with his parents. Hannah kept her eyes lowered. She watched his feet, enormous in polished dress shoes. She looked at her own flip-flopped feet and the bright red toenails there, and then quickly up through the oak leaves that dangled like limp, many-fingered hands. The sky today was too bright and clear. Hannah lifted her arms away from her sides to let hot air in there. Sweat stuck tendrils of hair to her neck and the sides of her face. The men in suits put big seat belts under Gabby's coffin and they lowered her slowly in, the way they had done when Mick died. All around the hole was dark, damp earth, smelling of watered gardens.

Right now she had the urge to fake her death, a thing she'd not done in a long time. When you faked your death you could just lie there, do nothing. You did not have to say one word, or even think. You could close yourself. Hannah shut her eyes. Now she could feel herself in Gabby's cold body, swaying, going underground. When they tossed the soil on, it was as though they tossed it on Hannah's skin. Moist but crumbly. It built up coolly around her and then on top, weighing her down. Soon there would be faceless worms crawling through. Did worms eat humans? Wren said they did; it was part of nature. When birds hit windows their bodies got carried off by cats, skunks, maybe raccoons, if raccoons ate meat, but something told her no, they did not. The swaying belts creaked and the dirt thudded onto Gabby's coffin. Hannah opened her eyes and looked at Gabby's crying mother, Gabby's crying father. It was better to think of raccoons, who had tiny hands like human hands with gloves on. They could unlatch the garbage cupboard in the backyard and pull things out one by one, picking and choosing. Vivian said things that were not pleasant happened every day in the wild world of nature, and no one got upset about it.

The next day Hannah sat on her father's marker. Moss grew on the stone, proving that now he had been dead for a long, long time. From here she could see the mound of dirt that was Gabby, fake flowers growing up out of it since real ones just died and drooped over. Death was part of life. She eased a blade of grass from the ground and chewed the spicy end of it. Grass was a living thing. It didn't have a face but neither did a worm. Could it feel us stepping on it? How could we know? She thought of Wren's bugs and of worms without faces. The eyes of potatoes. Potatoes kept your health up. A lot of people had died in the potato famine but at least there'd been a reason, a blight to explain things. Hannah thought of Pete, of Gabby Mirault. Of Lily Sinclair's missing Chinese mother, the disappearance like a death. She thought of Mick and traced the letters of his name with her finger. Death was something you got over, like any bad thing.

Vivian

Vivian passes through Barry's Bay, making her languorous way home. She wishes she had brought a man as a buffer, as she has done in years past. Having cacophonous sex in her childhood room. Darlene hated that. She never said, but Vivian knew. The things that most bothered Darlene were the things she never mentioned. You could count on her for that, at least. Nevertheless, she had scrawled *Vivian and Guest* on the envelope that contained the invitation. And later, over the phone, she had casually asked, "You bringing a date, Vivvy?" But just now there is no one worth the effort. Instead Vivian has cut her hair so short that her scalp shows through the white-blonde bristles. Darlene will hate that too. She might give off vibes mean enough to make Vivian set up the trailer and sleep there instead. Which would be no sacrifice. The trailer was the best thing Darlene had ever got for free, though she'd made no use of it. It had come from a man passing through. Darlene often joked that he'd stopped at the restaurant for dinner and left the trailer as a tip.

"I guess he was short on change," she laughed.

Who knew the real story? Vivian didn't care to. She only knew that with the trailer came new possibilities.

She was eleven that year. She had not been further west than Grandma and Grandpa Gillis's or further east than the Bonnechere Caves the morning a stranger arrived, pulling a trailer behind a new black Ford. He made three short toots with his horn and Vivian woke, peered out her window. With ease he backed the trailer into the driveway, disappearing from Vivian's view. She waited for him to appear again and drive off, realizing he had the wrong house, but he did not. She crept through the house and sunk to her knees when she reached the side door, so as not to be seen, but he had spotted her. How, she did not know, for he was working with his back to her when suddenly he spoke.

"Always make sure this is secure before you go anywhere."

Vivian didn't respond. She glanced around. There was no one there other than herself, and him.

He stood and faced her. Only her eyes appeared above the door's window frame.

"Come on out," he said. "I'll show you."

Vivian opened the door and stepped out. Up close he resembled Pierre Trudeau, bald in that handsome way. He had those same high cheekbones and kind flashing eyes.

The trailer was all the way free now, and the man stood holding onto it. He pointed to the round metal knob on the back of his car and said, "Hitch." Then he pointed to the matching cup that stuck out from the trailer and said, "Tongue." He looked at Vivian. "This part's obvious, no?"

Vivian nodded and let herself smile.

"But make sure these are perfectly lined up. That's the hardest part—backing the car into just the right spot. If you manage that with precision, the rest is child's play."

She liked the way he said that. As though she were no child.

Near the cup was a little lever, which he flipped up. "You'll never get anywhere if you don't do that. Once the tongue is on the hitch, pound it down with your foot. Don't be gentle about it. You don't want to take any chances. Losing a trailer on the road could cause any number of gruesome accidents. That's why you have these," he said, pointing out two chains that hung from the tongue. "Criss-cross them and hook them on here, by the hitch, one on either side." He pulled a bolt from his pocket, held it in front of her eyes and slipped it through a hole in the tongue. "That's about all," he said, "except for the jack. Here, you hold the trailer. Hold it just so and it won't tip back or forward. Balance is the key."

She could not fathom its lightness. She covered the black metal cup with her hand and watched as the man let down the stand that would hold the trailer in place without her.

"Okay," he said. "My work here is done."

He smiled and saluted. He climbed into his car and drove away, and Vivian saluted a belated goodbye.

Darlene laughed when she saw it. She stood in the driveway, in her pink kimono, with her hands on her hips and said, "Well, girls? Where do you want to go?"

Hannah right away said Florida, which was what she always said, but Vivian went inside and opened the Ontario map. All day she looked. There was not a place she didn't want to go. She chose a southwest route that led down through Manotick and Vernon and Winchester. On it went to New York State, ending finally in Hannawa Falls. Vivian showed Hannah, knowing she needed her on side. Hannah's eyes widened with delight, and together she and Vivian kept on and on until Darlene promised that trip. They would go all the way, trailing that trailer, setting it up each night, sleeping within the soft green walls.

"When?" asked Hannah repeatedly.

"Soon," said Darlene.

As soon as possible.

Sooner than you know.

Sooner or later.

They waited and waited. Hannawa Falls was on the Raquette River, and south of there was the Rainbow Falls Reservoir. That was where the map ended, so perhaps it seemed far, too far for Darlene. Vivian added the little red numbers that showed the distance in miles.

"It's not that far," she said one morning, trying to curb the edge in her voice.

"What's not?" asked Darlene. She sipped her coffee and left a lip stain on the mug.

"Hannawa," said Vivian. "Hannawa Falls."

Darlene sighed. "That again? What is it with you two and Hannawa Falls?"

Vivian felt herself heating up. She knew her eyes had hardened to that cold mean green and she tried to warm them again.

"You said pick a place," she told Darlene. "We picked one."

"Hannawa Falls," said Hannah, grinning. "Or Florida. That would be okay too."

"Shut up," said Vivian, too meanly. She smiled quickly to cover the meanness and said, "Florida's too far, Bee." She looked back at Darlene. "But Hannawa Falls is only—"

Darlene held her hand up. "Enough!" she said. "No American vacations. I know what I said but I hadn't quite thought it all through."

Vivian clenched her teeth. Her eyes narrowed and she felt her ears move back on her head.

"Don't you look at me like that, Viva. I'm making a responsible choice. It wouldn't be safe to drive in foreign territory without a licence. If they throw me in jail down there," she said, "I might never come out."

"Why don't you just get a licence?" said Vivian, one side of her top lip rising.

"And draw attention to the fact that I've been breaking the law all these years? I don't think so. Plus, why should I?" said Darlene. "I already know how to drive."

Vivian's anger hung around her, an aura.

At Angie's for a barbecue, Angie said, "Pass the buns, Darlene," and Vivian grabbed the bowl before Darlene could.

"Don't ask *her* for anything," she said, looking at Angie, who blinked and held the bowl. "She promised to take us camping and now she won't."

No one said anything. Charlie looked at Angie and Angie looked at Darlene, who flushed and laughed it off.

"Viva," she said, as though chiding.

A pulpy red-brown ant skittered along the picnic table and Darlene quickly squished it with her napkin. Wren winced.

"Of course I'll take you," said Darlene. She balled up the napkin and tucked it under the rim of her plate. "It's just a matter of when and where." She smiled at Charlie and Angie, then leaned towards Wren. "Want to come, Wrenny?"

"Yeah," she said. "I do."

Vivian looked at Wren. She had not once made eye contact with Darlene. "Don't hold your breath," she told Wren in her flat voice. "You'll suffocate."

Hannah

After Darlene goes to bed, Hannah flicks off the TV. The house is utterly quiet except for the small-town noises from the yard and the trees beyond. Hannah, still waiting for Vivian, moves to the window and looks out at the trailer, which may sell with the house. It had been given to them by Tim. No. By a man named Will from Napanee, she thinks now. He had showed them the difference between a red pine and a white pine, and they had secretly laughed because he'd got it reversed. Mick had taught them every tree in the forest. Will had known his birds, though, or seemed to. He pointed out one who sang the same short song over and over. "Don't whip poor Will!" he bird-songed, laughing. He had rolled into town with the camper and out of town without it. Darlene had a way of getting everything for free.

How they had longed to camp! The trailer sat alone in the backyard, making a patch of yellow grass. But Darlene was no camper. When they were still a family Mick had always said he would take them to Florida, which had appealed to Darlene, to be tanned in winter. All he wanted was to see the manatee, friendly as puppies, he said, but that had never happened. Hannah had waited for it and Vivian had waited too, not believing.

To Vivian, Hannah had said, "I want to visit It's a Small World After All."

"That's not the name of the *place*," Vivian had said. "It's only a line from the song." She had rolled her eyes at Hannah, who had looked on blankly. "Anyway, don't hold your breath," she'd said.

It was a good thing she hadn't.

But it was not as if they'd never gone anywhere. Instead of Florida they'd gone to Eganville, all four of them, and seen the Bonnechere Caves. The cave was a hole in the ground beside the brown Bonnechere River. The tour guide said that if you went in at the right time of year, in September or October, hundreds of bats hung upside down in there, or flew past you, so close you felt the air stirred by their wings. But they had not known that. They had come at the wrong time. There had only been one bat sighting in the whole month of July, the little chalkboard at the caves' gift shop said so, and added an exclamation point to make it seem exciting.

"Damn," said Mick, pinching Darlene's behind. "We could have seen bats! Hundreds of them!"

"Ha-ha," she said.

He was teasing, of course. He knew Darlene would hate to see bats. She said they were just like birds, who all had lice and also rabies from biting each other, but that they were actually even worse than birds because their wings were sticky and got stuck in your hair. Hannah didn't like the thought of that, a bat stuck in her hair. She knew there was the chance Darlene was exaggerating, but just the same she was glad they had come at the wrong time, though she did not say so out loud for fear of disappointing Mick. He wanted her to love bats, she knew, but the best she could do was pretend.

The ceiling was low in the cave, made from brown and dripping sculpted rock. Lights like patio lanterns were strung along each side, but still it was dark down there. They walked with the guide on a narrow plank further and further into the earth, and they listened as he recounted the history of the caves, of Mr. Woodward who'd floated in here in his canoe and dropped his flashlight in the water. It was then that the guide turned the lights out. It was so dark that Hannah could not even see the regular muted pink glow of Saturday, and for a moment everyone was silent.

Outside in the light, Mick said your eyes could never adjust to a darkness that dark. He said there was no telling where the caves really ended. That just because the tour ended didn't mean there was not more cave beyond it. Hannah imagined that ahead it might spread out everywhere, in every possible underground direction, just as, above ground, the road beyond Eganville might—to Renfrew, to Arnprior and far along to Ottawa, where they had never been but where there was the longest skating rink in the world.

Afterwards they stopped in the town of Eganville and bought fries from a chip truck. There was the smell of the vinegary fries and also of creeping thyme, which crept in purple flowers down the hill to the water's edge. They stood eating and looked at the Bonnechere River, and at the dam from which rushing water flowed.

"Look, Girly," said Darlene. "Have you ever seen a waterfall before?"

"That's not a waterfall, Dee," said Mick. "Don't teach her that."

"What's a waterfall then?" Hannah asked.

"Niagara Falls," said Mick without pause. He put his hand on Hannah's hair. "Someday I'll take you there."

⁓

Hannah was six when the trailer appeared, or seven. Because of the mishap with Hannawa Falls, she knew that any wrong thing might cancel Darlene's promise of a camping trip to Algonquin Park. She did not hold her breath, but she did keep the excitement low in her belly, and when it was mentioned, *the camping trip*, she felt a nervousness wash through her.

Even on the day of departure she held on to that shell of calm. She woke early. Sleep scabbed her eyes in two tiny clumps and some crusted her lashes. By the back door sat the cooler, cool blue and white, as well as a borrowed stove that looked more like a suitcase made from green tin. It was hard to believe you could cook on that. Borrowed too were four rolled sleeping bags, one Thursday blue with the lighter blue of Tuesday inside. She would sleep in that one, blue on blue.

Larger than ever they drove through the town and the camper followed. They drove past the Loblaws parking lot, which was filling up with cars and shoppers. For others it was an ordinary Saturday. Everyone watched them go by, pulling that trailer. Poor you, she thought. Poor you. She wanted to wave like the queen, moving just her hand, holding all her fingers close together.

The excitement inside her swelled as they reached the highway, the Trans-Canada, which could take you everywhere, to every province, even Prince Edward Island, though there was that gap between. The excitement grew and kept growing and pushed up through her stomach and chest. Wren and Vivian rode in the back seat, and Hannah rode up front with Darlene, leaned her head out the open window. She was hiding her smile, not opening her lips, so no bugs could get stuck in her teeth.

Outside smelled of hot, wet summer, a smell that hung in the air, and then at the gas station came the going-places smell of gasoline. When had she ever been anywhere other than Eganville? They dipped into Algonquin Park, and then they dipped back out to find some place more civilized. They ate their packed lunches of peanut butter and banana on squishy white bread, and two towns away they stopped for chip-truck chips, rolling all the windows completely down afterwards and squirting Darlene's lavender perfume so their hair wouldn't stink. It was late when finally they found a spot that suited everyone, a spot close enough to a town, in case there was some sort of emergency, a bear or a group of bad men. Darlene's lipstick had worn to a thin pink line encircling her lips. Sweat and wind had smudged her mascara, the smudges like pale bluish bruises beneath her eyes.

"Okay," she said, sighing. "Let's set this puppy up."

They unbolted and removed the hard top of the camper and began to pull at the canvas, but all of them jumped at the mass of centipedes that wriggled there. Darlene screeched and ran back from the camper, grabbing at a corner of the top that now lay on the ground.

"Get it back on!" she shouted, and they all stared at her. Her pinned-up hair had come loose and it hung now, covering one smudged eye. "I'm not sleeping in there!"

Vivian's face reddened. She swatted the centipedes with her bare hands, stilling some and making others slither more. They scurried with hairy legs over and under each other, moving in and out of the folds of canvas and sometimes dropping from the camper to the ground, where Vivian stepped on them.

"Get it back on!" Darlene screamed again, dragging the top in the dirt.

Vivian slapped Darlene's bare arm and slapped again at the centipedes, and Wren slapped Vivian with her mitteny hands.

"Don't!" Wren shouted, and flapped her too-long sleeves. "Stop it!"

Hannah watched Wren. Darlene had squished that ant on the picnic table when all it had done was be an ant, and Wren had felt it, Hannah could tell. What did Wren feel now? Hannah felt nothing. The excitement gone. She watched everyone slapping and screaming, and then she watched them slowly lift the top, not looking at each other, hating each other, and bolt it back on.

That had been camping.

They drove home in the dark with all the windows up because Darlene wanted no bug to have a chance to crawl out of the trailer, along its sticking-out tongue, and then along the car into a window. Near town Darlene flipped on the ceiling light, putting them all on show. She wiped the ring of pink from her mouth and pressed fragrant lipstick to her lips. She rubbed her lips together and smacked them, then turned off the light.

"Tomorrow we'll get up and I'll put makeup on everybody," she said cheerily. "You too, Wrenny."

She peered in the rearview and grinned, and Hannah thought, It's true what she says. Lipstick does make your teeth whiter.

Hannah turned and looked at Wren and Vivian, and then behind them to where the trailer followed. It followed them all the way back into town, retracing that route, past the Loblaws parking lot, empty now, and back along their own dark street.

In the morning Wren and Vivian left on their bicycles, before Darlene had the chance to make them up, and Hannah almost cried for Darlene, who, in her holey pink kimono, had tiptoed with her makeup tray past Hannah's room and down the hall to Vivian's. Hannah watched her cowboy curtains move in the breeze. Sunday was black, which was not a bad thing. She would sit on Darlene's bed and let her toenails be painted and that would make Darlene happier.

"Your toes are so long, Girly!"

Every time she said it there was surprise in her voice, as though she had never seen the toes before.

"Long as fingers. Even knuckly!"

Hannah wondered, Was this good or bad? Wrinkly elbows were bad, as was baldness, even small bald spots. Unevenness.

Darlene kept the camper hitched on all that day, and for many days afterwards, because it wouldn't pop off easily, and also because Uncle Tim had gone to so much trouble getting it on there in the first place. He had backed up repeatedly, aiming for the hitch, and then had spent hours with the pulled-out coloured wire, trying to hook up the blinkers. Vivian had laughed at him, which made Darlene angry, but even she said that it would never have taken Mick so long. Now she said it was a waste to unhitch the thing and stick it in the backyard.

"Plus it's a bit fun having it on there, don't you think, Girly?"

Hannah nodded but did not agree. The trailer made a show of them, there for no reason.

"Going camping, eh?" people said.

But they were not.

It was not asked as a question that required any answer because the answer seemed so obvious. After a while it was not asked at all.

On it stayed for weeks, reminding Hannah.

Darlene seemed to have forgotten about the bugs and no longer insisted the windows be rolled up. When she parked downtown she left that big half of them sticking out on the road with the hazards on.

Wren

It was hot the night they drove home from camping. From not camping. Wren longed for a breeze, a real one that carried the fragrance of grass and hot tar, but there was only the blower blowing stale air.

Everyone sat silent.

Vivian, with her arms crossed, clenched and unclenched her jaw, staring at the seat in front of her, above which floated a tangled wisp of Hannah's hair.

After a while Darlene switched on the radio and sang along to lighten the mood. Wren wished to sing too, because even crooning a song about someone dying or losing in love could make you feel good. She would sing if Vivian would, but, glancing at her, she knew Vivian would not. Vivian could know a song by heart even before she'd heard it all the way through, predicting not just the rhyme, which she said was always predictable, but the melody too. She must have got that from Mick because Darlene sang poorly. She could not mimic the tone of a singer the way Vivian could, and mostly she used *na-na-na* instead of the lyrics, so that a word, when injected, seemed an out-of-place sound.

She sang on regardless, in her solitary way. In this cocoon of deflated elation, they passed the towns they had more happily passed earlier that day. Two towns from home, where this morning they had eaten french fries from greasy paper bags, Darlene pulled off the highway at a gas station.

"Freezies, anyone?" she asked.

When she went in, Hannah turned around in her seat and asked Wren about the centipedes.

"Will they all be squished now, under the top?"

Vivian sighed and rolled her eyes but the other two ignored her.

"No," said Wren. "Not all of them." She said that even now the ones who had survived were laying new eggs in the folds of the canvas. "And if parts of them were amputated," she said, "they can grow those parts back."

"Like a worm," said Hannah.

"Kind of."

"So they'll always have a hundred legs?"

"Oh, look," said Vivian, interrupting. "Here comes the Bipede."

Darlene was crossing the parking lot, sashaying on her two long legs. She got in the car, flashed a smile at each of them, and passed the icy treats around. They drove on in the heat.

What Wren had wanted to say was that, no, a centipede would never have a hundred legs, it was just not possible: a centipede was made up of segments, each segment like a pearl on a string, and these were always oddly numbered. There might be fifteen or twenty-one or forty-three such pearls, each with two legs, and these could never add up to one hundred.

She could also have told how a mother centipede builds a hill of mud, scoops the top out and lays her eggs there. Then she curls her body all around the hill, there to save the eggs if needed. Right now there might be many curled mothers in the trailer behind them. When the babies are born, only seven pearls long, she stays close to them. Licks them clean the way a cat preens kittens.

Vivian

Even though his cars were often dented or missing pieces, Mick always said a car was a thing of beauty. It took you places you might not go without it, and it gave you the freedom to go any-where you wanted on your own. That Alfa had been rusty. With a tied-on muffler and leaking oil, leaving a trail wherever it went. The wipers were always broken, and in winter Mick scooped snow from the side of the road to clean the spotty windshield. He rubbed the shiny wood steering wheel as though he cherished it. The steering wheel of Vivian's blue Dodge is cracked plastic, covered in fake, blue, bath-mattish fur. The lit-up numbers of the radio glow green but no sound comes out. The Alfa had had no radio. Just a dark hole where the radio should have been. When Vivian and Hannah complained, Mick unrolled his window and bellowed made-up arias that both embarrassed and delighted them.

The Dodge is emitting low rumbles and a faint burnt-rubber smell that is not alarming but mildly disconcerting. Vivian passes the dark, nameless road that leads to Tim's. Town is five minutes from here. Past a stretch of thick black pine trees, and then the water tower that always reminds her of the boy who thought he could fly. He had been from Oklahoma but they had heard about him all the way up here in the Ottawa Valley, and even Mick, who shunned disgusting American news, stood riveted to the television. That such a thing could happen, he'd said, shaking his head. Yet, tragic or not, he said it was good the boy had died. You couldn't survive a fall like that and not become a vegetable.

When next they picked berries near the highway, Vivian had pointed to the water tower.

"He climbed all the way up," she explained to Hannah, "and then he tried to fly off but he landed—*thunk*—on the ground. He landed on his feet and his legs got shoved up inside his body, and he died like that, all midgety, still standing."

She squatted with her legs hidden in her sundress and mocked the fallen boy's dead face.

But Hannah wasn't watching. Stood looking high up at the criss-crossed metal, painted chipped mint green. Missing yet another good story.

Vivian rumbles past the dairy and the fluorescent gas station, where you can now rent movies. Then onto the road to town, downhill towards the river, black too. She passes the tiny home where Wren lives with Brie and a long-tailed dog, Delilah. She would like to go in and sleep there instead. Delilah stretched out alongside her in the morning, licking her face with that thick, wet tongue. But all the lights are off. Wren, Brie and Delilah, snug in their beds.

At Darlene's, Vivian parks behind Hannah's car and turns the engine off, and for a moment the Dodge keeps running, then shudders to a stop. It is so late that Darlene will be asleep, but angry in the morning, and age will show in the puff of her face until noon. Darlene is aging, finally. The skin on her face and arms has loosened, but it has loosened on Vivian too, and she is not yet thirty. As if she is catching up to Vivian, there's a hard look about Darlene that never existed before. Once, any wrinkle that appeared on her animated face had disappeared instantly, but this is no longer so. Her skin is lined and thickening, and there is a haggardness too, just emerging at forty-nine.

The key is under the pot of chives, along with shiny brown ants and grey-lined beetles. Vivian turns the key in the lock and a heaviness sets in. She can smell all of them in here, and also fruity shampoo from the uncapped bottle on the hair-washing sink. She can hear Hannah and Darlene sleeping. Recognizes their breathing the way she would their voices, a yawn or a sneeze. In the darkness she runs her hand along the wall on which their measurements are recorded. Darlene always liked to measure everything, especially on herself.

"Most people have one side a little bigger than the other," she'd say, laying the soft cloth measuring tape on Vivian's arm, shoulder to fingertip. "Not me though. Not you either, Viva. Not the Girl."

The measurements were recorded yearly on the wall beside the hair-washing sink. Darlene's height, the circumference of her head, chest, waist, hips, biceps, wrists, thighs, calves and ankles. The length of each arm and leg. Year after year the numbers the same. Beside is a column for Vivian, and beside that, Hannah's.

Vivian moves to the living room and lies on the sea-urchin sofa. She eyes the stacked boxes marked with Darlene's loopy writing. The window to the backyard is open and the dated orange curtains billow. The orange curtains and the orange shag carpet may be sold with the house, like the trailer. "A little bonus," Darlene had said on the phone, and Vivian had thought of the lurking centipedes.

Eyes adjusted, she rises from the sofa and moves down the hallway, past the ketchup stain and into Hannah's room. She sits on the bed.

"Hey, Bee," she says, nudging Hannah awake.

Hannah's eyes flutter open. She smiles and touches what's left of Vivian's hair.

"You got your hair cut," she says.

Vivian laughs. "You didn't."

Hannah looks more like Darlene as she ages. At twenty-three, she so closely resembles the Darlene of their childhood that Vivian is startled each time she sees her.

"I was dreaming about Dairy," says Hannah.

"Who?"

"Dairy," she repeats. "My imaginary friend."

She tells Vivian how she recalls thinking her heart might stop each time someone slammed the car door on Dairy or ran the mower over his tiny webbed toes. Hannah yelling, flailing bony arms.

"Dairy always survived," she says. "He had this flat, pushed-in face, red hair and dull brown eyes. He let me pull him along on a leash anywhere I wanted to go, and he never complained. Never flew away, even though he had these wings—" She reaches her hands around her back and flaps her elbows. "Stiff ones that jutted out from his sweater. I can remember him perfectly. His sweater was red. Cable knit. The sleeves were unravelling."

She tells Vivian that the first time she saw Dairy she thought he must be some sort of insect, small and peculiar. Part bug, part boy. But Dairy walked and talked and wore regular boy's clothing, and even had glasses. The thick lenses magnified his eyes, she says, which were sad and droopy. Their lids puffy, as if bee-stung. His wings up close were brown and brittle, and they made Hannah think of Fruit Roll-Ups, of raisins and umbrellas. She wondered, if she wanted to, could she poke a finger right through them, and would it hurt Dairy if she did?

"How come I never knew about this?" asks Vivian.

Hannah shrugs. "Mom knew, but she was always forgetting."

She tells Vivian that in the end Darlene ran over the boy. Wearing wraparound sunglasses and a spotty kerchief, she had climbed behind the wheel of that new Rambler convertible, sassy red, and shifted the handle to R. Hannah was at the edge of the driveway, squatting low, chalking lines for hopscotch, when a hissing sound made her turn to look. Dairy didn't say a word. Lay spreadeagled. The tire rolled slowly over him, and Hannah watched his flat face, turned towards the street. His mouth opened as the air squished out of him.

Vivian laughs. It has come to her now.

"That was Barry," she says. "Not Dairy. He was real—a retarded boy who lived down the street. He was small," Vivian says, "but not that small. And he didn't have wings. I remember the glasses though, and his sweater. You're right, it was shabby." Vivian shook her head and laughed again. "Only you could imagine an imaginary friend, Bee."

"But what happened?" Hannah wants to know. "What happened to Barry?"

"Nothing much," says Vivian. "His aunt backed her car over him, but he didn't die. He didn't even break a bone. Everyone called it a miracle. After that they moved to Sault Ste. Marie."

Hannah

Hannah lies awake, thinking about Dairy, whom she remembers so clearly she can see his glasses flash in the sun. Barry, his real-life counterpart, she does not remember at all. The thought is unsettling, that a whole person could have dropped so thoroughly from her memory. She has always worried that would happen with Mick. One day she'd wake up and not know him any more. And not care.

Mick loved the memory game of laying items on a tray, then covering them, and having Hannah and Vivian recall what was hidden beneath the cloth. Vivian always won.

"She's older," Mick would say, stroking Hannah's hair.

But it was not that. Vivian could look at a thing and know it inside out. For Hannah nothing was immediately clear. The only solace was that she had been able to ask him anything.

"There's no such thing as a dumb question," he would say.

But to Vivian there was. She sometimes rolled her eyes and told you so. Mick had patience and a crooked smile. There was nothing he didn't know. He knew that an aardvark's tail was white so that her baby could follow her in the dark. He knew that to kill a bat trapped indoors, you had to use a tennis racket, though there had been no racket—and no Mick either—when later they faced such a bat. He saw patterns in the stars that looked to Hannah like a mysterious game of connect-the-dots. They still look that way to her. With his finger he traced Ursa Minor and Ursa Major, and sometimes, for a clear glimmering instant, she followed his big freckled finger and saw those patterns too. She had just begun to catch on when all of a sudden he was gone for ever. She will always think of him when she thinks of stars, just as she will think of him when she eats corn because he knew that corn cooled off faster than meat and potatoes.

"Anything that comes in small pieces like that should be eaten first," he said, "or pockets of air get into the spaces and cool it all off."

And he knew about leeks—how rinsing them in cold water kept them new-leaf green. He preferred food that grew in the ground to food that came in a box or a tin, or even off of an animal. When Hannah complained of tasting dirt in mushrooms, he told her, "Not dirt. Earth. Earth's good for you," and in fact there was a healthy taste to it. Wherever they went he brought along a bag of shiny apples, and also arrowroot cookies, which were less good for you but equally delicious.

"Apples clean your teeth," he said. "The crisp of them scrapes off the plaque."

One blue Thursday they had gone all the way to Niagara Falls—Mick, Hannah and Vivian—the only time they had ever gone anywhere out of the Valley, and on the way they had eaten fourteen apples and thrown fourteen cores like bread crumbs out the opened windy windows. Giving nature back to nature, Mick called it.

When was that?

Hannah woke with the sun, anxious to go, because didn't he always say it was a waste to sleep in? When he'd lived there, weekend mornings he'd opened all the bedroom doors widely and bellowed, "Rise and shi-ine!" Without him they sometimes slept till ten, or even noon, waking with creased faces and the heaviness of too much sleep.

Hannah sat on the front porch and watched the yolk-yellow sun lift itself up from behind the mountains. Birds sang their mixed songs and a woodpecker pecked and pecked a metal pole, not realizing. Hannah tucked her legs inside her sundress, which was wrinkled and orange-juice stained. She crossed her arms on her knees and pressed her face there, breathed in the metallic smell of her skin. She would later ask him why that was, that smell of metal.

The sun was a full round yolk when finally she heard the Alfa. She heard it gear down for the stop sign around the corner, and then she heard it gear up again. She watched it pull into the driveway and park where once it had always parked.

Mick climbed out and mussed her messy hair, knotted in yesterday's ponytail, and she hooked her finger into his belt loop and followed him into the still-quiet house, tiptoeing behind him, obeying his *Ssshhh.* Vivian's door creaked open and they looked in on her, her white hair yellowish against white sheets. Together they moved down the hallway. He put his hand on Darlene's doorknob, turned and pushed lightly. Through the diamond space his arm made, Hannah could see Darlene, sleeping with her mouth open, no lipstick there. For too long they stood and watched her. She was not in her fancy nightgown, pale blue and nearly sheer. Instead she had on a big T-shirt, and socks on her sticking-out feet, not because it was cold, Hannah knew, but because there was Vaseline underneath, softening the hard skin. Hannah tugged her father's belt loop, urged him along the hall.

In his opera voice he shouted, "Rise and shi-ine!" and the sound was so familiar it hurt to hear it.

Right away Darlene emerged, tying her pink kimono. She ran her fingers through her hair and looked at Mick, stood close to him. Hannah watched her father's hand rise slowly, slip under Darlene's arm, where there was a hole in that old kimono. He stood with his hand in the hole, touching the big T-shirt. Just looking at Darlene. And when Darlene moved towards him, wrapped around him, Hannah's own single body felt like their two bodies pressing together. For a long time no one said anything. Hannah thought of the time he'd brought flowers for Darlene's birthday. They were wild, gathered from the side of road, a ladybird resting on a leaf.

"You can't do this any more, Sweet Boy," Darlene had whispered. "It's too confusing." She'd held the weedy bouquet between them and said, "We have to let go of each other."

Just why they'd had to let go was still unclear. Didn't they have two whole people in common? But Darlene had made Mick go away with his flowers, and she had cried and cried, not in her loud breaking-down way, but silently, which was worse somehow. And they drove off towards the Falls and left her behind, crying on the porch.

Hannah turned around in the back seat of the Alfa and watched Darlene until she was out of sight. She didn't care any more about Niagara Falls, the American or the Canadian side, and she didn't care about the people who'd gone over in barrels. For breakfast she could have made Darlene an open-faced cheese melt, with a blob of ketchup and a quartered dill pickle, and she could have gently combed the sleep knots from Darlene's hair, combing in little bits, easy does it, bottom to top because that was the way to best avoid split ends.

Hannah moped for a while, thinking of Darlene. She lay in the back seat watching the sky go by and wishing time backwards. She could hear Mick's mumbled voice, and sometimes Vivian's, but mostly she heard the growl of the falling-off muffler. She could smell the fresh juice of the apples they were eating, and though she wanted one of her own, she refrained from asking. She saw Mick's core whip by the side window, and then Vivian's core too, and she heard their muffled laughter.

She thought she might remain lying down the whole way, saying nothing. Even when they got there she might refuse to get up and out of the car. She might hold her breath. She might refuse to eat or even pee, and when Mick saw that she meant business, he would turn the Alfa around and go back for Darlene and they would start the whole trip over, the proper way.

But that did not happen. What happened was that her neck became sore. And her head hurt from leaning up against the hard armrest, and so she sat up again, alone in the back seat. Mick slid his arm back between the seats and held an apple in his palm. She could see he had shined it a long while and so she ate it in silence, looking sometimes out one side window, sometimes out the other, and sometimes out the front, between Mick and Vivian. Soon she was mesmerized. She wished she had wraparound eyes, so that she could see this side and that side at the same time, so that she might not miss anything.

She said it out loud. "I wish I had wraparound eyes."

Mick laughed.

"Turn around," he said. "Look out the back window. That'll give you your best view."

It was true, what he said. She sat that way a long while, looking backwards, and it felt weird, not knowing what was coming next, and then, upon seeing it, knowing it was already gone. It was as though they were driving *from* a place rather than *to*.

Still, this was going somewhere. This was really going somewhere. Niagara Falls was not Eganville or the Bonnechere Caves. It was not anywhere near the Ottawa Valley. It was not Florida, no, but it was also not camping and coming right home again. Niagara Falls was far enough away that you needed a map to get there. It was practically in the States. In fact, part of it was, Mick said. People from all over the world went to it, both the Canadian and the American side. Mick told her there would be people from Europe there, even Japan. All to see the Falls, which were truly a wonder of nature. Hannah had never seen a wonder of nature before, not that she knew of anyway. It was possible that the caves were a wonder of nature, but certainly people from Europe and Japan did not clamber to see them. Hannah herself had been enthralled, but all she remembered of them now was the batless bat wall and the wood-stick lettering that spelled BONNECHERE at the entrance. It had been too dark inside to really see anything. Niagara Falls would not be that way. It would be lit up, Mick said, even at night.

And yet, when they got there, it was already dark. Hannah looked in the blackness for the Falls but she could not hear or see them.

They stayed in a real motel called the Edgecliffe, because it was just that, on the edge of a cliff. It was not close to the Falls, Mick said, but it was close enough. Plus, this was where the Falls used to be, according to Mick and to a plaque that said so. Mick had been here when he was a boy, so he knew pretty much everything there was to know about it.

"Right there," he said, bending to Hannah's height and pointing out the window, where she could see night and her own reflection. "If this were 1600 B.C., the Falls would be right there."

"How could they just pick up and move like that?" she asked. Vivian rolled her eyes.

"They didn't pick up and move," said Mick. "They *receded*."

Hannah thought of hairlines. Mick's was receding, Darlene had often said so. In the reflection she looked at his forehead, which was high anyway, like hers. He might lose his cowlick if he lost any more hair at the front, and then she'd look less like him. They were the only two in the family with cowlicks.

"Do you know how long ago 1600 B.C. was?" he asked her.

Hannah nodded. A long time. *B.C.* meant "Before Christ," she knew enough to know that much.

Vivian rolled her eyes again and sighed. "How can you mark time by Christ if you don't even believe in him?"

"Who says I don't believe in Christ?" Mick asked.

"Oh, please," said Vivian. "Give us some credit."

Hannah's heart was pounding. Which was true, that he did or that he didn't?

"As a matter of fact," Mick said, "I don't believe in God, but I'm pretty sure Jesus was a real guy. A nice one too, from the sounds of it. I just doubt he was conceived by immaculate conception, and that he died and lived again."

But you always say anything's possible.

"Yeah," said Vivian. "Once you're dead, you're dead. Anybody who believes any different is stupid, if you ask me."

"Well, I wouldn't go that far."

Hannah twisted her hand in the curtain and pretended to look out the window. Instead she looked at herself, at her freckled nose and her lips, which were chapped from the sun. Who was God and who was Jesus? Weren't they connected? If you didn't believe in both, you didn't get into Heaven, that was that. She hadn't been to Sunday School, but she knew a thing or two.

Because it felt better not to listen, she tuned them out. She noticed now that the room smelled of smoking and recirculated air. Outside there was a lit-up pool, which she could see from the window. It might be filled with Falls water, who knew? You couldn't swim in the Falls but you could swim here. The water was turquoise, undangerous, and all around was white pavement and plastic-banded lawn chairs, not just like regular lawn chairs but extra long, so you could lie with your legs stretched out. At home they had only one of those. Hannah wanted to jump in the pool and then lie on a chair in the sun, letting the heat dry the drops on her body. But it was night, and you couldn't sleep outside overnight in a lawn chair, not in a city anyway, which Niagara Falls was. Not at a motel, where you didn't know who your neighbours were. Instead they would sleep in these two beds, each with a quilted brown bedspread. Hannah and Vivian in one, their father in the other.

It was late enough for that now, so they brushed their teeth in the motel sink and washed their faces with the doll-size soap, and readied themselves for bed. Hannah looked forward to sleeping. She would not think of Godlessness or Darlene, who right now might be crying alone. She would say a silent prayer, the only one she knew, which was, "Now I lay me down to sleep, I pray the Lord my soul to keep; and if I die before I wake, I pray the Lord my soul to take." That was a prayer she'd say from here on in, every night before sleeping. She wouldn't be able to kneel by the bed, not tonight. Not in front of Mick and Vivian. It would have to be enough to say the words in her head. God heard what was in your head anyway. He had the ability to be everywhere at once.

When Hannah pulled back the brown bedspread, there was a large moth, brown too, lying on the bright white sheet. She stood looking at him, feeling surprisingly unsurprised to see him, as though she'd known he'd be there. He did not move either, but she could see him breathing. He lay with his flat velvet wings covering his body. That was the difference between a moth and a butterfly. Wren had said so. A moth lay with his wings flat like a blanket, and a butterfly held them up and away from her body, showing off beauty. Wren had once told her that butterflies were like ballerinas, graceful even when standing still. She'd said that moths were beautiful too, in an eerier way, and this had come as a surprise to Hannah. Moths were hairier than butterflies, and they had bigger, clumsier bodies. But what was wrong with hairiness? Wren had asked. Was it bad to be big? She had learned from Wren that butterflies smell with their antennae and they taste with their feet. It might be true of moths too. This moth's feet were touching the sheet just now, so did that mean he was tasting the cotton? Or could he turn his taste buds on and off whenever he wanted?

"Gross," said Vivian.

She reached forward with a tissue in her hand and cupped the moth. Hannah saw his wings begin to spread as Vivian's hand closed over him, and before Vivian could squish him Hannah knocked the tissue from her hand and the moth flew away and rested on a tuck in the curtain.

Hannah looked at Vivian, who was once again rolling her eyes.

"Why can't you leave him alone?" she asked Vivian. "He's only a little old moth."

"Exactly," said Vivian.

In bed Hannah mouthed the prayer for all of them, because she knew they would not do it for themselves, perhaps not ever. She could smell the doll-size soap on her own skin and Vivian's. She listened again for the Falls but the only roar to be heard was the low, constant one of the air conditioner, a box in the wall. Also with that was a chirping, and she wondered, Was there a bird in the room? She lay a long while, just listening, waiting for the chirp, and when she heard it again she whispered, "What's that?" but Mick and Vivian had fallen asleep.

All night there was that chirping. She heard it in her sleep and in her dream it became the moth she had seen, making bird sounds. It didn't seem strange in the dream, only natural, and in the morning when she woke she thought that perhaps it was a wonder of nature, that a moth might chirp like a bird.

It was light but it had to be early. Mick and Vivian were still sleeping. Hannah lay in the motel bed, a double, and eyed the brown curtains for the matching brown moth. Wherever he was he would be sleeping. Butterflies slept at night, like people, but moths slept in the day. She looked around the brown room, on the beds and on the carpet. That may have been why he had come here, the brownness. Butterflies and moths believed in camouflage; this was another thing she knew. One kind made its cocoon look like bird poop—Wren had shown her that, and Vivian had scoffed, peering closely at the blob of black and white.

"Maybe it looks like bird shit because it is bird shit," she had said.

"No," Wren had calmly replied. "That's how it protects itself."

Again there was that sound, three short chirps and a long one. If she had a bionic ear she might be able to tune it in, tell where it came from. She slipped out of bed and crept across the room, peering behind the brown curtain. There seemed to be no bird anywhere, nor a moth. She thought of the time a bird had been trapped in the Ferguses' chimney. It had died in there. But here there was no chimney. There were two chairs and two beds, a dresser and a big TV, and also that box in the wall, blowing smelly air. She pulled a chair over to the humming air conditioner and peered into the long black slats that were rimmed with dust. There was nothing inside but darkness.

Being so far from the Falls was not a bad thing. In the morning it meant they got to walk along River Road, where there was a low stone wall that kept them from tumbling into the river. The wall and the trees beyond prevented Hannah from seeing the river, but she knew it was there. She watched Vivian and Mick watching it as they walked, and from time to time Mick lifted her. His hands hurt her armpits, but it was good, to be up high. He said the river was called Niagara, like the Falls and like the town. It was unlike the river at home. This one barely moved and the water was a thick chalky green. As yet, there was no sign of anything falling.

When he let her down again, the wall was once more at eye level. She listened for the roar of the Falls and she looked in the air for the mist. It was hot, and it seemed they'd been walking for ever. Vivian complained of the heat, which she did not usually mind. She was what she herself would call *cantankerous,* a word that always made Hannah think of canker sores. It made sense— canker sores could make a person cantankerous. And Vivian had a point: it was even hotter here than at home, and home was hot enough.

"It's supposed to be hotter here," said Mick. "We're closer to the equator."

"Please, Dad," said Vivian, rolling her eyes. "I know where the equator is. We're still miles away from it," she said. "As if I'm stupid."

"As if," said Mick, grinning and rolling his eyes in imitation.

Hannah knew where the equator was too. It was not a real line, but imaginary. It showed on maps and on globes at school, separating one half of the world from the other. Probably there were people living right on that line, not knowing. No, this was not that far south, but it was southern Ontario, and hot. Hannah thought she could feel her hair sweating but she did not know if that were possible. She could ask, because there was no such thing as a dumb question. But there was a silence hanging.

It had been in the air when they'd left the Valley, and it had followed them all the way here, no matter how many songs had been sung in the car or how many jokes had been told. It might not ever leave them.

So right then it seemed wrong to ask the question, *Can hair sweat?* And yet she hated not knowing. Instead she asked, "Where are the Falls?" though she knew what the answer would be.

"Not far," said Mick.

Yes, she knew he would say that. She did not doubt they were nearby. She never doubted anything he said. He stroked her sweaty hair, and she thought again, *Can hair sweat?* and then she heard her own voice asking, and Vivian's answer.

"No, Stupid."

Her response like a punch.

"Vivian!" said Mick.

He stopped so abruptly that Hannah walked into him, bounced off. Now they were all standing on the sidewalk. Mick had Vivian by the shoulder, and she was sneering at him.

"Why are you being so miserable?" he said plainly, as though he were asking any old question. "Don't you want to have fun?"

"Not particularly," said Vivian.

Hannah looked at Mick and then at Vivian. Between them she could finally see the white mist of the Falls, and as she looked at it she began to hear it too. She tugged lightly at the hem of Mick's shorts but he didn't notice. How could the green water below be so still while the Falls poured wild? Were they not attached?

Yes, Stupid.

But how then?

Mick was calm but his big fingers were pressing into Vivian's skin. Hannah could see white spots there.

"You don't?" he said. "You don't *want* to have fun?"

"Maybe I do, maybe I don't," said Vivian.

Hannah didn't think it could be possible, that Vivian didn't want to have fun. Didn't everyone want to, deep down? Perhaps it was just that they had left Darlene behind, standing there crying. That had been a wrong thing. It sat wrong in Hannah's belly and possibly the wrongness was weighing on Vivian too. Since arriving, Hannah had thought less often of Darlene, her red-splotched face and her messy bed hair. Now, when the image came, the sick feeling was worsened by the awful fact of forgetting.

It was possible that Darlene had not stopped crying. She had been known on more than one occasion to cry for days, and this might be one of those times. Hannah wished she knew a more general daytime prayer, one that might make everyone happy, but she did not. Last night's prayer had been said improperly, in silence and not kneeling, so perhaps it had not worked. Then again, it had only been about dying, and none of them had died. Not that she knew of anyway. Again there was that sickness. Could Darlene have died in the night? It seemed more possible for bad things to happen when they were separated. Plus, people could die of heartbreak, she knew that, and yesterday Darlene's heart had seemed more broken than ever. She'd like to ask Vivian once more about why they were not together, but today would be the wrong day for that. Today was not a day for questions of any kind. It was a day for walking and looking and thinking happy thoughts. She was wearing her happy-face backpack and she thought of that face now, the yellowness and the black-spot eyes, the half-circle smile.

She tugged again at the hem of Mick's shorts, and now both he and Vivian turned to her. Hannah pointed.

"Look," she said.

Already the air seemed cooler. The mist was like a cloud. Perhaps it was a cloud, she didn't know. In the tiny space between the trees it moved and swirled in the air, blocking their view of the actual falling Falls. Though in a way the mist *was* the Falls—the sheer power of the rushing water was what caused it, Mick said. He told them they'd go on a boat, the *Maid of the Mist*, and they'd get so close to the Falls that they wouldn't even be able to see them.

Now there was something to walk towards. Even Vivian seemed cheerful, as though she had decided she did want to have fun, after all. Together they walked further along River Road. Hannah ran her finger along the low stone wall, trying to calm herself. Over and over in her mind she whispered, I can hardly maintain myself. It was what Darlene said when a good thing was happening. *Like mother, like daughter.* She said that too.

Ahead loomed the Rainbow Bridge. Though Hannah could not see any rainbows upon it, it was shaped like one. It stretched from Canada to the U.S. of A. in one long arch, and Mick said you could walk across it. He had done so as a boy, and there were people doing that now. Hannah could see their heads bobbing above the railing. Imagine walking to the United States, she thought. That would really be going somewhere. Not that this wasn't. They had already come somewhere. They had driven all through the Ottawa Valley and whatever came south of it, in order to get here. And now that they were here, even if they only stayed on the Canadian side, it would still be an adventure. But to think of herself going to a whole other country wearing just her flip-flops and her sundress and her happy-face backpack, that was exciting. Not that this wasn't.

Now they'd gone under the Rainbow and come out the other side, which meant they were finally at the Falls. And instead of noticing the water, Hannah noticed the people. There were more of them than she had ever seen in one place at one time. Perhaps there were more people here than lived in their own whole town. Even at the Canada Day parade there had never been a crowd like this one. Mick put his hand on Hannah's neck and held Vivian's elbow.

"Wow!" said Vivian. She was smiling now.

But Mick's face fell. He said it was not at all the way he remembered it, and that he should have known. "Nothing ever is," he said. He squeezed Hannah's neck lightly and tugged her ponytail, and when she looked up at him, he shrugged and said, "C'est la vie."

She wished he would not be so dejected. It would spoil things, if he kept it up. Plus, Hannah liked the look of the place. She liked the telescopes all lined up and the long railing, which was open and see-through, unlike that low stone wall. She liked the speed and the sound of the Falls and the fresh feel of water in the air, and she liked looking over at the United States. From here she could wave to an American and he might wave back if he happened to be looking her way at the right moment. It was true that the seagulls seemed ruder than the ones at home, and bigger too. But she had never before noticed their yellow feet, like rainboots, or the stripe of black on their beaks, so there was something worthwhile to be found even in them. It looked like an elastic, that stripe, and at first she'd thought it was. She could see why someone might want to keep their crying beaks closed. They were loud, a bit frightening, but the fright was a good thing too: Hannah's too-hot skin went cold and tingly when one flew by, so close she could hear the flap of its wings.

They continued along the path that followed the river, heading for Horseshoe Falls, which were the Canadian waters. They were better than the American ones, she could see that from here. They were curved—though not quite so curved as a horseshoe—and bigger too. The closer they got, the more it seemed to be raining. She looked in the sky for clouds but there were none. The sky was bright blazing blue, so those drops were the Falls spraying her.

But when they got to where they needed to be, there was nothing to do but look. The Falls were the same thing happening over and over again, nothing but a constant stream of water. So they turned their backs on them and headed up Clifton Hill, where there was the Haunted House and Ripley's Believe It or Not and more than one wax museum. The excitement inside was whirring again. Hannah stared at the fake candle bodies that stood outside, checking for movement. She would like to see a body made from wax up close, because what were its eyes and teeth like? Its hair and its wax eyelashes? But Mick was groaning. She could tell now that they wouldn't be going inside, not here or anywhere fun.

"Oh my God," he said.

That was swearing, but it didn't count if you didn't believe. *Believe it or not.*

"Oh my God," he said again. Everywhere he looked brought out an Oh-my-God.

Hannah wished he would stop his moaning.

"What?" she asked, tugging his wrist.

"It's so—" he searched for the word. "*Awful.*"

To Hannah it seemed anything but.

Mick called himself a bit of a naturalist, and he said it made him sad to see candy floss here. But what was wrong with candy floss and souvenirs? If she could she would buy one of everything—a pen that had the *Maid of the Mist* inside, travelling up or down the river depending on which way you tipped it. Most of all she wanted a picture of herself and her happy-face backpack going over the Falls in a barrel, which of course she had not yet done and probably would never do, but it was possible to buy such a thing anyway. It seemed that, in Niagara Falls, it was possible to buy anything.

"Let's go," said Mick.

He took their hands and led them through the crowd and back down Clifton Hill towards the water.

In sweaty black raincoats with hoods they boarded the *Maid of the Mist*, where life jackets hung from the ceiling. Cool white spray touched their faces, and an endless wall of water roared down. Here was something that never stopped. Hannah leaned laughing towards the Falls and the mist beaded her skin. There might be fish in that wall, not in barrels but just in their own speckled, rubbery skins, twirling and tumbling. Funny-eyed sole with their weird flat bodies. Or blobbed jellyfish that could sting you. Moving so fast through the roar you'd never see them or hear them screaming. Who knew if fish could scream? Anything was possible.

Back at the Edgecliffe Motel, Hannah unzipped her happy-face backpack and slid wrapped soaps into it in place of real souvenirs. When she saw the moth inside, she had that same unsurprise, and she stared at the spots on its wings. She watched it fly out of her backpack and disappear into the curtains.

Mick said that long ago Niagara Falls had been a different place. He said it had been formed by a melting glacier, which seemed impossible, because why would it keep on falling once the glacier was gone?

Hannah didn't ask that. She didn't ask anything. She lay on the motel bed, picking the balls on the bedspread and listening to Mick.

He said it had been called Onguiaahra.

"What?" said Vivian.

He wrote it down and Vivian and Hannah leaned closer to look at the word on the page. On paper it looked a bit like Niagara, but not.

Anyway, she didn't care about Onguiaahra. She wondered what Darlene was doing, if she was crying or painting her toenails. This was the longest she had been away from Darlene in all of her life, and just now she couldn't picture her face, though she could clearly see the hole in her kimono, and Mick's hand there.

"Onguiaahra, Niagara," whispered Vivian, as they began to doze off.

All in all they were gone four days. A day driving, two days there and a day driving home. It was the longest vacation Hannah had ever had. It was in fact the only one—not counting Eganville and camping, which she couldn't really count because Vivian said a vacation was not a vacation unless you stayed overnight. Three nights was not so long to stay away, she supposed, but still there was a sick feeling driving home, as though anything might have happened in their absence.

Something had. There was a lobster trap on the front lawn, and when they pulled up beside it Mick got out and stared at it.

"Where did this come from?" he asked as Darlene emerged in a halter top and short shorts.

"Why, P.E.I., of course!"

She said Uncle Tim had taken her there on a whirlwind trip. She called it "spur of the moment," and claimed she'd had a glorious time.

"*Oh,* it cheered me up. I was a bit blue, you know, with my girlies gone."

She did not seem blue now. She pressed lipstick kisses into Hannah's cheeks and then Vivian's, and flashed a smile at Mick, but he did not smile back. In silence he unloaded the bags from the Alfa, brought them into the house and drove away.

Hannah looked at the trap. She wondered if there were lobsters in the Falls.

"Like it, Sweet Pea?"

Hannah nodded. She guessed she did. It had a nice little door. "But what's it for?" she asked, running a finger along the thin slats of slivery wood.

Darlene laughed. "For flowers, Girly."

But flowers were never planted in there. In the winter it got snowed on and the next summer Mick and Uncle Tim took turns mowing around it. The grass underneath grew up through the slats, and still does. It will sell with the house and the trailer.

That first night home Darlene tucked Hannah in and kissed her forehead, and just as she was about to pull away, Hannah touched the soft sleeve of her kimono.

"Mom?"

"Mmm, Girly?"

"Do you believe in God?"

Darlene blinked. "Sure I do!"

"Is it bad not to?"

"It's *silly* not to, is what it is." She smiled and pressed a finger to Hannah's nose. "Night-night."

Hannah watched her move to the doorway.

"Mom?"

"Mmm?"

"What are they called, people who don't believe in God?"

Darlene smiled again. Her silhouette shrugged. "Silly," she said.

"No, they're not," called Vivian. Her voice carried across the hall. "They're called *atheists*," she said. "Dad's one and I'm one too."

"Vivvy, please!"

"What?" said Vivian. "It's not a swear word."

"I know perfectly well what it is, thank you very much, Viva."

"It comes from the Greek word *a,* which means 'not,' and *theos,* which means 'God.' *Not God.*"

"Did Daddy tell you that?"

"No," said Vivian. "Anybody can look it up. It's in the dictionary."

It seemed wrong to Hannah that something like that should be in the dictionary. Vivian was always reading the dictionary. There was no telling what else she might have found.

"They're just being silly, Sweet Pea," whispered Darlene. "You go ahead and believe. Pray, if you want to. Why not? If there's a God, he'll hear you. And even if nobody's listening, what have you got to lose? You're better off covering your bases, don't you think? There's no point shooting yourself in the foot. That's what I always say, anyway." She flicked the light on and grinned, then flicked it off again. "Night, Girly. Sweet dreams."

It wasn't true, that part about "That's what I always say." Hannah had never heard Darlene say such a thing.

⁓

Now, lying awake, Hannah cannot remember when she stopped praying, only that for a long while she did pray, religiously. And then some nights she forgot altogether, or didn't care to, because what difference did it make? Other nights she prayed longer, adding *Onguiaahra, Niagara,* after *Amen.* After Mick died she thought it may have made God angry, her adding her own words. She lay awake many nights after the funeral thinking that it was both her fault and his that he wouldn't get to Heaven. Because he was an atheist, he'd ruined his chances. If there was a God, he wouldn't let Mick in after all his years as a non-believer and all his talk about religion being a load of baloney. She wondered, and still wonders, if Mick is regretting that now, wherever he is, because whatever he's told her, she cannot believe he is nowhere.

Vivian

Down the hall Darlene is snoring like a man, which she has always done, but if you told her she'd never believe you.

"Mom, you snore."

"Don't be ridiculous." Laughing. "I do not. You want to hear snoring, listen to Tim."

Which could no longer be done. He'd had his adenoids removed to prove his love for Darlene.

"It'd never work between us, Timmy," Darlene had said in her teasing voice. "All night long your snoring wakes me up."

Hannah and Vivian shared a surprised look.

"And there's this little click that comes from the back of your throat," she told him.

Tim made a sound like a laugh to show that he knew she was joking, but he was bruised by the comment, Vivian could tell. Surely Darlene could tell too. So transparent a man was Tim that it had to be her sole intention to hurt him.

"Once every couple of weeks I can stand it," she told him. "But night after night till death do us part, I don't think so."

The year of his operation was the year Vivian turned seventeen. By then he had loved Darlene for seven years, long enough that he would try anything. And anyway, adenoids were like the appendix, like wisdom teeth and tonsils; people didn't need them any more, and one day they wouldn't have them. That was evolution, Vivian knew. Probably there were already babies being born who didn't possess them at all, or had just the faintest trace, the way a whale had hair in the infant stages. Even Wren might not be a freak of nature but an evolutionary throwforward to a time when humans will no longer need fingers. She had her opposable thumbs. Maybe those were all that would be necessary. Eight wiggling separate digits might one day seem fussy and excessive, like pleonasms.

But Tim was not coping well with his streamlined self. They didn't know for certain if his new demeanour was related to the operation—none of them had known anyone who'd had adenoids removed. But he was more sallow than normal. He was quiet and lethargic. Vivian joked that the doctor had misunderstood, had removed his adrenal gland instead, and though Darlene abhorred any teasing of Tim, even she laughed.

To Angie she confided, "I hope he doesn't act like this for long. It's really tiresome."

"What's the matter with you?" said Angie. "The man just had a part of his body removed to please you."

"Oh, he did not. He didn't do it just for me, Angel. They were bothering him, too. They were swollen or something. He said his throat hurt a lot."

"That's tonsils, Darlene."

Whatever was wrong with him, it only made him more pathetic in Vivian's eyes, and he'd been pathetic enough already. Through everything that he did for Darlene, he must have known it would never work. In fact, the more he did, the less chance there was she could love him. He would have to walk away, as Mick and Dare had done, for Darlene to long for him at all. And he could never do that with conviction. She would see right through him. And he would be looking back to make sure she'd noticed him go. Any time he tried getting angry with Darlene, she changed tack.

"Oh, God, you're right," she'd say, letting her eyes fill up. "I don't deserve you, Timbo. I don't blame you a bit if you never want to see me again. I'm a big fool, taking you for granted the way I do. You have to know it was never my intention to hurt you."

With Tim, she knew exactly what she was doing every step of the way. How to keep him and also how to keep him at bay. But he had hung on so long now, he had to know it was futile. It astonished Vivian that someone so hopeless could be so full of hope.

Vivian hoped only to be gone from that house. But even this, she knew, could not be called hope. Rather, she *waited* to be gone. Hope was for the frightened and the desperate.

This was her final year. She had soared through school without ever trying, and now, recalling the private terror she'd had when she'd skipped Grade Four, she was thankful. It had moved her that much closer to getting away.

Already she had chosen what to take with her and what to leave behind. Only the plainest, most comfortable clothes would come, and only the one book she was reading right then. There were plenty of books in Toronto. From under her mattress she pulled her childhood treasures, and one by one, without pausing, she threw them away. Until she came to his blue canvas shoes, flattened by the weight of the mattress. She placed them on the floor and tied the laces. For a long while she sat looking at them, and then picked them up by the bows and put them in the garbage. From now on, she would not be a keeper of things.

Darlene would have let her go on the bus and Vivian would have loved that. Hoarding the front seat and watching the road signs fly by, the numbers to Toronto ever-dwindling. But Angie had been appalled.

"You mean you don't even want to see that she gets settled in?"

"It's not that I don't *want* to, Angel," said Darlene. "But it's far. And there's my licence and all. I've never driven in a city that size. I just think it would be more sensible if—"

"Oh, come on," said Angie. "Surely Tim—"

"No," said Vivian.

Both of them looked at her.

"No, thank you," she said. "I'd rather take the bus."

There was an awkward pause.

"Anyway," said Darlene. She shrugged. "I'm no doctor, but I can tell you right now that Tim is not fit for travelling."

"He just seems depressed to me," said Angie. "Getting out of town might be good for him."

"I said it's all right," said Vivian. "I can take the bus."

Oh, how she would love that long trip.

But Angie wouldn't let up.

"*We'll* take her," she said. She looked from Darlene to Vivian. "Okay?"

Vivian shrugged.

"Oh, Ange, you don't have to—"

As she left the room Vivian heard Angie's hard whisper.

"For crying out loud, Darlene."

That final night Tim set up the trailer, and Vivian slept there with Hannah and Wren. She should have slept there every summer night since that eloquent, elegant man had delivered this gift. She felt herself dozing off almost immediately, once the talking and singing had subsided. She wished to be awake longer, that she might savour the musty smell and the breeze that filtered through the fine green screen, but she could feel herself going, strangely conscious of sleeping soundly. And then she woke. It had to be three, at least. She could tell by the placement of the moon. She needed to pee. She crawled out of her sleeping bag, across Hannah's sleeping body, and out of the trailer.

Inside, she walked quietly through the kitchen and down the hall, and when she passed her own room, she saw Darlene. Head down, she sat on Vivian's bed, sobbing. Vivian stepped out of view. She stood in the hallway, flattened herself against the wall. Unsure what to do, she waited and waited. Darlene was crying in that soundless, genuine way, thinking no one was watching. Vivian slid down the wall and sat with her head on her knees. After a very long while she crept outside again and peed behind the garage.

Hannah

The day Vivian left, Darlene rearranged the furniture. She dragged Vivian's empty dresser across the hall to Hannah's room, and Hannah's dresser to Vivian's room. She said this was the perfect opportunity for a little pick-me-up, a change of pace. She dismantled the living room, moving the orange La-Z-Boy into the chesterfield's place, angling the chesterfield where the television had sat, pushing the television into the stereo's spot, and making everything unlike the way it had been before. Now she was kneeling, rubbing the furniture footprints exposed on the shag carpet. Hannah knew it was heavy work for her fragile state of mind, and that she bustled through it with the artificial cheerfulness that sometimes overcame her in difficult times. Hannah wished for some cheer of her own, feigned or otherwise, but none would come.

She transferred her socks and pastel underwear and nightgowns from her own dresser into Vivian's, unburying old, smooth soaps that had lost all their fragrance. She lifted the layers of nightgowns and panties, and beneath found the coasters and Mick's passport, and the shock of having forgotten they were there ran through her. She held the passport in her tingling hand and closed her eyes, trying to picture the serious photo of a father so rarely serious. She opened her eyes and slowly turned the crisp, important pages, pausing to look at him with his long nose and cowlick. There was the date of his birth in thick black letters, just like on the gravestone, but without the date of his death beside. She thought again of how every year that date had passed, with no one ever knowing it was coming. Just as every year the date of Vivian's departure had passed.

Tonight they would dine without her. They would eat apple-and-cheese sandwiches, it had already been decided. They would sit on the couch with trays, for a treat, and they would watch TV and settle into their new twosome life.

Only yesterday, dinner had been a party. A barbecue to which Wren, Angie, Charlie and Uncle Tim were invited. Darlene's old-sheet banner hung from the clothesline and flapped in the wind. With leftover green housepaint she had hugely scrawled, *Au Revoir, Viva!*, and at the corners of the sheet she'd drawn green daisies, as though this were something to celebrate. Everyone acted happy.

Hannah had watched Tim form the pink and white meat into patties with his bare hairy hands. In the meat was raw egg, flakes of onion, Mrs. Dash. She watched him lay the patties on the hot grill, flip and flatten them. She watched him poke them, lift them open to check for blood inside.

They gathered around the picnic table, and the green-daisy sheet snapped and flapped. Hannah ate her carrots. Picked at warm potato salad, a cob of corn. Ignored her burger hiding in its bun, because even burnt black on the barbecue, meat tasted of blood. The blood would squish out of it and into Hannah's mouth, filling it, swelling her throat closed. If she chewed it to mush, the meat would still not go down easily. The little reflex inside would kick in and she would gag, need to spit it back out, and that could only cause trouble. But there were twice as many people today, and laughter: her uneaten meat might not be noticed.

"What's the matter, Girly? Not hungry?"

Hannah shrugged one shoulder.

The horrible cheerful chatter continued, and Hannah heard only their mixing voices until Darlene's clear one pushed through again.

"Not eating your burger, Banana?"

Hannah shook her head.

"Have a little bite," coaxed Darlene. "You could take it out of the bun if it's too filling."

Hannah shook her head. She did not look up. With her fork she pierced a corn kernel and eased it from the cob. Rage brightened the green in Darlene's eyes, and Hannah did not have to look to see it. She did not have to look to see that Angie, Charlie, Uncle Tim, Wren and Vivian were also not looking but had seen it.

"Do you know what you could be doing to your health?"

Hannah said nothing.

"Those lovely teeth of yours could be eroding as we speak."

Which was silly. Hannah kept her lips closed and ran her tongue secretly along her teeth. Did meat have calcium?

Darlene reached across the picnic table and grabbed Hannah's plate. With a steak knife she angrily sliced the grey meat of Hannah's patty, even her small-enough potatoes and cubes of carrot. She slammed the plate back down in front of Hannah, and a warm lump of burger splatted onto Hannah's lap.

"Eat."

Hannah looked up at Vivian, who continued eating. She looked at Wren, then down at the food that smelled of dead flesh the way leather coats and shoes did. People wore peeled-off skin and they ate dead bodies. What was the difference between a cow and a cat? A human? Didn't they all have eyes and lashes, nostrils that breathed air? One by one she swallowed the carrots and felt Darlene's hot stare.

"Eat the *meat*," said Darlene. "It's the most expensive part."

Hannah pushed the meat around. Slid potatoes on top of it. She eased a tine into another halved square of carrot, and, as she lifted it to her mouth, Darlene's arm shot out, grabbing Hannah's wrist, and though she was shouting and shaking Hannah's arm and her own head, Hannah heard nothing. Only the slow-motion clang of her fork on her plate. The waning, snorting sobs of Darlene. The slam of the screen door.

Uncle Tim coughed. He stood and his lightweight lawn chair fell backwards. "I'll go see," he said. "Excuse me."

Hannah watched him move across the lawn and into the house. In there he would comfort Darlene, stroke her hair.

Hannah looked at Vivian, who cut her food and continued eating. She took a swig of milk and a morsel appeared on the rim of the glass where her mouth had been. Hannah stared at that and then at her fork in the middle of the picnic table, still with a carrot stuck on.

It was twilight when Darlene emerged, red-eyed. Tim carrying the blazing *Au revoir, Viva!* cake behind her. She squeezed in beside Hannah at the picnic table and burrowed her face in Hannah's neck, butterfly kissing with stiff, freshly coated lashes, and Hannah watched Vivian, lit by the sparkling cake.

She was no longer hungry but she had been. She had wanted bananas, noodles with butter and sugar, orange-juice popsicles, jellied salad, rhubarb, all of her favourite things.

Afterwards, for a treat, Uncle Tim set up the trailer, and it seemed all of a sudden like something they should have done long before. There it was, faded green, not in a hard box any more but stretched out, parts of it flapping in the fresh breeze. Uncle Tim said there were no centipedes this time, only an old earwig and a blanched, dry inchworm. He held them in the puffy palm of his hand, two empty shells, and he showed Darlene.

"See?" he said, grinning. "Nothing to be afraid of."

Darlene found even dead bugs repulsive. She pushed his hand away, squealing, and the bugs tumbled.

That night they slept in the trailer, Hannah with Wren and Vivian, breathing in the mustiness of cooped-up cloth. It was not camping, they knew that, but it was like camping. Their bodies in damp sleeping bags, three cocoons. Hannah's body long enough that her toes touched the cool zipper at the bottom. Vivian said she wished she had made this her home, and Hannah could see how she might want that. After all, it had a soft door, two soft windows. A canopy out front like a roof over a patio, which even their real house did not have.

They kept all the flaps open and the air and moonlight spilled in through the fine screens. Outside the crickets played music with their sticky hind legs, and inside a mosquito buzzed, the buzz near, then far. Vivian wanted to find it and swat it, but Wren said no, that mosquitoes lived for just one day, born from a puddle, and it wasn't fair to shorten a life as sadly short as that. And oddly, Vivian stopped her search.

She began instead to sing radio songs, which she knew by heart, and Wren and Hannah hummed along. Vivian had all the *ooohs* and *lah-lahs* in their right places because there was nothing she could not remember. She still knew which star was which in the sky, and he had been gone three years now.

Through the screen Hannah could see the sky, lit up and blotchy. Those stars wouldn't show in the city. Too many lights, Vivian said. Too much smog blocking the view. She seemed to look forward to that. From here on in their skies would be different.

White Friday and Hannah woke sweating in her sleeping bag, hemmed in but not wanting to move. She looked at Vivian. Tangled white hair, dark with sweat. Wren's black hair, long and hot, sprawled everywhere in thin locks. Hannah softly blew cool breath into her sleeping bag. Today would be so humid it might be hard to breathe. The sky hot white like the day.

Across the lawn and through the window came the peal of Darlene's alarm clock, the same short scream repeated. Not a sound that makes you pleased to wake up. Everyone opened their eyes.

Breakfast was lumps of cereal that Hannah couldn't swallow, with long red rhubarb from the garden, delicious. Vivian's face was pink with excitement. The excitement glowed in her eyes too, and Hannah forced her face to smile.

Too soon Angie and Charlie arrived, and Tim came too, wanting to say goodbye. Hannah sat on Vivian's hard grey suitcase until the last minute. This was the suitcase he had carried when he left the first time. Inside was worn yellow lining and the long, gathered pockets that had held his precious things. Now they might hold Vivian's. The secret mementoes she kept under her mattress.

"Bye, Bee," said Vivian.

Hannah said nothing because no sound would come out. Vivian hugged her, but how strange it felt: both foreign and familiar. Vivian's skin had a tangy smell of sweat and borrowed perfume, and Hannah breathed it in, a smell she might remember.

"Oh, Viva!" cried Darlene. She lunged at Vivian, sobbing, butterfly kissing, combing Vivian's fluffy hair with her fingers.

Uncle Tim looked on and Hannah looked up. At the sky. At the water tower, which spelled out the name of their town. Uncle Tim squeezed Hannah's shoulder, and when he took his hand away she could still feel his palm and fingers.

Vivian climbed into the car. Everyone waved goodbye, and Charlie backed slowly down the driveway. There she went. Hannah could see her puff of white hair and her waving white hand until the car was out of sight.

Wren

Wren has often wondered how different her life would have been had Vivian not skipped Grade Four. Up to then they had moved through the levels together, and if they had continued to do so,

Wren may have been spurred on by Vivian come graduation, filled with the need to be elsewhere. As it was, she felt unsure about where she should be.

When she graduated the year after Vivian left, she had still made no decision. Charlie was dismayed. He was an educated man.

"You can be anything," he told her. "Anything at all."

Perhaps that was it, the choices were too numerous.

"You could go anywhere," said Angie. "You could be with Vivian."

But while she missed Vivian, Toronto was not for Wren. On that long drive she had smelled the smog miles before they reached the city. It came through the cracked open windows and the vents, and formed a membrane on her skin. And in among the tall, lit-up buildings she had grown short of breath. She had not breathed relief until the next day, driving home, when the multitude of trees had reappeared, and the polluted layer of yellow turned to clean white clouds.

That was not the path for her. What was, she did not know. She had the need to wait. Something would come.

When they came in style, Angie made Wren twenty flouncy blouses in varying colours and fabrics, some trimmed with ribbon, some trimmed with lace. Each with the belled sleeves too long, so Wren's hands could nestle unseen. Wren felt angelic in the white eyelet one with its tiny see-through holes. Exotic in the deep purple with scarlet poppies. She was wearing the plain yellow one the day she got the job at the Snack Bar. Her hair looped in a half-ponytail with yellow yarn, making her long ballerina neck appear even longer.

Everyone came to the Snack Bar, where milk was more expensive but available when you needed it if the grocery store was closed. Here was a large selection of chewing gum, candy and chocolate, some of which could be bought singly at affordable prices. Also hockey or baseball cards, depending on the season. And magazines that showed what was beautiful. Thin women with tanned velvety skin, teeth even as bathroom tiles. Wren sometimes flipped through the magazines and stared at the long arms and legs, at the gentle slopes of breast and belly. Beauty was a crazy thing. Everyone chasing it. In school, as part of home ec, they taught you how to hold a hair dryer in one hand and a brush in the other, to achieve big swooping curls, and how to put on makeup so it looked like you hadn't. Wren never wore makeup. Her skin was so pale the veins showed through, and her eyes, grey and narrow, looked stretched, as though she was straining to hold them open as widely as possible. She used to dislike this look, until it came to her that perhaps she appeared vaguely, exotically Asian. She stared more and more into mirrors. Sometimes she stared and cried. Other times, though rarely, she thought that, at certain angles, she might be almost as lovely as Darlene, who was to Wren the pinnacle of beauty, like the luna moth. The chances seemed out of this world, that another person might be put together as perfectly as Darlene had been, in fine, graceful pieces with delicate bones and skin.

At work, when she stood at the cash, Wren could see herself in a mirror on the opposite wall. She could see the customers there too, seated on stools at the counter. Today there was only Stuart Fergus. He was opening a package of cigarettes and burning the thin paper from the foil. On the counter beside him was a large foil ball, and every day at lunch he bought his cigarettes and added to it.

He worked for the town now, paving roads, planting baby trees. He wore a vest with a fluorescent orange X on the back.

On hot days he wore nothing underneath, his T-shirt hanging from the pocket of his jeans. When the vest fell open Wren could see that there was muscle not only in his arms and shoulders, but in his chest and stomach too. His stomach was brown and rippled, and a deep line ran up the centre, where before had been pale, flat skin. He seemed a whole different person from the disturbing boy who had been Hannah's childhood friend. Now he was the boyfriend of Lily Sinclair. Disturbing still, but electrically so.

For lunch Wren served Stuart pre-formed burgers that must have tasted like rubber, the buns thin and stale. He sipped pop and she watched him in the mirror, and when she wasn't watching she felt his eyes on her. Sometimes he smiled. He rarely spoke but left her tips, which here were unusual, and he looked too long at her before leaving. She hid her hands in her flouncy sleeves where he wouldn't see them.

One night he was outside when she left work. He was leaning against the rough brick wall of the Snack Bar, tossing his foil ball from hand to hand. His T-shirt was stained with sweat under the arms, and an image flashed in her mind of her hands on those wet patches.

"Hi," said Wren shyly, and started to pass.

Stuart smiled. One long leg was bent, foot flat on the wall, and that leg swung out and stopped her. He held it there, pressed against her own legs.

"I could walk you home," he said. "It's on my way."

Every night that week Stuart waited and walked with her through dark back lanes, and down to the beach, where he held her so tightly it seemed she might move right through him and out the other side. On her legs she felt the imprint of his corduroys, too warm for summer. She had never been kissed before and maybe she would never be kissed again. His tongue was stiff and pointed. His mouth was hot and wet and tasted of cigarettes and unflossed teeth. Without clothes, his thick tawny skin was softer than she expected, no moles, no freckles, no scars except one faint squiggly one on the pale underside of his arm. He thrust doglike in and out of her, spreading her open and bringing forth a hot, sharp pain. It was over before she knew if it was something she had wanted. She watched the stars and the moon, which was said to be the size of Africa. Tonight it was fat and low-slung, brighter than normal. She listened to water spill up on the shore.

From the beach they followed a long path through the woods. He held her hand and led the way, which was kind but not necessary. She could be blind and make her way here. The woods were mapped in her memory.

At the top of the path he stood and looked at her.

"Well," he said. "See you."

He had the blank face of someone she did not know.

Right away she could feel the baby inside. She may even have felt it forming, coming together in two pieces, but that could have been gas, a pocket of air. She began to touch her breasts and belly often, expecting change, but for a long while there was nothing. Only something vague. A bruise she could feel but not see. And then her breasts, too, felt bruised, swollen, and she imagined feet forming, and hands. Real feet and hands like Stuart's, with individual toes and fingers.

Soon she felt sick. In the mornings she heaved waves of nothing into the toilet bowl's blue water, and sometimes she heard a thick silence she knew was her mother pausing, listening at the door.

All the while the baby inside grew eyes and ears, and holes around which a nose would soon appear, and it occurred to her that people were not unlike bugs in the way they began and transformed. Scorpion mothers brought forth not eggs for hatching, but live, tiny, colourless babies who otherwise looked just like them. They emerged in a skin-thin cocoon from which the mothers released them, and for a time they rode everywhere on the backs of their mothers. As adults, they were loners. It was thought to be a miracle that two, a male and a female, came together at all. What he did was stare her down. He pinched her claws with his own and dragged her off, but all that happened next was that he scooped a little hole in the ground and put his sperm in there, hoping she would take it. Sometimes, after she had gotten what she needed, she ate him.

Wren wondered about the baby's hair, if it would lengthen, if it would tickle. And would it be black like hers? She thought of Stuart's hair hanging towards her as he moved. His toes splayed in the sand, so evenly angled from smallest to largest, as though with a ruler. The pockets beneath his arms, where long hair grew and where there was a faint smell of tomato soup. His mouth, whose full top lip matched his bottom lip exactly. He had not walked with her since that night. He had not come for lunch. He waited in the car while Lily came in to buy cigarettes, and Wren peered out at him, but there was nothing on his face that showed any feeling. Wren looked at Lily's glittery eyeshadow, at her pockmarked face. She watched Lily leave and then stood in front of the colourful tabloids. A woman in Utah had captured one thousand butterflies, just so she could set them free at her wedding. It was instead of confetti, Wren knew. People could be ugly in ways no one seemed to notice.

In her parents' wedding album, Wren's mother smiles with teeth that gleam and have since become yellow in places. Her eyebrows, plucked and redrawn, arch in constant delighted surprise. Wren's father, in bare feet, rests his big hand at her slim white waist.

Wren touched the rippled edges of the photographs. She traced the curve of her mother's bobbed hair beneath the veil. Folded in the back of the album was a mauve napkin with the names of the bride and groom, *Angela Gillis & Charles Hill*, and also a clipping from the newspaper, which made her mother seem like some sort of celebrity or society girl, though of course she was nothing of the kind.

The dress she had worn hung beneath blue plastic in the closet of the spare room. Wren pulled the zipper slowly open, slipped her hand inside. She unbelted her housecoat and let it drop, and pulled first the cover, then the dress, from the hanger. There were many tiny buttons up the back of the dress, and she sat on the bed unlooping them with a partial finger, wondering how she might loop them all closed again once the dress was on.

The dress fit more tightly than she'd expected it to. Fine white stitches stretched open at the shoulders. The bouffant skirt rose high on her ankles, and she looked at her feet—thick, flat, ungraceful. Patterned from a tan in sandals.

And then the door whined open and Angie was there, seeing Wren, and Wren noticed how her mother's hair had dulled, how there were springy white hairs that coiled away from her head, giving her an unkempt, unpolished look that matched not at all the photos of a radiant bride.

Upon discovering the pregnancy, Angie made arrangements. They drove to the city and let Charlie believe they were shopping for school clothes.

"He'd be so disappointed," Angie told her.

All the way Wren stared at her reflection in the passenger window, turning her head in small movements to find her prettiest angle. She liked her head tilted low, which made her face heart-shaped, and her eyes, looking up, large and gloomy. Mostly she stared at herself because it was embarrassing to look at Angie, knowing she knew what had happened. Wren having sex. Wren naked.

Ahead of time there was an appointment with the doctor, not at the hospital but in an office where other girls waited—some with mothers, some without. They glanced at each other and away. They looked through magazines. When it was Wren's turn, the doctor put something inside her to spread her open. He said it would make her feel crampy, like with her period. He said a lot of other things but she did not hear him. She was having trouble even seeing him. She was thinking of soft bees buzzing from flower to flower, unrolling their tongues and sipping sweet nectar. She was thinking of the combs and brushes on a bee's front legs, used to scrape the pollen from its fluffy body. She was thinking of the tiny baskets behind a bee's knees, which the bee fills to overflowing with golden pollen, pollen that might rub off and fertilize the next flower the bee sipped from.

In the hospital Wren was glad to be away from Angie. She was on a stretcher, covered up, and around her there were others on stretchers, covered too, and she wondered if they were all here for the same reason. If this place, which seemed more like a hallway than a room, was just for people waiting to have babies removed.

She wished Vivian would appear. On her head there was a hat like a shower cap, and Vivian would laugh at that, make a joke and say, "You look *loo*dicrous," and everything would feel less awful. She pulled her heavy hand out from under the sheet and tucked her fingers beneath the elastic because she could not remember—did they shave her head? She tried to feel the baby inside, but instead she felt the foreign object cramping, spreading her open. Would they take that out too or would it become part of her, like the fine grey sliver from the backyard fence that went into her hand and never came out again?

She felt strange. Not unhappy, really, but unlike herself.

In a brighter room, people in white and blue and pale green stood over her, their mouths covered with patches of cloth. She was embarrassed by her shower cap, which could not be attractive. She thought of her mother, passing the time smoking in the smoking room, one after another, adding wrinkles to the edges of her eyes. Drinking thick black coffee that came out of a machine. She thought of dragonflies, a less painful image. The muscly, veiny, iridescent wings of a dragonfly move it both backwards and forwards, or allow it to hang suspended in the air like a helicopter. *P-t-e-r. Pteron.* Wing. She would tell Vivian that. Beautiful dragonflies have ugly, ugly babies. The adults skim the water, dip into it and emit bubbly eggs that hatch into nymphs. The nymphs move slowly among the water weeds for years, then one day climb a stem, breathe air, split skin and fly.

Wren looked into the friendly eyes of a masked woman.

"Stop," she said. "I've changed my mind."

Angie and Charlie asked questions.

"Who *did* this?"

"Who is responsible?"

"Whose baby is this?"

And Wren said, "*I* did. *I* am. Mine."

Angie chewed the skin around her fingernails and said, who knew, the baby might not be normal.

"The baby will be beautiful," said Wren serenely.

What hurt were the sad eyes of Charlie, red from crying and lack of sleep. Each night he came home from work and moved directly to the bedroom, lay there in his clothes, tie loosened. But Wren could not pretend to be unhappy. In truth she was ecstatic, rapturous. Radio songs floated through her mind, and she hummed and whistled, soothing sounds for the baby inside. She remembered what Lily Sinclair had once said about Mozart, about mothers teaching babies who were still in the womb.

Angie softened first; and Charlie, she knew, would follow. Wren woke sick and ran to the bathroom, heaving. She was leaning into the toilet, waiting for the next wave, when she sensed her mother behind her. A hand in her hair. Two hands, fingers combing through. Wren vomited again and Angie held her hair, ponytailed it with her hands. She walked back to the bedroom with Wren and then brought a tray with crackers and ginger ale, a fancy cloth napkin and a vase with two orange poppies that yawned open in the summer heat, exposing black centres. Wren would not be a mother who snapped in and out of loving her child.

Inside, the vast emptiness was filling up. Love was hit and miss. Everywhere you looked it hung in the air, longing to be invited in. She could put that love into this baby. All the loose love that floated around, missing the people it aimed for, she could grab it up and give it to this baby.

Hannah

Stuart's wooing of Wren had lasted only one week, but Hannah had seen them. She had seen Wren rounding a corner and turning into a back lane, and she had run to catch up, wondering at Wren's odd route home. Then she had seen Stuart. His arm grazed Wren's as he walked, and Hannah slowed and turned away.

Brie was born with a mouth just like his, the strange top lip. Hannah couldn't hold her. All her awful secrets had to do with Stuart Fergus, and each one, called up, stirred a sickness in her. He could get away with anything, and she had let him.

When she was alone with Wren, she asked, "Is it his?"

"It doesn't matter, Hannah," Wren answered calmly.

But it did, it had to.

"Is it his?" she asked again.

"I said it doesn't matter, okay?"

Hannah looked at the baby, at its mouth and dark eyes. He had killed a kitten and a girl, and all she had done was watch.

"Whatever you say, I'll deny it," Wren told her. "This is something I want, Bee."

"So it *is* his," said Hannah.

"*She,*" said Wren. "Not *it.*" She took Hannah's hand and touched it to the baby's fine hair. "Her name is Brie."

That made a sudden surprising difference, this reminder and the touch.

"Hi," Hannah whispered.

Brie's baby skin was warm beneath her hand. Hannah thought of the long-ago day that Stuart had swelled from the hornets.

"You saved his life," Mrs. Fergus had said.

If she hadn't, there would be no Brie.

Angie

Without hesitation, Angie loved her. All the built-up, bitter disappointment vanished when she looked at the baby, a girl. She had the red scrunched-up face of a newborn, and bent legs and arms that made her seem cramped from being inside so long.

Granddaughter.

"What will you call her?" she asked Wren.

"Brie."

Later, when Angie passed that on, Darlene laughed.

"That's not a name, Ange, it's a cheese," she said. "Try to talk her into Brianna, at least. That's got a ring to it."

"No," said Angie. "I like Brie."

"Me too," said Darlene. "On crackers."

Angie smiled, unperturbed. She had already found the name book beside Wren's bed. Turning to the one folded page, she had scanned each column and finally seen *Gabrielle. Feminine version of Gabriel, angel of God. Gabby, Gaby, Brie.*

Hannah

White Friday, the day before the wedding. Hannah surface-sleeps while far away a mower buzzes. She hears the squeals of children. Brie, maybe, pulling cats' tails, squeezing blood from raspberries. She opens her eyes to her sad pink room, mostly packed into boxes, and is drawn to the one that holds the camera, a Polaroid, still with pictures inside. It is heavy in her hands. Now they make things lightweight and perfect. She looks through the viewfinder to the cowboy curtains.

"You have to wait for just the right moment," he had told her. "Then capture it."

He'd stood behind her, crouching, his hands on her hands holding the camera. Hannah blinked her lashes against the viewfinder, waiting.

"You'll know it when you see it," he said, talking against her ear. "It's magic."

She looked and looked for the magic, but everything she looked at stayed the same unmagical way. She could hear him breathing behind her, feel his palms sweating on the tops of her hands.

Was that Mick or the man with the postcards? She can't be sure, but it must have been her father. The Polaroid was his, and then hers, no one else's. When she thinks of him her stomach turns over, even though she only knew him for nine years.

Hannah loops the long strap of the camera around her neck and leaves her pink room for the living room, where Darlene in her kimono is sipping coffee.

"Morning, Girly," says Darlene.

She looks up and sees the camera, Hannah holding it to her eye, and she squeals and shoots her hand out.

Hannah presses the button that makes the picture slide noisily forth, and with the whooshing-out of it comes brief joy, relief. She pulls the mysterious black picture out and places it on the table, and she and Darlene watch it. It smells of chemicals and looks sticky, but there she is, coming slowly. A blur of colour at first, then clearer, her hand pale and big, out of proportion, covering half of her unmade face, which is both laughing and not.

"What's up?" says Vivian, and Hannah turns and takes her picture too, straight on, white bristled hair sticking straight up.

.

After breakfast they walk downtown, Darlene walking briskly, a step ahead in new sandals. From behind she looks girlish. Her shoulders thin and bony, her neck slender. Her hair is twisted into a chignon, which to Hannah seems a silly way to wear it with shorts and a tank top, but it's true Darlene looks lovely, always lovely. Only at her elbows is there any sign of aging. There the skin puckers and folds like too-big sleeves. Darlene herself is aware of it.

"If I had to live life over again," she once admitted, "I'd bend my arms less often. That's what does it. Too much bending stretches the skin."

She straightened Hannah's arms then. That whole visit she tapped on Hannah's elbows whenever she saw them bent. She pinched the skin, which pulled out easily, and showed Hannah.

"See?" she said. "It's happening already."

Downtown Darlene slows and steps between Hannah and Vivian, linking arms.

"Let's surprise Reg," she says, which is no surprise to Hannah and Vivian. Why else would she want to walk downtown?

The shoe store is just the same. Even the shoes don't look that different.

"Hello, hello-o!" Darlene calls. "I brought my girls!"

Reg in pressed navy shorts and a golf shirt with the collar turned up emerges smiling from the back room. He is a large pale man with a perm and the strangely hairless shapely legs of a woman. Hannah thinks at once of her own father, long dead but handsome, of Uncle Tim, Dare and Ned Norman. Of poor Mr. Onion, whom she had almost forgotten. She and Vivian had peered at him through holes cut in the newspaper, laughter escaping through them.

Hannah and Vivian go to the deli to pick up sandwiches for everyone because Reg can't leave the shop. They laugh all the way, turning heads, and some of the laughs come out like snorts and that makes them laugh more.

At the deli they take their time, order the sandwiches and then sip sodas until the giddiness subsides.

"I wonder if this will be a *permanent* relationship," says Vivian, cackling. "She's never dated anyone with a perm before."

"No," says Hannah. "But there was Ned Norman. Remember his bangs? They kind of curled under, like with a curling iron."

Vivian looks puzzled.

"You don't remember Ned?" says Hannah. "He almost killed me. And then he saved my life."

Hannah and Vivian and Darlene had been out walking, and Ned Norman was there too. Being the man he carried the picnic basket. Inside were layers of egg-salad sandwiches on soft white bread and a Thermos of iced tea. They were on a mountain, and Hannah could see through the trees that the cliff beside them was steep. Ned Norman was huffing and puffing, going too slow in white shoes with curled tassels, and Hannah tried to pass him. There was just enough room on the cliff side, but right then he swung the picnic basket out to change hands and it hit her, knocked her down, and she felt herself rolling, tumbling, sand in her shoes and her mouth, and too late she knew she was falling. She could hear Darlene screaming, and all of a sudden Ned Norman grabbed her, so hard she felt her shoulder pop out of its socket. He pulled her up and laid her on the path, and all of the sandwiches were strewn there too, lying in the dirt in shiny Saran Wrap. Ned Norman stepped on one with his cracked white shoe, and Hannah watched the egg ooze out and smear against the plastic.

"Phew, Girly," said Darlene. "Are we ever lucky Ned was here!"

Which was not the way Hannah saw it. She stood and looked at her knees. Smears of blood seeped through the dirt. She looked at Ned, puffed proud as a bird.

But Vivian says Ned wasn't Ned, he was Joe. Joe was the one with the curled bangs and the basket, and Ned had the Batmobile car, black, with pointy wings above the tail lights. Vivian says Hannah didn't fall and tumble. Only tripped on a root thrusting out of the ground. And there was no cliff. Just a big old dirt path with grass on either side. Vivian says Hannah tripped on the root, landed flat on her face with her skirt up and her flowered panties showing. Joe had laughed, Vivian says, and poked Hannah's bum with the toe of his shoe, which, yes, was white with curled tassels.

They sit in the back of the shoe store, in Reg's office, with chairs pulled around Reg's desk. Reg crosses one hairless leg over the other and tucks a napkin into the V of his golf shirt. How peculiar that Darlene will marry him. Shoe-Store Man. As strange as marrying the dentist, whose thick-fingered hands had been in Hannah's mouth.

On Reg's bulletin board there's a photo of Darlene riding a horse. It's a Polaroid, which means that Mick took it. And there she is cupped in Uncle Tim's hammock, and again climbing into the basket of a hot-air balloon. The pictures have been peeled out of Darlene's own album, maybe put here to insert Reg into Darlene's past, or Darlene into Reg's. Is this the way memory becomes reality? There are also photos of Lily through the years, and one with Stuart beside her. Bizarre, the lot of them coming together.

Darlene pulls half the stringy pastrami from her sandwich and slips it into Reg's, pretending she couldn't possibly eat so much, and Hannah glances quickly at Vivian. Will marriage to Reg mean Darlene will stop eating cold ravioli from the tin? Stop snacking on raw wieners? It's hard to picture Darlene married, living away from the green house where inside there is orange shag carpet and a lampshade Darlene made herself during her arts and crafts phase. Hard to imagine Darlene living instead at Reg's place, where snooty Lily grew up speaking fake Chinese. Darlene with a basement and a pool. Roaming around the plush sunken living room in her pink kimono with the hole under the arm. This might be what she's always wanted.

After lunch they go their separate ways. Darlene to Angie's for the final fitting of her georgette dress, Vivian out with Wren and Brie, and Hannah to gather flowers for the wedding.

She drives to The Flower Shoppe and stands looking at the sad carnations in the cooler, red with blackened edges, one dyed blue. There is wrinkled freesia also, perhaps two weeks old. Flower shops are sorry places in small towns. Nothing to choose from, so no one buys anything. No one buys anything, so there is nothing to choose from.

"Can I help?" asks the florist. Her voice momentarily hides the buzz of fluorescent lights.

"I don't think so," says Hannah. "I'm looking for flowers for my mother's wedding."

"Oh!" says the florist, motioning to the wall. "I've lots of artificial."

Fake flowers cover the wall and hang from the ceiling, and Hannah, glancing at them, recalls the plastic daisies on Mick's grave, and then the wild bouquet he brought for Darlene's birthday, a ladybird on the leaf. Hannah's own tiny bracelet made from Indian paintbrushes.

"No," says Hannah. "But thanks anyway."

She drives up and out of town, along the Trans-Canada, and down a gravel road that ends in a meadow, and here she gathers whatever grows wild. Bull rushes and goldenrod and black-eyed Susans for the church. She makes the bouquet all green, in varying shades, using unripe raspberries, gently curling ferns and the fine new shoots of cow parsley. Around the edge she forms a collar of maple leaves and also keys that have twirled from the trees. She has never made a more perfect thing.

That evening they drink wine while Hannah makes the corsages and boutonnieres. Vivian is helping Darlene pack, and Hannah works and watches them.

"Don't give that away," she keeps saying.

She'll take the toaster home with her, the faded cowboy curtains and the A to Z fridge magnets. Certainly the camera.

Darlene gives them their baby books, a touching moment until she adds, "I can't hang on to all this stuff—Reg just hasn't got the room."

"Reg," says Vivian, "must have a very small place."

Which makes Hannah think of Tim and his square-box house.

"How is Tim?" she asks.

Darlene shrugs. "Tim's Tim," she says. "He'll be okay."

To Hannah this seems unlikely. She pictures Tim's sad face. The yellow whites of his puffy eyes.

"He drives a pick-up now," says Darlene, brightening. "He's offered to move my stuff, can you believe it?" She makes a clucking sound with her tongue. "Sweet man."

Hannah runs a hand over the marbly pink book, which says *Our Baby* in scripted gold on the cover. She was born at 8:50 p.m., and she came out so quickly and easily that the doctor arrived after the fact. She was nine pounds, two ounces, huge and healthy. Her hair was reddish-gold—there's a curved lock of it taped to the page and there's also the scab from her booster.

"I couldn't just throw it away, Girly," Darlene once said. "That scab's a part of you—a milestone!"

Throughout the book there are more locks of hair, changing from red to blonde and back again. Darlene clipped the locks regularly, from underneath so no unevenness would show. It was comforting to pull on the hidden short piece.

"Pull too hard and you'll pull it right out," Darlene would say, gently slapping Hannah's hand. "Bald spots aren't pretty."

The curves of hair remind Hannah of bats. That once a bat had flown towards the light inside the house through a rip in the screen, and a cat, marbly orange, had followed him through the hole. Suddenly trapped, the bat hid behind the bureau, wedged the back half of his tiny body between the floor and the baseboard and screeched. Hannah and Vivian and Darlene, in bare feet and nightgowns, screeched too, bending to look beneath the bureau, alarmed, pale-faced. "Get a tennis racket!" Hannah had yelled, but there was none, and if there had been, what would they do with it? "Get sheets!" cried Darlene, and Vivian did, pulling a crisp white, a floral blue and a soft, worn flannel from the closet. Thinking ahead and also grabbing three clothespins, with which to fasten the sheets, cloaklike, beneath their chins. A bat's wings could get stuck in your hair, Darlene said, and it would just flap and screech there until you cut it loose, chopping a big chunk of your hair, and maybe by then it'd have bitten you and you'd get rabies and foam at the mouth and die.

"If only Chuck were here," said Darlene. Chuck with his black motorcycle gloves that reach right to the elbows.

Wrapped, they bent in unison, kneeling and peering. The bat screamed wildly and looked right at them, though it had to be blind. It writhed but could not break free. The marbly orange cat peered too, even stretched a paw out as if to swat, but didn't. Colour appeared on Darlene's face, a circle of red on each cheek. She covered her hand with a corner of the sheet and stretched it forward, panting as if in labour. When her hand had closed around the quivering body of the bat, she gave a quick tug and screamed, but the bat remained stuck and only screeched louder, as though a limb had been broken. Touching him so unnerved Darlene that she stood and ran, and so did Vivian, sheets trailing behind them.

Hannah stayed, wrapped and watching, and the cat stayed too.

"*Ssshhh*," she said. "*Ssshhh.*" She said it over and over for a long time, and then she reached forward and slowly pulled on the bat, holding her breath, hoping its legs would not be left behind, wriggling and bleeding at the breaking point.

When finally it came loose, intact, it screeched and writhed so much it frightened Hannah, and she felt her heartbeat in the tips of her fingers, but still she held the bat wrapped in her hands. She walked outside to set it free in the darkness, and the cat walked too, wending around and in between her legs, in meowing figure eights, and almost tripping her. When the cool of night touched her exposed parts—her circle of face, her feet and ankles—she wanted to fly with that bat on brittle Dairyish wings. Opening her sheeted hands she wondered what it sounded like, inside, when you flew. If the wind was like the ocean in a seashell.

Vivian laughs. She refills their glasses.

"That was *me*," she says. "Not you. *You* ran with Mom to the kitchen. You were petrified. It was pathetic! *I* took the bat outside. And as for a cat, I don't remember any cat at all."

"Too true, Banana," says Darlene, clinking her glass to Vivian's. "Viva wore the pants that day."

"And I didn't set it free," says Vivian, grinning. "I squished it with a rock. I can still remember the June-bug crunch it made."

In the night Hannah wakes half drunk, her pink room spinning. She slips her foot out from under the sheets and presses it on the cool floor.

She can hear the lilting murmur of Darlene's voice in the hall. A man's voice too, and the sound of an engine running in the driveway. Hannah crawls to the end of her bed and peers out the door. Darlene in her pink kimono is wrapped in Tim's curly-haired arms. Tim clings and sobs, kissing the top of Darlene's head, kissing her eye and cheek, her forehead, and Darlene holds him up. His sloping shoulders slope more with the weight of his sadness, a sadness Hannah can feel across the top of her chest and in her throat too.

Darlene slides her hands up inside Tim's dingy T-shirt, squeezing him hard. She pulls away a little and touches his face, placing a finger at the top of his forehead, where lines now show. Hannah watches the finger run slowly down Tim's gloomy face, along the large bumpy nose, over lip and lip and stubbled chin. Darlene turns her finger and lifts Tim's head.

"Hey," she whispers. "Chin up, Sweet Boy."

Hannah lies back in the bed, suppressing the sweep of sickness that might just be the wine.

It was Tim who taught her to grow an avocado tree from the pit, propping the pit up on toothpicks in a glass of water. The plant grew up out of the pit like a weed in a sidewalk crack. Each day the stem curved taller until a new leaf unfolded.

"Look, Girly—something blue!"

It is morning now, the day of the wedding, and Darlene dangles her lacy blue bra with panties to match. She unbelts her kimono and shrugs it off, revealing a glorious smooth body despite age, peanut butter, canned ravioli, no exercise. She steps into the panties and clips the bra's front closure.

"Something old is Reg," she says, laughing, though he cannot be much older than she is.

Something new is the sheer georgette dress Angie has made, finer than anything Hannah has ever seen, lined with rustling taffeta. The spangles are tiny random gems, white stars in a white sky. The dress lies spread out on Darlene's bed, and Hannah touches the gauzy fabric that will be wasted on Reg Sinclair. This dress should be for true love only, but what is love? Hannah thinks of Darlene's finger tracing Tim's sad face. He was a decent man. Had Hannah and Vivian kept her from him? Forever they had wanted only Mick for Darlene. Only a dead man was good enough for their mother.

With a puff Darlene dusts powder under her arms and then mists her neck and chest with perfume. Her smell is everywhere. She pulls the dress over her head as though it is any old dress, as though this is any old day.

"Zip me?"

Hannah pulls the long zipper slowly closed, hiding Darlene's tanned back and the thin blue strap of her bra.

Something borrowed is Angie's veil of silk illusion, which now Darlene attaches to her hair. She turns and looks at Hannah through the veil. She looks beautiful.

"You look beautiful," says Hannah.

And she does, but somehow she also looks got up, silly, like a large, aging Barbie. The tiny clothes of Hannah's own Barbie dolls were like this. Too fancy to be anything but make-believe.

Outside Charlie takes photos of Darlene near the Hannah Tree, and then in the Ferguses' yard, where there are more flowers. Hannah's camera hangs on her shoulder. The heavy heads of the sunflowers look on with their brown velvet faces, mingling with all the other faces. Wren's and tiny Brie's. Vivian's. Hannah closes her eyes. She feels dizzy and strange, not from last night's wine but from sorrow. From too many things gone wrong.

Mrs. Fergus moves across the lawn towards her, so lit up, so happy to see her. She embraces Hannah, and when Mr. Fergus sees her, he does too. He smells freshly of aftershave. Hannah looks around for Stuart, wanting and not wanting to see him. And then there he is.

"In a way we'll be related," Stuart says, laughing.

The comment shocks Hannah and for a moment she stares at him. But he's referring to Lily, of course, Reg's daughter. He doesn't know it is Brie who already connects them, though how can he not? Hannah knew the moment she saw Brie, whose dark hair sprang roosterlike from her head. When she saw Brie up close it was her top lip, like a bottom lip, that frightened her. Could evil be passed down?

Stuart has turned away now, but still she watches him. He is puffy, too old for less than thirty. He has eaten too much meat, she thinks, but it is more than that. She recalls Princess Tiara and the queer pale blue of Stuart's eyes. Once she thought he could get away with anything. Now she believes he has gotten away with nothing at all.

Brie buzzes by in her flower-girl dress, which is stained at the knee. She weaves through the people, brushing her hand against skirts and pant legs. Hannah lifts the camera and presses the button, catching that blur.

In the front row, on Darlene's side, Hannah sits with Vivian. Everyone is here now, waiting for the bride. It occurs to Hannah that the last time she was in this church was for Mick's funeral. He had always said he wanted to be cremated. Because he didn't believe he'd been created, Hannah thought then. That was how she'd remembered the word, *created* plus an *m*. But Darlene went against his wishes when he died. She wasn't his wife any more, not legally, but she referred to herself as the widow, and so it seemed natural that she be the one to make the decisions. If she went outside, even in the blistering heat, she wore dark glasses and a scarf tied over her head. She said she was in mourning, that she wanted to be left alone. Uncle Tim followed her, though, and she didn't mind that.

"Thank God for Tim," she said, leaning against him. "He props me up."

She needed propping, Hannah could see that. She lay on the couch, scarfless, with a cold cloth on her forehead, hoping to calm herself. Hannah wanted to lie there too, with a cloth, but instead she sat on the kitchen stool and watched Angie mix salmon and mayonnaise in a bowl. It was horrible, the way she left the bones in.

"What if we choke?" asked Hannah.

"You won't," said Angie. "It's good for you. Adds calcium."

Fishy fumes rose from the bowl and turned Hannah's stomach. Those little wheel-shaped bones were fish spines, she knew that, though she didn't see how they could be. A spine was straight in a person. These made her think of guinea pigs or hamsters, whichever spun around on a treadmill, getting nowhere.

"Come have something to eat, Dee," said Angie as she put the platter on the table.

There was a moan from the couch.

"What did you say?" asked Angie.

Another moan.

Vivian rolled her eyes.

And then Darlene started. She wailed and sobbed, and once she got going there was no telling when she might stop.

"Eat your sandwiches, girls," Angie said. "Eat up."

She rose and moved to the couch and wrapped an arm around Darlene, who now was like Raggedy Ann.

All through lunch Darlene flopped and cried.

"I was crazy for that crazy guy," she burbled.

"I know," said Angie, stroking Darlene's hair. "I know."

"No, you don't. I mean *really* crazy," she said. "I loved him like I never loved anybody."

"Ssshhh," said Angie. "I know."

"*No, you don't.*" She was moaning now, and rocking with her arms wrapped tight around her body.

Hannah thought of a question.

Why did he leave, then?

She looked at Vivian and Wren, eating, and then at her untouched sandwich, which stank. Salmon swam in the river. Maybe not in the Ottawa River, but somewhere. Maybe further south, near Niagara Falls. She didn't think she would ever be able to swim again, or pick up dead minnows for fun, or dig in the sand, or ride in a boat or look at a wave rushing in.

Vivian was livid.

"He wanted to be cremated," she said, "because he believed it didn't make any difference what happened to your body once you were dead."

Hannah wanted to ask, If it doesn't make any difference, what difference does it make? But there was no one left who would answer such a thing.

Those days after the death all happened so slowly, as though there were weeks between the day he died and the day he was finally buried. With every day that inched by, Hannah worried about him decaying. It was hot, and she wondered, Did dead bodies sweat? Because that was what he was now, a body. The body. Vivian said so.

"He's not Dad any more," she said. "He's just a body. The shell of Dad."

That made him sound like a walnut, which he could crack in two more perfectly than anyone she knew, splitting and never crushing the meat inside.

Hannah wanted to ask if he might be sweating, but she knew what Vivian would say.

"That's a stupid question."

Which Mick never would have said.

The death and the pending burial had made Vivian more cantankerous than ever. She would not speak at all to Darlene, and even referred to her as "her" or "she." Those words had seemed nondescript before now. Suddenly they were nasty, even vulgar.

"Tell her," said Vivian to Hannah, "I'm not going to any fancy funeral."

Hannah looked at Darlene. "She says—"

"I know, Sweet Pea. I heard."

Darlene looked tired, Hannah thought, but more beautiful than normal with the scarf on. Hannah wished for a scarf just like it to wear to the service, and at the last minute she came upon her snowsuit hood, which was too warm and less glamorous but had a similar effect. She didn't care what Vivian said about it, how ridiculous she thought it was. With the hood on she could hardly hear Vivian's angry slurs, or Darlene's wailing moans.

On the morning of the funeral, Vivian said nothing about not going. She didn't speak to Darlene and she refused to sit beside her in the church, and though she made it obvious how much she hated Hannah for wearing the snowsuit hood, she held her hand all through the service, and later stood with her hands on Hannah's sunburnt shoulders as they watched his coffin being lowered into the ground. Soon he would be in a darkness to which his eyes would never adjust. A blackness as black as the Bonnechere Caves.

That was the last they saw of him.

Together the congregation stands and turns to see Brie fly down the aisle too fast, the opposite of Darlene, who approaches slowly in her georgette dress, needing the moment to last. The church aisle is not carpeted, and even though the organ is loud, Hannah hears grit crunching beneath Darlene's specially dyed shoes. Dog-eyed Tim, in a rumpled suit, leans into the aisle and snaps photos with Darlene's Instamatic.

The look in Darlene's eyes is convincing. Her lids heavy, hooded. She blinks slowly, peering in a sultry way at Reg and Reg only. Hannah has seen the look before. With her own father, certainly with Tim, and even with Darren—Derek? Darwin?—who appeared one Canada Day weekend and disappeared shortly thereafter.

"Do you, Darlene Miranda Gillis Oelpke, take Reginald Joseph Sinclair to be your lawful wedded husband, to have and to hold from this day forward, for ever and ever, amen?"

"I do," says Darlene, and then, whispering, leaning closer, "I really do, Sweet Boy."

Vivian turns to Hannah. "That's that," she says flatly. "The ultimate anti-climax."

Afterwards, in the parking lot, there are more photographs and confetti that sticks in the hair. Brie holds some in her hand and looks baffled.

"All it is is paper," she says incredulously.

Hannah holds her own hand out and lets the pastel rounds of paper fall into her palm. There had been confetti at Mick and Darlene's wedding too, she knows from the pictures, which are black and white, dramatic. Confetti falling like snow in July. Hannah is sure her parents' wedding had been something more than this, something grander. At least it had always been made to sound so, with the marquee and the bathtub and everyone waiting. Not like today. Hannah holds the camera in front of her face and looks up. The sun streams through the poplar leaves, colouring them silver. She can feel Mick in the heat of the rays. The eye she sees in the viewfinder is just the reflection of her own, but it looks like his, creased and smiling, and she has to concentrate to look past it, past herself and him, to the others. She pans the crowd. Least happy is Tim. He smiles a sad, welled-up smile, and his dog eyes follow Darlene as she twirls in her glorious dress. Hannah looks long at Tim. She would like to take his picture—cropped, close up, so the sweat in the lines of his face shows, glistening. She pans to Angie, presses the button, and then to Wren beside her, pressing again. She slides the black pictures into her pocket, knowing they're changing in there.

Later, at the reception, Hannah sits with Wren and Vivian, showing them the pictures, which are all coloured strangely, perhaps because the film is so old. They are also swirled and fuzzy in places, distorted, as though taken of TV. They have the eerie, false look of tinted black-and-white photographs. Vivian's cropped hair is yellow, and Wren's face is blue, undefined, slightly frightening. It reminds Hannah of the time Darlene painted her with makeup, all of them looking on, wanting to witness metamorphosis.

"My God," says Vivian, pointing to one of the photos. "Look at Tim. He looks just like Jay here."

Hannah peers closely at the photo. It's a shot of Angie, really, but Tim is behind her, his face red and blurry.

"Who," asks Hannah, "is Jay?"

Both of Vivian's eyebrows rise. "You're the one who saw them," she says.

Vivian

That was the summer their brown home slowly turned green. A man named Jay came to paint it, and Vivian abhorred him at first sight. Every morning he was there when they got up, scraping off paint and preparing to paint it back on again.

"Hey," he said instead of hello.

What? Vivian wanted to ask. *Hey*, what?

He obviously didn't know what *hey* meant. And he was not only moronic, he was squalid as well. Not the kind of redhead she trusted. His hair was coppery, straight and thick, and his eyebrows were that way too. His eyes were an uncertain brown, and this, really, was what threw her. She did not approve of red hair and brown eyes, uncertain or no. It looked wrong and it felt wrong too. Whoever he was, she could see right away he was dishonest.

Darlene took to Jay immediately.

"Hay is for horses," she sassed, giggling, and Vivian could not believe she'd said that.

Jay neighed and whinnied. He flared his nostrils at Darlene and showed his top teeth, which were short and uneven, unlike a horse's. Every couple of hours Darlene brought out an icy drink for him, and sometimes a snack, and once, when Mick had come home from work and seen all the glasses and plates lined up on the front step, he said to Darlene, "He's not a house guest. We pay him by the hour, you know."

The hours dragged on. During the hot ones Jay scraped and painted shirtless. He was almost maroon from the sun. And all the while the house grew shabbier. Beside the pristine white of the Ferguses' home, with its soldierly flowers and lawn ornaments, the Oelpkes' home looked worn and tired, beaten up. Little chips of paint littered the unwatered garden, where Jay had crushed petunias with his large splattered running shoes. Vivian loathed him for that. She had never much cared about the garden before, but she was appalled by his disregard for it.

"He's stepping all over the flowers," she said to Darlene.

Darlene shrugged. "He's got a job to do, Viva," she said, waving to Jay through the kitchen window. "Besides, you're supposed to pinch the flowers back. It encourages new growth."

Vivian lifted an eyebrow.

"Oh, come on," said Darlene. "Soon he'll put the green on and then you'll see how glorious it's gonna look."

That happened, finally. After all the scraping came the fiddly work of the trim, and for days Jay's too-tanned face appeared in window after window. Vivian pulled the drapes closed to be rid of him, but Darlene opened them up again.

"Don't be rude, Vivvy," she said. "Plus, we need a breeze in here."

Which was not true. The breeze was a hot breeze, and when the drapes were open the sun came in too, heating the inside. Worst was Jay's face, though. Sweaty and with globs of paint in his thick hot hair.

"Why does he always have to look in here?" asked Vivian.

"He's not *looking*," said Darlene, smiling out at him. "He's *working*."

That did not seem to be work, the eyes he made at Darlene. And even when he started painting the actual wall of the house, all he was doing was covering over the shabbiness he'd created. When the fresh coat of green was on, the patches of brown and white were still beneath it. Just because something was invisible didn't mean it wasn't there.

Once he had done the front and the sides, Mick said it had taken forever.

"He's going too slowly," he said, and Vivian agreed.

"That's because he spends all his time voyeurating," she said.

Mick held his fork in the air and looked at Vivian, then at Darlene.

"What?" asked Hannah.

"Voyeurating," said Vivian. She knew it wasn't a word but she liked the sound of it. It had a vulgar ring, like *urinating, defecating*. She grinned inwardly, and said to Hannah, "It means spying."

Mick chewed and swallowed and continued to look at Darlene, who shrugged and kept eating.

"I'll finish the back of the house myself," he said. "We've given that kid enough money already."

The next day when Jay pulled into the driveway, Mick had already left for work. Hannah and Vivian and Darlene were seated at the dining-room table, eating cereal and gazing out the picture window. Vivian watched Darlene wave as Jay climbed out of the truck.

All day he painted in his easy, lazy way. Nothing seemed different. Darlene brought him coffee and lemonade, and for lunch a sandwich stacked so high that the fancy cocktail toothpick got lost inside it. Vivian looked at the thick layers of meat that made Jay's sandwich, and then at hers and Hannah's. Soft white bread and a thin smear of peanut butter and jam. She cocked an eyebrow at Darlene, who was decorating the rim of Jay's plate with a fan of sliced pickles.

"What?" said Darlene.

Vivian said nothing.

"He's a man, Viva," she said. "He needs to eat."

Vivian did not think that was necessarily so, for although Jay was reasonably slim, he had a slight belly that sloped over his jeans and seemed to pull his shoulders forward.

"Look at him sweating up a storm out there," Darlene continued, clucking her tongue. "You have no idea how much work it is to paint a house."

But Jay's long arm moved slowly. Rollering up, rollering down. Vivian had the uneasy feeling that he was circling them, moving around the perimeter of the house, closing in for the kill.

Darlene set Hannah's and Vivian's sandwiches on the table and returned to the kitchen for Jay's plate. She bent and peered at her face in the toaster, pinching her cheeks for colour, and then she headed for the door.

"Are you going to tell him?" asked Vivian.

Darlene paused in the doorway. She pushed the screen door open with her toe. "Yes," she said, moving outside. "Of course I am."

Darlene sat with Jay on the porch while Vivian spied. She was waiting for news of the firing to come, for Jay's face to fall. But Darlene did not seem to be breaking the news. They sat side by side with their legs stretched out to catch the sun. Jay's beside Darlene's looked even less appealing than they did on their own. Maroon with that disturbing red down on top. Darlene's legs were golden brown, shining with oil. Not a hair showed because she had smeared them with Nair the night before, which burned all the hair off and left the skin unnaturally smooth and buttery.

Vivian looked again for signs of the firing. She strained to hear their voices through the screen, but other than laughter, she could make nothing out. Jay had eaten every last crumb of his mammoth sandwich and now there were only the pickles left. Darlene lifted one and held it above Jay's open mouth for too long. Finally she lowered it in and Jay's lips closed on her finger. Vivian shuddered and looked away.

Jay was barbaric, dim-witted. He had the small ears and hairless face of an orangutan, and his orangey-brown hair was fine and downy in that same primal way. On his upper lip there were not even the lines that extended down from the nostrils, and the skin there was bloated and round, monkeyish. He was strangely under-developed. And yet Darlene did not seem able to pull herself away.

It was not until late in the afternoon that she came back inside and took out her cheque book. She wrote Jay's full name with extra care and signed her own with an added flourish, and then she went outside again to join him.

He was in the driveway now, packing up for the day, and Vivian sat on the floor inside the side door, listening to their conversation.

"Hey," he said when he saw Darlene.

"Hay is for horses," she said.

Jay neighed and whinnied the way he had done too many times before, and Darlene laughed as always. There was a long silence during which Vivian could only wonder, and then Darlene spoke.

"This has got to be goodbye, Blue Jay," she said.

Vivian groaned inwardly.

"What?" he said. "But I'm not finished."

"I know," said Darlene. "But Mick's a wild man when it comes to other guys lurking about."

She paused, and Vivian longed to stand and peer out at them but didn't dare.

"Especially guys like you," said Darlene more quietly.

Another long silence and then a low Neanderthal moan. Jay's door slammed shut and he drove away.

Once he was gone Vivian didn't trust that he would never appear again. She glanced peripherally at every window as she walked through the house, expecting to see him there, but he did not come. She lay in a lawn chair in the backyard, soaking up sun and reading, gazing now and again at the messed-up wall of the house, which she knew might long remain unpainted.

On Saturday Mick rose early and bellowed, "Rise and shi-ine!" He said that today was a day for a trip. It was too nice a day for painting, and anyway, who ever looked at the back of the house except them?

"Oh, great," said Darlene, emerging from the bedroom and tying her kimono closed. "Now it'll never get done."

Mick pinched her bottom.

"Relax!" he said with a smile. "There are lots of days left in the summer."

"No," said Darlene. "There are not."

It was easy to see she was angry. Her green eyes flashed and darted, looking into one of Mick's and then the other. Vivian held her body stiff and waited.

"Yes," said Mick. "There are."

Mick and Darlene stood staring each other down.

"There are, Mom," said Hannah. She was standing in her bedroom doorway.

"What, Sweet Pea?" asked Darlene, switching off her anger.

"Lots of days," said Hannah. "There are lots of days left in the summer."

"No, Sweetie, there are not." And though she kept speaking to Hannah, she looked back at Mick as the words came out. "Because, you see, I know Daddy better than you know Daddy. Daddy's never painted a wall in his life and he could care less about painting one now."

"*Couldn't*, you mean," said Vivian. "You mean he couldn't care less."

Darlene glowered at her.

"Because if he *could* care less—"

"Whatever," said Darlene, holding a hand up to silence Vivian. She turned back to Mick. "He'll leave it that way today, and the next day, and the next, and before you know it, the whole summer will have passed, and you know what else?"

She looked at Hannah. She had worked herself up the way Vivian knew she would, and there was nothing to do but let her roll on.

"What?" said Hannah.

"I'll tell you what." She turned to Mick now. "All of next summer will pass too, and the one after that, and in fifty years, when I'm too old to care any more, that'll be when he picks up that brush!"

Mick laughed and rolled his eyes. "You're being ridiculous," he told her. "Besides," he said, "I think I'll use a roller. It'll be much quicker that way, don't you think? Since I'll be on my death bed and all."

"Shut up," hissed Darlene. "I am *not* being ridiculous. I am sick and tired, mister! For how many years have I been asking for a green house? I do not want a brown house any longer. Not even a *partially* brown house. I have *never* wanted a brown house and I have always *hated* brown. DO YOU HEAR ME?"

She was breathing heavily now, her chest and shoulders heaving. Vivian longed to slap her. *If I acted that way, you'd slap me,* she thought. She wondered sometimes how Mick kept his temper. And he was right anyway. Who cared about a stupid back wall? She would rather have the horrible patches of brown and white than that orangutan Jay swinging from the eavestrough.

Hannah

Hannah, sipping her third rum and Coke, looks intently at the photo, and finally she begins to see Jay in Tim. How she could have blocked something so entirely from her memory is inconceivable to her. It was like with Barry, or Dairy, whoever he was. She wonders what else has happened in her life that she can no longer see.

They left Darlene on the step that day, Hannah remembers that. She had stood in her kimono with her hands on her hips, watching them drive away. Without her they would go on an adventure, Mick said, perhaps to the Rolphton dam or Rapides-des-Joachims, which was all the way to Quebec.

"So?" he said, once they were on the road. "What'll it be?"

This was meant to be exciting, but soon came the queasy pink churn of Saturday. Something was wrong, something was off. There was a false tone in his voice that she had not heard before. She looked at his eyes looking back at her in the rearview and thought that, just now, he did not look at all like himself. And so she stretched in her seat. Straightened her back and lifted her head so she could see more of his face, simply to be sure it was him. There was his nose, straight and long.

Roman. She wanted to hear him say that now.

I've got a roamin' nose, my girls. It roams all over my face.

But he would not. He was smiling, even winking, but he was in no mood for joking around.

"Well?" he said. "Where to?"

Vivian shrugged. She lifted her legs and pressed her bare, dirty feet on the glove-compartment door, leaving toe prints there.

Mick was waiting. They sat at the stop sign at the end of their road, and he kept his hand on the stick shift, wobbling it back and forth. Hannah glanced back at the house, and then at the other houses on their street. If they sat here much longer someone might think something was wrong.

"I know," she said. "It's a Small World After All."

Vivian groaned, but Mick, laughing, said, "How about Storyland? Close enough, don't you think?"

And because she couldn't really know the answer to that, never having been to either, Hannah said, yes, it was, and Mick steered the car up and out of town, east towards Renfrew on the Trans-Canada Highway.

Storyland was just that, the land of stories. Walking through the woods they came upon Snow White and all her dwarves. Hannah longed to love them, but they were stiff and painted, not real at all. She peered too long into the weird, flat eyes of Dopey, who looked just past her no matter where she positioned herself. He was exactly her height, and she felt a chill run through her body. Because he was plastic, he had to be creepy.

"Oh, look," Mick said, pointing. "There's Dumpy."

Perhaps he was mixing him up with Humpty. He got all the names wrong, and Hannah didn't know, Was that a joke or not? She would have liked to laugh, but nothing seemed funny today.

She wanted to go away from here, back to Darlene, and then to have it be as though they had never left in the first place. But she did not say so out loud.

When it grew dark they began to drive home. It seemed they'd been gone a long time. They kept the windows down and in came the cool night air and the insect sounds, all different. Hannah was tired. There was something about driving. The hum of the motor, the street lamps passing, all at the same dancing pace. She could sleep and sleep. Her lids fluttered closed and open, closed and open.

And then, when she woke, she realized they'd stopped. She felt a transport roar by and shake the car, which was parked on the highway's shoulder. She gripped Mick's seat and pulled herself up and forward.

"Where's Daddy?" she said to Vivian.

Vivian pointed.

There he was, lit up in the phone booth. She had never seen him in a phone booth before.

"Who's he talking to?"

Vivian shrugged.

"Let me out," said Hannah. "I want to see—"

Vivian turned and stared hard at Hannah.

"No," she told her. "Stay here."

In her tired state Hannah did not immediately recognize the house they pulled up to. It was green, and theirs had forever been brown. The windows were dark, and it looked as though no one lived behind them. She wondered at the hushed roll of the tires on the driveway, and she realized, Oh, we're playing a trick. Mick had done that before. Turned the car off and let them roll silently down Townline Road. But this seemed different. She peered between the seats at Vivian, and saw that she was sleeping. The car came to a stop and Mick sat there, his head pressed back into the headrest. She had to pee and she wanted to go inside. Hurry up, she thought, and her willpower worked. Mick slowly opened his door, and Hannah crept out from behind his seat and rushed inside, hearing his hissed "Wait!" but not waiting.

For a moment all there was was confusion. How could those be Mick's feet dangling over the edge of the couch, when Mick was outside with Vivian? How could that be Mick on top of Darlene?

Darlene's face went white, as though she wore no makeup.

"Girly," she whispered.

Darlene was naked, lit up by the moonlight that streamed through the window, and so was the man named Jay. He was red-haired, red-skinned. Hannah looked up and away until, all of a sudden, Mick was there. She stood behind him with Vivian and watched his fingers stretch open, curl closed. Over and over he did that. He was calming himself.. Hannah knew that, though she had never seen him do it before.

Darlene began to speak. "I thought you were staying—"

"You should get dressed," Mick told her. His voice was flat, too even. "I'll take the children for a drive."

That's us, Hannah thought. *The children.*

In the car Hannah sat in the back seat, too aware of the puffed-up leather. It stuck to her legs and she could feel each stitch of the stitching. For a long time they drove, until she was delirious. So tired but she could not sleep. Awake, she dreamed that the stitches on the seat popped open and then resewed themselves, sewing her skin too, until she was sewn to the seat.

⌒

Hannah sips her drink and looks at Vivian, then turns to look at Wren.

"We went to your place, didn't we?" she says, and Wren nods.

Hannah is astounded. She is trying not to cry, which would be ridiculous right now. The rum and Cokes are making all this mean more than it should. Beyond Vivian and Wren, Darlene is whirling around the dance floor with Reg Sinclair. She looks as though she might never tire. If she could wear her georgette dress for all time, be the star from now on, then she might finally be happy.

Wren

Far off, the bog was burning. Charlie had told her that day about the fire, but Wren had known already. She had smelled the peat in the air and known that this fire was unlike the calm controlled burns at Charlie's work. This was part of nature. Bogs blazed all the time. They were slow fires, and they spread beneath the sprawling peat, searching for a hole through which to escape. She thought with growing alarm of the flora and fauna there. Of the black bears who may have been visiting the bog, eating crowned blueberries and velvety bog holly. The deer and the snowshoe hare, four-toed salamanders and leopard frogs, birds that warbled. She tried to fathom how many butterflies and moths might reside in that place, but the number would be so big it wouldn't really be a number, not one you could understand, and so Wren thought instead how quickly their thin wings might burn, licked as they were by flame. *Flutterby*. That was Hannah's first word for *butterfly*—wrong, but a nice mistake.

She lay in bed, unable to sleep for the thought of all that burning, and finally she crept outside for relief. Outside was an orchestra, and the sounds called her. The hotter it got, the more the crickets chirped. She had noticed that on her own, and later it had been proven to her by a book, *The Insect World,* which said that if you counted the number of chirps you heard in fifteen seconds, then added forty to that number, you would know what the temperature was. Sometimes it worked and sometimes it didn't. She always allowed for the possibility that she'd counted wrong, because in truth it was late the nights she sat outside, and her mind was probably not as alert as it could have been.

She came close, some nights, to catching a cricket of her own, because she'd read in *The Insect World* that crickets were pushovers— they could be easily coaxed from a meadow to a cage, and if you set them in the sun and fed them moist bread and lettuce and some sweet ripe fruit, they'd play on as if they'd never left nature. Though she longed to sit and stare, studying eyes and wings and veins and antennae, she left the insects where they belonged. It was wrong to confine them, no matter what the book said. Even if you treated a cricket royally, it did not belong in a cage.

Now she was lying in the tall grasses at the edge of the back-yard, just listening. She wished she had not worn this night-gown, which glowed bright white in the dark. Too obvious, she was. She would take it off but the feel of grass on bare skin was unpleasant to her, no matter how much she tried to like it.

Concentrate, she told herself.

Yes, it was hot tonight.

She rolled onto her stomach and stared at the yellow back-door light, and at the moths that fluttered around it. From here she could see four, of varying shades of brown, and also an apple-green luna. People didn't believe in luna moths, not around here. Anything that beautiful, they said, had to be exotic. Once she had brought a dead luna moth to her mother. Its wide pale wings more than covered the palm of her hand. Along the frontal wings were delicate smudges of mauve, and the long curving tails of the hind wings looked as though they'd been dipped in the faintest of yellows.

Wren held the luna up to Angie. It was so light that if she looked away she could not even tell it was there.

"Oh, my!" said Angie. "Where did you buy that?"

"I didn't buy it," said Wren. "I found it in the backyard."

Angie smiled and shook her head, a non-believer. "Oh, sure," she said. "Are there peacocks back there too?"

"No," said Wren.

Angie smiled at her serious face. "You're a real joker, aren't you?"

Nothing could have been further from the truth. Wren had never been a joker and never would be. She took the luna back outside, where it belonged, and cupped her other hand over it to keep the wind from blowing it away. She placed it in the crook of an oak branch because she knew that, as caterpillars, oak leaves were the lunas' favourite food.

Now she could hear not only the crickets but a bullfrog too, and another one answering. From far off came a less pleasant sound that grew louder and louder until it chugged to a stop in front of their house, and that was when Wren knew it was the Alfa.

She could not immediately understand why they were there, all of them except Darlene. She stood with them under the porch light and waited for Angie to come to the door. No one seemed to find it strange that there she was in her nightgown. There were too many moths in the air, and Vivian swatted at them. Wren looked at Hannah. Her hair was wild with knots, and her mouth hung open. Her eyes were glassy and red. Wren thought she might be sleeping standing up. Vivian was not sleeping, but wide awake and angry. Wren saw the gleam in her eyes.

Mick shifted nervously. He avoided looking at Wren. Instead he looked at the screen and pressed the buzzer again and again.

When Angie came to the door, she seemed alarmed to see Mick and Vivian and Hannah, and then more alarmed to see Wren outside in her nightgown. She pushed the door open, still looking at Wren.

"What are you—"

"Angie," said Mick. He took her hand and squeezed. "I need you to watch my girls."

And that was the last they knew. Upstairs they were all put in Wren's room, Hannah on a cot and Vivian and Wren in the bed. Wren lay still, waiting for Vivian's version. Hannah slept immediately, as though she truly had been sleeping all along.

Vivian

Vivian wakes with the sun. In adulthood she has reset her internal body clock, which now runs on a circadian rhythm in tune with Mick's. She stretches out on a lawn chair and smokes two cigarettes. All she wants is the trailer. She would trail it right across Canada and the States too.

No one wakes as she loads her car. No one wakes as she backs out of the stained double drive. She thinks she is leaving but in a moment she is driving back in, this time in reverse.

She pulls the trailer to the car and stands looking down at the tongue. Near the cup is a little lever that she flips up. She puts the tongue on the hitch and pounds hard with her foot, not desiring any gruesome accident. She criss-crosses the chains that hang from the tongue and hooks them up, one on either side of the hitch.

That's about all, she tells herself.

Now she goes, doubled in size. In her rearview mirror she spots Hannah, stepping out the side door. Hand flying to her laughing mouth.

Vivian pulls onto the street and waves, knowing the rule—that you have to keep waving until you're out of sight, invisible, as soon she will be. They played this game with Mick, waving their mad-fool waves every time he drove away. Vivian had played more for Hannah than herself. It made Hannah delirious, the waving. If their view of Mick was blocked by a tree or a passing car, Hannah would hold herself completely still, her hand stopped in the air. And then, when they could see him again, she'd jump up and down and wave insanely.

He's still waving! she'd say.

And Vivian could see that, yes, he was.

Wren

Wren, too, wakes early, smothered by Delilah and Brie. Today is ballet. Brie is already in her pale pink leotard, and on her own she's put a sloppy bun in her hair. She is no dancer, Wren knows, but she loves it. Not just the dancing but the costumes and the shoes, the hardwood stage, and Wren recalls that wondrous .

feeling: awaiting the creak of the piano bench, the rise of a thick crimson curtain. Garlands of autumn leaves, blackberries, blown roses, circled their heads, their tiny waists, even their wrists and ankles. Lily Sinclair out front, prima ballerina, blue-black hair brushing thin shoulders. Wren tucked far back, off to the left, hiding her hands in the leaves. The smell of the fresh outside hanging heavy, the berries wet, cool, some squashed and staining the hairline where no one would see. Sprigs of ivy sprouted from necklines, slippers, anywhere there was a place to tuck. Their bodies were covered by brown leotards that stretched over flat chests, round bellies, making them look like the trunks of trees. To their backs were stitched tulle wings of green and yellow, colours of nature. The wings had been coated stiff with hairspray, and each face brightened with dots of rouge, lipstick, smears of glittery eyeshadow. On their feet were gold slippers that flashed and sparkled when they moved and rendered them magical, ethereal. Wren watched hers as she waited, and the others watched theirs. Twelve pairs of eyes on twelve pairs of feet. They kept their brown legs together and their feet pointed outwards, at ten to two, and they waited that way, hardly breathing, so still they could no longer hear themselves or the rustle of their many garlands. Eyes downcast, they watched their slippers, chewed their bright lips, which tasted of mothers. The smell of the makeup and the hairspray on their wings mixed with the outside smell of the garlands, smells that escaped through the tiny space between the curtain and the floor, a long crack where light shone.

Hannah

Hannah drives up to the highway, away from home, back home. She passes the population sign that faces the other way, and then the no-name road that leads to Tim's. She passes a school bus heading into town, loaded with wild bus kids, the kind who always have to go to summer school. Their faces pressed against the tiny top windows. Tongues swirling spit on the glass. Just briefly she sees a red-haired boy with a finger in each nostril, his eyes bugged open as though the fingers are pushing them out, and then the bus is gone, visible only in the rearview, and Hannah thinks of poor Ricky Lewis—or maybe Dicky—who brought head lice to school in his bristly hair, and of the scarred face of Dodie Hay.

She continues on the Trans-Canada, which is two lanes here, and dangerous, people passing when they shouldn't, spiraling out of control, but further on there are four lanes, smooth pavement, freshly painted yellow lines.

Once they had an accident. Darlene and Hannah and Vivian, driving back from Uncle Tim's in the old green Nova. It might have been after that that he gave them the Rambler. Late at night, when the sky was navy blue. Hannah lay in the back seat, one hand pocketed in a rip in the plaid upholstery. She was counting the dots on the ceiling and thinking how, with a pen, she could connect them. She heard the tires rolling on the gravel, pebbles kicking up behind them, and then the car slowed and sped up again onto smooth pavement, and there was a gasp, the squeal of tires, a flood of white light that brightened the interior. Hannah saw in a flash her own body in stretchy yellow shorts and an orange tank top, her bony, dusty knees, one with a scab, her pocketed hand pulling away, tearing the plaid further, and then she saw the green AstroTurf floor mats up close, so bright they hurt her eyes, and she felt the rough itch of them against her skin, scratching her face, her elbow, her already sore knee. With the last roll she was propelled to the dotted ceiling. Stillness. The steady rasp of crickets. Hannah looked around. Their three pale heads were stuffed against the ceiling. Together they looked outside, which now was upside down, the sky a river. They looked at each other, not speaking or blinking, and barely even breathing, but half laughing.

Was that right or wrong? She no longer trusts her memory and wonders if, perhaps, the purpose of memory is not to be an accurate account of a life but rather to convey the way whatever happened in your life made you feel.

In Eganville she stops at the dam and sits at a picnic table, looking out onto the rushing water. This is where she has stopped before, on rambling trips home over the years, and also long ago, on that trip to the Bonnechere Caves. She can smell the creeping thyme and the water.

It may have been Mick who told her about the monarchs, but more likely it had been Wren. Each fall they fly south in flocks of thousands, resting nightly with their wings upraised. Year after year they land on the same trees, lured by a secret male butterfly fragrance that seeps into the wood and stays there, calling to the ones who come after.

ACKNOWLEDGMENTS

For inspiration, encouragement and answers to endless odd questions such as, Do raccoons have fingers? my sincere thanks to Robert Boyd, Denise Bukowski, Bonnie Burnard, Paula Fullerton, Pamela Goodwin-Pray, Janet Hardy, Gene Kasaboski, Siobhan Maloney, Diane Martin, Rosemary Nixon, Jeremy Rawlings, Caitlin Russell, Reed Russell, Jamie Sinclair, Joan Thomas, Julie Trimingham, Rick Warden, Kate Yorga and Noelle Zitzer.

Thank you to the Canada Council for its generous financial support, and to the Sage Hill Writers' Experience for providing the serene setting in which this novel began.

Kristen den Hartog's work has been published throughout Canada in literary magazines and short-story anthologies, including *The Journey Prize Anthology* and *The Turn of the Story: Canadian Short Fiction on the Eve of the Millennium*. *Water Wings* is her first novel. She was born in Deep River, Ontario, and now lives in Toronto, where she is working on her second novel.